Readers love
J.S. COOK

Skid Row Serenade

"…a very intriguing mystery with lots of twists and turns."
—MM Good Book Reviews

"…I really liked how it was executed and was even surprised by the couple of revelations."
—Dear Author

The Quality of Mercy

"A recommended period story of atonement, hurt/comfort and renewed hope, which left me with a big smile on my face."
—It's About The Book

Stranger at the Door

"*Stranger at the Door* is a little sad and eerie and wonderful love story written by J.S. Cook. The plot is very creative… and kept me intrigued as the story developed."
—The Novel Approach

By J.S. Cook

But Not For Me
Come to Dust
As JoAnne Soper-Cook: The Eye of Heaven
Famous Last Words
A Little Night Murder
The Lovely Beast
My Man Walter
Oasis of Night
The Quality of Mercy
Sixteen Songs About Regret
Skid Row Serenade
The Stranger at My Door
The Winter Dark

Published by DREAMSPINNER PRESS
www.dreamspinnerpress.com

My MAN WALTER

J.S. COOK

DREAMSPINNER PRESS

Published by

DREAMSPINNER PRESS

5032 Capital Circle SW, Suite 2, PMB# 279, Tallahassee, FL 32305-7886 USA
www.dreamspinnerpress.com

My Man Walter
© 2016 J.S. Cook.

Cover Art
© 2016 Catt Ford.
Cover content is for illustrative purposes only and any person depicted on the cover is a model.

ISBN: 978-1-63477-030-9
Digital ISBN: 978-1-63477-031-6
Library of Congress Control Number: 2015916313
Published February 2016
v. 1.0

Printed in the United States of America
∞
This paper meets the requirements of
ANSI/NISO Z39.48-1992 (Permanence of Paper).

For Sheppie: 1999-2013. You were my sunshine.

ACKNOWLEDGMENTS

Thanks to everyone at Dreamspinner who made this book possible.

Can you butle? We're fresh out of butlers. The one we had left this morning. (My Man Godfrey, 1936)

PROLOGUE

New York City: August, 2014

BRIAN SCHRADE hated waiting. He wasn't the kind of man who could possess himself patiently until the appearance of whomever or whatever he was waiting for. Split-second decisions he could deal with. Lengthy negotiations with pimps and drug dealers, he ate for breakfast. This? This was beyond irritating.

His "office" was located directly across from the precinct's ancient and very weathered door, so he had a clear view of whoever passed the desk. It was twenty-seven minutes after nine by the big clock on the wall, and twenty-eight minutes past by Schrade's wristwatch. Little bastard was late again. Nearly half an hour late.

He went to get a cup of horrible coffee out of the dispensing machine over by the water cooler, just to have something to do. The precinct was unusually quiet this morning because it was Monday and the guys who'd pulled the weekend shift were off, but also because of the funeral. Detective Vincent Casiano had been staking out a suspected meth kitchen when it blew up in his face—literally. Schrade wasn't sure how bad the damage was, only that the funeral home had strongly recommended a closed casket. Some of the boys down in Vice said there was nothing left of Casiano from the neck up, but Schrade knew better than to believe anything that came out of their pie holes.

Schrade took a sip of the plastic-tasting coffee, sighed, and went back to his desk. He took the long way around, weaving past clacking keyboards and agitated phone conversations. Harmon was showing pictures of his new baby, even though the kid was as wrinkly as an elephant's ass and looked like Winston Churchill. Schrade nearly tripped over a box of spilled pencils, the hot coffee splashing over his hand and wrist. *Oh for fuck's sake.* He reached his desk and fumbled in one of the drawers for something to clean up with. Twenty-nine minutes late now, by the big clock on the wall. Schrade was beginning to think—

"Good morning, Detective Schrade. I apologize for being late. I experienced some difficulty locating a cab." A young man, perhaps closer to Schrade's thirty-eight years than he initially appeared, slid into a chair and offered Schrade an insincere smile. "I sincerely hope you weren't waiting overlong." He squared the desk blotter and laid Schrade's pen across the bottom, directly in the middle. Something about its position bothered him, because he picked it up, turned it around, and laid it back down again in a flurry of nervous gestures. Just watching him was enough to make Schrade twitch.

"It's fine, Alec," Schrade replied. "I wasn't doing anything important."

Alec fell into a profound silence and glanced around the room. To Schrade it looked like he was pretending interest in the daily workings of the precinct, which was bullshit. The only thing that interested Alec Pratt was Alec Pratt.

He looked back at Schrade, offering another of his fleeting, nervous smiles. "Sorry." Pratt raised social awkwardness to the level of an art form.

"Would you like some coffee?" Schrade asked. He couldn't imagine anyone actually wanting anything that came out of that machine.

"Thank you, no." Pratt's smile came and went, an irritating simper.

"Still running errands for Fatty Veranda?" Schrade asked lightly.

Alec skewered him with an "oh please" look. "You know I can't tell you that."

"So you're still involved," Schrade said. And, when Alec didn't reply: "Humor me. It's my best guess."

"I don't know why you're asking," Alec said quietly, "especially when you already know." He traced the edge of the blotter and didn't look up. "Maybe you want to hear the old clichés one more time? 'It's safer if you don't know.' 'I could tell you, but I'd have to kill you.' 'What you don't know—'"

"That's enough," Schrade said. Christ, his nerves felt shredded and it wasn't even ten o'clock yet. He suspected the bad coffee wasn't doing him any favors. "You're probably wondering why I called you here."

"They always say that in movies, don't they?" Alec clasped his hands together on top of the desk, released them, then clasped them again, this time so hard his knuckles showed white against the skin. "Sorry," he said again. "I'm all right now. I promise."

Schrade doubted it. It was kindness that made him think of Alec as "unusual"—an iconoclast, a genuine individual. In reality, Pratt was simply very, very odd. Schrade had no idea if there was an official diagnosis on file, but he suspected Pratt had some kind of anxiety disorder, with perhaps a smidgen of OCD in the mix, and whatever his lunatic family had done to him in between times.

"If you need to move things around, it's fine," he said, as Alec lined up a pair of ballpoint pens end-to-end. "I don't mind." He turned at the sound of approaching footsteps. "Here's Detective Mendes now."

Alicia Mendes, honey-blonde-haired and green-eyed, had the height and looks of a supermodel and an expression that said *fuck with me at your peril.* Like Schrade, she'd worked with Alec before, but where Schrade tolerated him, Mendes couldn't stand the sight of him. It galled her that Schrade had decided to make use of Alec's specialized input. She despised snitches as a rule; she definitely despised Alec Pratt.

Alec stood, his manners impeccable. "Detective Mendes, you can't know what a pleasure this is, seeing you again." He reached for her hand, and instead of shaking it, clasped it gently between both of his.

Mendes shot a look at Schrade. "Let go of my hand," she said, "or I'll shoot your goddamn fingers off."

"Yes, well...." Alec raised a sardonic eyebrow. "Let's try and behave in a civilized manner."

"Alec has agreed to help us," Schrade put in.

Mendes yanked her hand away.

"Detective Mendes has doubts about your ability to carry out this assignment," Schrade said.

Alec looked crestfallen. It was an expression that he wore particularly well. "Oh." He glanced at Schrade. "If you'd prefer that I—"

"It's fine," Mendes said. She took the other chair in front of Schrade's desk.

"Alec and I go way back," Schrade said. "Years." He tossed a newspaper onto the desk. "I assume you've seen this."

"Yes," Alec said, scanning the page. "I remember reading it." He drew the paper toward him. "'Masetti Construction Kickbacks: How Much for Whom?'"

"The guy who wrote that freelances for several area papers," Mendes said, "including the *New York Times.* He must have a death wish, because this isn't the first time he's named names. It's like he's trying to get a pair of cement shoes."

"The Masettis are gunning for him," Schrade said. "He's nothing to them, except he won't shut up about their various business deals. Nobody knows how he gets the leads he does. Either he's a good reporter or he's a goddamn idiot."

Alec nodded. "And you want me to…?"

Schrade told him.

"Uh-huh," Alec said carefully. "Does he know?"

Mendes shook her head. "Probably. I don't know. It's common knowledge he's in bed with several underworld scumbags. How deep, nobody's real sure."

"And it goes without saying," Alec said, "that he would be…." He glanced from Mendes to Schrade. "Useful?"

Schrade slid a photo across the desk to Alec. The photo showed a massive early-twentieth-century mansion, probably in the Palisades or on Long Island. It seemed to squat on the landscape, glowering at everything around it with a barely concealed malevolence. "We're going to stash him here, at least for now. He'll get hired as a butler to keep him away from the Masettis."

"And he'll agree to this because…?" Alec raised both eyebrows.

"Walter Godfrey thinks he's going undercover to get the scoop," Schrade said. "You know, the *big* story."

"*The Great Gatsby* goes to hell," Alec mused. He laid the photograph down, carefully squaring the picture so it and the edge of the desk were flush and parallel. Then he shifted the photo slightly to the left, adjusting its location so it was directly in the middle. He tapped the photo with his index finger. "I'm sure he could find dozens of places to hide in this… mausoleum." He examined the picture intently, his chin cradled in his palm, elbow on the desk. He looked like someone perusing a dinner menu. "Why don't you stick him in some witness protection program?"

Schrade exchanged a look with Mendes. "I need him where I can get to him in a hurry. If things go south with the Masettis…." He left it there.

"All right," Alec said, after a period of silence. "I'll do it." Without further discussion, he stood and nodded to them both. "You'll hear from me." He gave them a strange little smile. "Eventually." He reached to take Mendes's hand, but she leaned away from him. "You owe me," he said, glancing from Mendes to Schrade. "Both of you."

Mendes waited till Alec was out of earshot. "Are you out of your goddamn mind? Him? That's your big idea?"

"Alec has been very helpful in the past," Schrade said. "Don't let his appearance fool you."

"I don't trust that snitch as far as I could throw this building," Mendes said. "Are you sure about this? Seems to me you have something in mind."

Schrade smiled, the secret little smile of a sphinx. "You have no idea."

CHAPTER ONE

CHASE GORDON turned forty on a cool day in late October, without fanfare or celebration. From the back patio of Gordonstoun, his Long Island home, he could see an occasional sailboat tacking into the wind, fighting the waves to make its way back to relatively dry land. The massive oaks and maples surrounding the Gordon property effectively screened him from casual onlookers—that and the twelve acres separating him from his nearest neighbor. Chase wasn't interested in friendship or congenial discussion. His personal worth amounted to some forty billion dollars, but what he wanted more than anything was to be left alone.

A shadow fell over him, the figure of a woman he knew almost as well as he knew himself. "You must eat something." The shadow reached out and turned the soup bowl on its tray, so it was closer to him. "By the way, happy birthday."

"I'm not hungry." He spoke reluctantly, the words dragged out of him on the end of a long sigh.

"You've not been hungry all week."

"Please, take it away." He turned soft brown eyes on her, not quite pleading. "It's cold now anyway."

"Master Chase, I must insist—"

"Juliet, *please*." He raised his hands and let them fall onto his lap. His legs and the lower part of his body were wrapped in a thick plaid blanket against the autumn chill. Only a very keen observer would have noticed Chase Gordon was unable to move below the hips. The chair he sat in—the chair his butler, Juliet Lavish, had obediently brought out here into the sunshine—was the very latest in assistive technology, but it was still a wheelchair.

"At least try a little."

"No."

"You really are a trial sometimes." Her crisp English accent crackled at his ears. "Are you planning to starve to death? Or is this some new project of yours that I'm not privy to?"

"No… no new project." Out there, on the Sound, someone was rowing a tiny wooden boat painted a bright and unmistakable orange. He—or she—battled hard against the wind but was beaten back again and again. Chase wondered how the rower's hands could take it. He himself had rowed in college, part of Harvard University's prestigious eight, but that was years ago, and he was able-bodied then. *And now I'm a cripple in a chair*, he thought sourly. *All hail the great Chase Gordon, playboy billionaire and international sportsman.* It annoyed him that he still felt sorry for himself, even after all this time.

"Would you like some tea?" She allowed her hand to linger for a moment on his shoulder. He shook his head. "Well, don't stay out here too long." She picked up the tray with his untouched soup and turned to go back into the house. "George said it's going to rain."

"That should make George very happy," Chase replied. "He's been complaining how the rhododendrons are dying for a drink."

He watched the birds for a while, dipping and swooping down to claim a peanut or a sunflower seed from the feeder set to one side of the huge stone patio. He liked watching them; birds, unlike many other things in life, made sense. He'd read somewhere that birds mated for life.

What was that like? he wondered. What was it like to have someone to come home to, or someone to wait for at the end of a long workday? People mated too, often for life. His parents had been very happy together. Theirs was a real love story, from start to finish. Even as a very young child, he had known there was something unusual about their bond, the way they'd finish each other's sentences and how his father almost always knew what his wife was thinking. On long weekend afternoons, Elliot and Marilyn Gordon would steal away together, to some secluded corner of the house where they could be alone without the audience of servants or even Chase himself. His father had once claimed it wasn't enough to only court a woman while you were dating. The courtship ought to continue throughout life, if the marriage was to be successful.

Later, when Chase grew old enough to understand his own sexual orientation, he wondered if this applied to men as well. Did decades' worth of close, affectionate attention guarantee a lifelong love? He'd always assumed he'd have a chance to find out for himself, but he never had, and it was no longer possible to ask his father.

The sun had disappeared, hidden from view behind a bank of thick clouds. The rower had disappeared as well. To dry land, Chase hoped, although one could never be too sure. Life was whimsical like that: without warning, it could just jump up and bite you in the ass.

The patio doors clicked open and Juliet appeared with a glass of water and his capsules. "Time for your medication, Master Chase." He wished she'd stop calling him that, but Juliet insisted on maintaining the master-servant divide, even though she'd cared for Chase since the day he'd been born.

He swallowed the small capsules and handed her back the glass. Chase had paid a very famous doctor a lot of money to come up with a diagnosis. It didn't really matter, since money was one thing Chase had plenty of. The famous doctor's determination—that Chase was suffering from intractable depression—didn't mean a whole lot. Chase could have learned that from a fortune cookie.

"Come inside now," Juliet said. "It's starting to rain." She unlocked the wheelchair brake, turned him about, and guided him through the hallway leading off the patio. "Did you get wet?"

"I don't think so." He touched his hair. He'd caught a few drops, but it was nothing serious. He opted not to tell Juliet, on the off chance she might hustle him directly into bed with a mustard plaster and a hot water bottle. "I'd like to watch a movie, I think."

"Very good, sir." Her voice was sardonic in its intonation. "In your study or the screening room?"

"The screening room."

She wheeled him down a smaller, secondary hallway and stopped in front of the elevator he'd added for his personal use. The screening room was in the basement of the vast Gordon mansion, down a long flight of stairs that for him were no longer an option. For ages he'd resisted having a lift installed, until Juliet had advised in her usual pointed fashion that she had far too much work to do and couldn't spend all day "hauling sir about the premises," and if Chase wanted to spend time in the screening room—or anywhere else in the house—he'd best "get off his arse and do something about it."

I can't exactly do that, Juliet.

You know what the doctor told you, Master Chase. It's all in your mind.

The elevator bumped to a gentle stop and they both got out. Juliet wheeled him into the room and positioned him directly in front of the enormous screen. The room was the size of a hotel penthouse and equipped with all the latest in cinematic media technology. The walls were painted a tasteful and unobtrusive midnight blue and featured paintings done by several of the more preeminent modern artists. Instead of the usual movie-theater seats, there were luxurious leather chairs, each with its own side table for snacks and drinks. A fully stocked bar ran the length of one wall and boasted every kind of alcoholic beverage known to man. It was designed for ease of use, with a dual-level counter that could accommodate a standing bartender or someone in a wheelchair. Chase could have used it to entertain his friends—if he'd had any friends.

"What do you want to watch?" Juliet asked. "There's a new Superman film."

Chase made a rude noise in response to this suggestion. Generally he loved what he called "comic book movies," but the actor they'd cast as the newest Superman irritated him. Couldn't people leave things well enough alone?

"Something old. Maybe…." He thought for a second. He'd been on a classic movie binge lately, working his way through the careers of people like Cagney and Bogart. But he wasn't in the mood for anything too serious. "Do we have that William Powell movie? The one where he's a butler?"

"Of course, sir." She loaded the Blu-ray into the little tray and started the machine. "Is there anything else, sir?"

"He always reminded me of an older brother," Chase said, gesturing at the screen. "The family scoundrel who ran away to South America and made a fortune, like they did in those days."

"You could run away to South America," Juliet pointed out. "I'd even go with you."

"Really?"

"I'd have to, sir. You can't even boil water."

WALTER GODFREY sat at an empty desk in a huge room full of ringing telephones and stared moodily at the computer screen. He was thirty-eight, dark-haired, and blue-eyed, with an innate slenderness that would have been gauntness without the taut buffer of his well-developed muscles. He'd worked hard for them, first as a firefighter with the FDNY and now as a devoted lifter of heavy things at a small neighborhood gym. He seemed to be perpetually smiling even when he wasn't, his lean face fixed into an expression both professional and droll.

"Fuck."

"Language." The man leaning on the corner of Walter's cubicle reached out to tap the top of his head with a file folder he was carrying. His name was Billy Newman; he'd worked at the newspaper almost as long as Walter and boasted a long and impressive list of credentials. "Who pissed in your cornflakes?" When Walter merely grunted, Billy peered over his shoulder at the monitor. "Jesus. You some kind of masochist?"

"I must be." Walter scrolled up to a newspaper headline from thirteen years before: MISSIONARY COUPLE DIE IN HONDURAS PLANE CRASH. "It's a weird story from beginning to end. They were on their way to Central America when the plane just… disappeared. It's like it fell off the radar. Some local people found the wreckage and alerted the authorities. That was it. No further discussion, no investigation. It's like they deliberately buried it." What Walter didn't say was that he was desperate for a story—any story—that would pay the rent. His landlord had paid him a visit several days ago, with a team of movers in tow. *Either you pay me the rent or every goddamn stick of furniture goes out.* Walter had been able to buy his landlord's forbearance with a few hundred dollars, but he knew Mr. Hough wouldn't stay quiet very long.

"Chase Gordon," Billy said. "Nobody's seen him since. He's a virtual recluse in that big old house of his."

"I heard he lives with some old lady," Walter said.

"He's a granny grabber?" Billy reached to tilt the monitor toward him. "There's a picture from the funeral." A small group of people in black stood around two open graves in the incongruous sunshine, while a minister read from the Bible. A slender figure sat nearby, slumped in a wheelchair, probably some older relative who didn't want to be left out of the proceedings. "Jesus, he buried them in the yard."

Walter tilted the monitor back. "It's a family graveyard on the estate," he said scornfully. "They all get buried there." He shot Billy an annoyed look. "Don't you have work to do?" He nodded toward the pile of folders tucked under Billy's arm.

Billy ignored him. "Man, you really planning on digging up Chase Gordon?" He shook his head. "It's your funeral. I wouldn't touch that with a barge pole. Besides, he doesn't let anybody in the house. You can forget about getting an interview. Not gonna happen. The last guy who tried it was dragged away in handcuffs."

"I'll get an interview," Walter said. "Just you watch me." He looked as confident as he felt. A source had recently confirmed his suspicion that the Gordon family—rather, what was left of it—shared some common business interests with the mob, the Masettis in particular. It was an open secret, but until now nobody had managed to gather confirmation. Walter had, and he was going to pump it till it was dry.

"Uh-huh," Billy said. He grinned. It did nice things to his face. Tall, athletic, sandy-haired and blue-eyed, he was very handsome and he knew it. "Watching you is something I enjoy. You ought to know that." He winked.

"Don't let Lance hear you say that." Walter reached for his desk phone. "He's the definition of jealous boyfriend."

"Seriously," Billy said. "How are you going to get in there? Pretend to be the delivery man?"

Walter smirked. "Something like that."

He left Billy to his own devices while he called the Gordon house, a sprawling Gold Coast mansion built in the early 1900s by one of the old railroad robber barons. In every photograph Walter had ever seen, it looked like something out of the Roaring Twenties, a veritable monument to wealth and excess. He waited patiently while the telephone rang and rang, and he was just about to hang up when an English voice—a woman's voice—answered.

"Good morning," Walter said, trying hard to be his affable best. "I wonder if I might speak to Mr. Chase Gordon."

The telephone connection hummed between them. When the voice spoke again, it was very, very frosty. "Where did you get this number? It's supposed to be unlisted."

"I'm calling from the *New York Times*," Walter began—and was promptly interrupted.

"I regret Mr. Gordon is unavailable to members of the press. Don't call here again." The call disconnected with a sharp click.

Walter debated whether to call back and risk the English woman's wrath, or to leave well enough alone, at least for the time being. He got up from his desk and strolled over to the wide bank of windows overlooking the busy street below. At this time of day—just past one in the afternoon—8th Avenue teemed with traffic both vehicular and pedestrian as much of workday Manhattan went to lunch. Walter's stomach had been growling since noon, but he didn't bother going out. Like as not, he'd grab a sandwich from some small corner deli and eat it on the drive to Long Island. Where he was going to look for Chase Gordon.

You got brass balls, his pop would say. *Go stick your head in the lion's den. See if I stop you.*

Two of his internal lines were lit up, but he ignored them. Whatever it was could wait, unless it was something serious like the building being on fire and then he'd run down the stairs with the rest of them… run down the stairs in the midst of smoke and falling debris, trying to hold his breath until he made it down to street level… *if* he made it. The smoke alarms would be shrilling in his ears, the noise almost painful, and he would hear the sirens of approaching fire trucks, police, and other first responders as they raced to the scene. Maybe they wouldn't get there in time. Maybe he'd be trapped on his floor, unable to make it to any of the exits, with his heart pounding bloody murder in his ears….

He stopped, made himself breathe.

Like most of New York, Walter would never forget September 11, 2001. The patent shock and horror at seeing airplanes—actual goddamn *airplanes*, for Christ's sake—slicing into the World Trade towers, then the towers themselves collapsing, was forever imprinted on his consciousness. It had looked like scenes from a bad movie, some disaster flick from the 1970s, with things burning and people screaming and jumping to their deaths. Only it wasn't a movie and the people screaming and jumping really were going to their deaths.

He glanced around, checking to see if he was being observed, then dragged a file folder labeled "honeymoon_pix" out of his e-mail and onto the desktop. He knew the file he wanted, had clicked through to it so many times he could literally do it in his sleep. It was a picture of the two of them sitting on the Australian beach they'd visited for their "honeymoon" trip. Gary was sitting to one side of him, his hand on Walter's shoulder; they were both grinning like fools. Behind them stretched an expanse of faultless sand and the sea in the distance, quiescent and serene. That they weren't able to be legally married in the state of New York meant little. They'd committed to each other and exchanged rings, and as far as he and Gary were concerned, they were married. Gary was twenty-seven at the time; Walter was twenty-four.

Why wait? Gary had asked. *Nobody lives forever. Carpe diem, already.*

Walter remembered everything about that day, as if it had happened earlier in the week and they were just now getting back from their

vacation, settling into their new life together as a couple. For weeks—
no, months—afterward, he found himself admiring his "wedding" ring
under various environmental conditions: in light and in darkness, while
walking down the street or hailing a cab on a busy Manhattan street. A
simple gold band with three tiny diamonds. *Nothing too fancy*, he'd said.
Gary liked bling and had a tendency to go overboard. Walter had had to
argue him into getting the plainer bands for them both, but in the end,
he'd capitulated. *Anything to keep you happy, babe.*

They'd arrived home to a sumptuous reception hosted by Walter's
best friend, Kate, a wedding planner who'd arranged everything with
her usual efficiency. There were buffet tables groaning with food, and a
flower-laden arch under which the newlyweds walked on a floor strewn
with rose petals. "You wouldn't believe the trouble I went through to
get rose petals," she'd said. "Rose petals on the floor, you'd think it was
kitty litter. We're having roses, I said. You can just get over yourselves,
I said." Kate never let anything or anyone get in the way of what she
wanted. She had a helluva lot of chutzpah. It was her compassion that
saw him through those first few horrible months after Gary's death, when
he wanted to crawl inside a bottle and just stay there.

*You can't hide from the world, hon. You gotta get back out there.
You think you're the only one who feels this way?*

Six months later, Kate herself was gone—ovarian cancer. And
people expected him to believe in a just and loving God?

Walter sighed and closed the file.

More lights appeared on his desk phone. Billy went by and made a
throat-slashing motion.

Walter steeled himself and picked up the receiver, punching the
nearest button. "Godfrey."

"What the hell are you doing here?" A pause. "I'm positive I
fired you. Did I not fire you?" The voice was feminine and beautifully
modulated, the product of first a private prep school and then four years
at Vassar. Eleanor Rigby ("Yes, it's my name, just like that goddamn
Beatles song") held several degrees, but mostly what she held were
Walter's balls, in her hand, ready to be crushed when and if she chose.
"You said you'd bring me something good." She sighed loudly into the
phone. "Goddammit, you owe me, Walter. For Christ's sake, you don't
work here anymore. You're lucky I even let you into the building."

Walter made a noncommittal noise. "You said I could freelance, El. You said as long as old man Pratt didn't find out, no harm done."

"What bullshit are you giving me? Have you written something?" She paused, and Walter heard her light a cigarette. She was one of the few holdovers left in the building who dared to smoke on the premises. "Or are you choking?"

"I'm polishing it," he said.

"Darling, save your spit. I'm coming down there." *Click.*

Billy went by, making the approaching-shark noise from *Jaws.*

Walter flipped him the finger and turned back to the computer. *Better look busy,* he thought, *before she gets here.* Eleanor was right: that he was even allowed in the door was some kind of miracle. It was important that he stay on her good side.

INQUIRY HEARS DETAILS OF CONSTRUCTION KICKBACKS. Just recalling the recent headline made Walter cringe. It was the third—and final—error he was ever to make while on salary at the *Times.* His printed accusations of money laundering and crooked politicians had caused such a fuss at City Hall that he was banned from the premises for life.

Eleanor had practically taken him apart. *What the fucking hell are you trying to do to me, Walter? You named names, for chrissakes, without any real proof.*

Some of the names mentioned belonged to close friends of the Pratt family—the same Pratt family who owned the *Times*… the Pratt family who had ties to several prominent New York "businessmen."

Do not drag me down with you, Walter. I swear to God, I will eat you for breakfast.

When Walter pointed out that she was in fact the editor-in-chief (and therefore responsible for final content before the paper went to press), Eleanor had come within a hair's breadth of having a stroke. *Fact checkers, El.* He had, foolishly, tried to defend himself. *They're called fact checkers. Look into it.*

After she'd had Walter escorted out by building security, she'd called Payroll and had his salary suspended. She sent an e-mail and a text, left phone messages, and wrote a formal notice on *Times* letterhead, advising him that his services were no longer required. She wanted to make sure Walter knew he was fired.

Only a significant amount of persuasion—helped along by Walter's native guile—had persuaded Eleanor to let him write for them freelance. It didn't hurt that he'd seen city councilman Paul Lamoreaux sitting in the lap of a particularly gorgeous drag queen one night, in one of Manhattan's better dance bars. Speculation had been swirling for weeks about Lamoreaux's new love, but nobody was able to get anything concrete. Walter did, and it landed him in Eleanor's good graces. The lap in which Lamoreaux had been sitting belonged to the Lady Chastain; they'd met at some official City Hall function and it had been love at first sight. What Chastain had been doing at City Hall, Walter had no clue, and he wasn't about to phone up and ask. As for Lamoreaux, Walter had only met him once, and the memory of that meeting had stayed with him like the remnants of some botulism-ridden sidewalk buffet.

He pulled up the story he was working on, well aware that he was probably wading even deeper into what had turned out to be a pretty nasty morass. At first glance the story seemed like a puff piece: Sister Perpetua O'Something, head of an after-school drop-in center in the Bronx, upset because the building that housed the center was slated for demolition. Walter sighed. The woman was as dull as ditch water, dedicated to God and the Church and the good of everyone, a friend to orphans and drunks and stray kittens. She'd appealed to the construction company, the developers, even City Hall, and got absolutely nothing for her trouble, with good reason: the building was being razed to make way for a brand-new nightclub.

A nightclub, Walter strongly suspected, that was to be a front for the Masetti crime family's latest foray into drug trafficking and prostitution. Masetti wanted to up the ante, so he and his top man, Fatty Veranda, had been sniffing around for the kind of girls you couldn't get locally, and he was planning to bring them in from South America, Bosnia, and Africa. That many of them didn't speak English hardly mattered—Veranda and his cronies weren't hiring them to talk. The girls were essentially abducted from their home countries and pressed into sexual slavery. When they were no longer any good—when they couldn't provide their usual services—they were usually taken somewhere, shot in the head, and buried in a shallow grave. It was beyond sickening.

Walter could say such things in print, of course; he just couldn't name *names* (God forbid), which wasn't to say he couldn't drop a series of very broad hints. Or very narrow ones, for that matter.

A pair of teal-green Gucci pumps with gold toe-caps stopped by his cubicle. A small woman, her dark brown hair pulled back into a bun, gazed down at him. She wasn't smiling. "Well?"

"Um." Walter's hand went to his necktie. "Nice shoes, El."

She slid a pair of glasses on and leaned over his shoulder, reading the screen. She straightened up and nodded. "Let it go the way it is. It's fine."

"Are you sure?" Walter asked. He wanted to make reference to the Masetti property, but he'd put that in after Eleanor had gone back upstairs. What she didn't know wouldn't hurt him.

"Let it go, goddammit! You can always fluff it up in rewrite." She saw there was a second tab open on his Internet browser and clicked it. "What's this?" She read aloud, "Chase Gordon, only son and heir of Elliott Gordon, billionaire philanthropist...."

"That isn't anything." Walter moved to close out the page, but Eleanor stopped him.

"Chase Gordon, huh?" She peered at him over the tops of her reading glasses. "I remember this guy. Used to be you'd see him every Saturday night, tearing the hell out of some hotel or fancy restaurant." Eleanor shook her head. "It's a damn shame."

"I'd like to write something about him," Walter said. "He's in charge of a humanitarian project in Honduras, trying to combat local poverty. It's a good angle."

Eleanor laughed nastily. "Stop wasting my goddamn time."

"No, seriously." Walter cast about for suitable evidence to bolster his argument. "I know him from school. We went to school together."

"What school?" Eleanor asked.

"Uh, boarding school," Walter replied, warming to his subject. "In Switzerland."

Eleanor stared at him so hard, Walter could practically feel his insides melting. "You went to boarding school. With Chase Gordon. In Switzerland." She rolled her eyes. "You'll have to do better than that, Walter."

He was reminded of a line from one of his favorite pulp novels, *I Wake Up Screaming*: "She was as white as marble, but she looked lovely." Maybe El didn't look lovely, exactly, but her expression just then was every bit as unmalleable as marble.

"Seriously," Walter insisted, well aware he was skating on extremely thin ice. "We go back a long way."

"Bullshit." Eleanor spread her arms wide in her usual melodramatic style. "What kind of idiot do you think I am?" She was practically shouting. Several people in the immediate vicinity stopped what they were doing. The pimple-faced boy from the mailroom stepped gently backward, easing his cart away from the impending debacle. "When are you going to get it through your head, Walter? You don't work here anymore. I'm still wondering why I even let you in the goddamn building." She turned and walked away.

"I can get this story." Walter got up and went after her. "I'll really go to town on it, El. I swear."

Eleanor stopped midstride and turned, so she was looking right in his face. "You don't have a goddamn thing," she said. She flicked a dismissive fingernail against the knot of his tie. "Listen to me, Walter. Stay away from Chase Gordon. It could get really, really ugly." She started toward the elevator.

Walter called after her, "I can do this, El!"

She didn't turn around.

IT ALL started with a bottle of mustard.

He'd wanted some mustard for a sandwich he was making in the kitchen of his tiny apartment at three minutes past midnight on a rainy Wednesday night. The rain in Manhattan wasn't like rain anywhere else: it was sideways, driven by a ferocious wind and striking the skin like daggers. The only place open was a grungy, rundown little store on the corner of West 86th and Broadway. People—tourists, especially, and others new to the city—went there because *hey, it's right there on Broadway, gotta be classy*, and people like Walter went because it was close to where he lived, just off Broadway, which wasn't classy either, even though everybody thought so.

The store was open practically twenty-four hours a day, seven days a week, run by two Iranian brothers whose only conversation consisted of nods and grunts. The interior was maybe six by nine feet, with minimal lighting and a trap door leading into the basement, where the brothers stored crates of canned food, candy bars, and a limited amount of fresh produce.

"You got any mustard?" Walter asked, stepping out of the rain and pulling the door closed behind him. "Doesn't matter what brand." One of the brothers found it, took it off the shelf, and handed it to Walter, who stood there reading the label. He had no idea what he was looking for. Mustard was mustard, wasn't it?

Walter was reaching for his wallet when the door burst open violently, swinging hard on its hinges. Two men in ski masks grabbed the man behind the cash register and hauled him over the counter. One held him while the other quickly and efficiently shot him twice in the head.

The second man turned, saw Walter, and brought the gun up to fire. There was a short popping sound, like firecrackers, and the bottle of mustard exploded in Walter's hand.

Get out, he thought. *I gotta get out. They shot me in the mustard.* The gunmen were between him and the door. At this close range, they couldn't miss and they would almost certainly shoot him, shoot him till he was as dead as the store clerk, lying on his face with half his head blown away. Behind him, the trapdoor to the basement yawned open. Walter made a split-second decision and dove in, slamming the trapdoor behind him and slapping the lock closed. *Padlock on the inside of a trapdoor, who the hell does that?* Overhead, he could hear the two men walking back and forth, and someone tried the trapdoor, yanking hard. *That lock can't possibly hold. It'll never hold. I'm a dead man.*

The basement was roomier than he'd originally thought, and divided into several sections for storage. At the far end of the space was a narrow door leading God knows where, but Walter didn't have a whole lot of choice. He slipped inside, closed the door behind him, and saw a short flight of stairs going up to a second door. He went through that and found himself in the space behind the building, hemmed in on all sides by dangling fire escapes. There was a locked gate at one end, taller than Walter, and the other was blocked by a dumpster. Walter chose the dumpster. He clambered over it, panting and sweating, and took off at a dead run, pounding blindly through the pouring rain until he was—finally—standing in the lobby of his building.

His hand shook as he opened his apartment door and slammed it shut behind him and fumbled with the locks. He went around and pulled all the blinds down, then crawled on his hands and knees to the kitchen. *The phone on the countertop....* He yanked it toward him by the cord, dumping the receiver into his lap. He dialed frantically and waited in an agony of suspense until—

"This is Newman."

Walter sagged with relief. "Billy, I'm—these two guys—I went to get mustard." Until now he hadn't noticed the jagged cut in the center of his palm, raw flesh showing underneath a slow trickle of blood. Until now, it hadn't even hurt. Adrenaline, Walter supposed. Most likely adrenaline was what had propelled him through the trap door and into the basement.

"Whoa, slow down. What the hell are you talking about?"

Walter told him. "They saw me, Billy. They saw my face."

"Were they wearing ski masks?" Billy asked. "If they had their faces covered, it doesn't matter. It's not like you can identify them in a lineup." He yawned. "Do you know it's after midnight? Where are you, anyway?"

"Home," Walter said. *On the kitchen floor, scared spitless, waiting for them to come and get me.*

"Don't worry," Billy said. "They're not interested in you."

"You sound awfully sure."

"You didn't see their faces," Billy repeated. *How does he know?* "They'll never know you were there unless somebody blabs. Kinda hard to do, since you don't know who they are." He paused, like he was trying to figure something out. "There were two of them?"

"Two." Walter was shaking hard enough to make his teeth chatter. "One was tall, kind of lanky, long arms and legs. He didn't say anything. The other one was shorter, kind of stocky."

"But you didn't see their faces."

Walter tried to draw a deep breath, but his chest felt like it was encased in iron bands. "I didn't see their faces."

"That's good," Billy said. "These guys don't like it when somebody gets in the way of their wetwork."

Walter spent the night lying curled against the cupboards in the kitchen, cradling a baseball bat. In the morning he called the police. Two disinterested detectives named Schrade and Niedermeyer spent twenty minutes asking him for a description of the shooters, then sighed and closed their notebooks.

Call us if you see them again.

For a long time, Walter convinced himself that he was perfectly safe. This was Manhattan; it was clean (relatively), wide-open (more or less), and civilized. Except civilized people didn't shoot other people for the hell of it, and other civilized people didn't crawl through somebody's filthy basement because two masked lunatics with guns were coming to kill them. He slept with a hammer under his pillow and his cell phone near his hand.

"You should see somebody," Eleanor said, when he told her. "Doctor or somebody. Get yourself fixed up."

But Walter, who'd been literally on the doorstep of 9/11, didn't think a doctor was going to help, but he did think it would go away on its own. He did his best to forget, to put the entire incident behind him.

It worked… for a while. It worked until the afternoon Walter was warming a bar stool in Divvy's, a favorite spot for many of the *Times* reporters. He'd been having a great time, trading witticisms with Billy and Jared from Sports, when Lou Lou the bartender tagged his sleeve and said, "Looks like you got a secret admirer, Walter."

He seemed to rise out of the shadows, a big man with his arms crossed over his chest and a tiny smile quirking the corners of his lips. He was beautifully dressed—too beautifully for a dump like Divvy's—from his tailored suit to his very shiny, custom-made shoes. He nodded at Walter and raised one beefy arm to beckon him closer. "How you doing, Walter? Good to see you again."

Walter buttoned his coat in anticipation of the chill outside. "I don't believe we've met," he said. It was the sort of thing the detective heroes in his favorite books said, squint-eyed and gritty: *I don't believe I know you.* He made to brush past, but was restrained by a big, warm hand that reached to cup his shoulder, not quite painfully. Not yet.

"Sure we have," the man said. He was affable, handsome in a heavyset way, Walter thought, and probably cried during sex. His kind always did. "It was a rainy night. You were buying mustard. Our eyes met across a room. Don't you remember?"

Walter's heartbeat thundered in his ears. "You must have mistaken me for somebody else," he said.

The hand tightened on his shoulder. "It was you, Walter. I never forget a face." He moved closer. "Now you…." He grinned. "You have a really bad memory, am I right?"

"What…? Uh, yeah, sometimes, I guess."

"You need to have a bad memory from now on, Walter." The big man's fingers dug painfully into the muscle of Walter's shoulder, clamped so hard now that his arm was going dead. "You don't see nothing. You don't know nothing. Nobody else was in that store but you. Anybody asks you something, you don't know." He released his grip. "You don't even like mustard. You follow me?"

"What did he look like?" Eleanor asked, when Walter got back to the office.

"Tall, kind of heavyset, but handsome," Walter told her. "Really well dressed." Really polite, really civilized, really articulate. Really deadly. There'd be no next time. Walter brought up a fresh page on his laptop and typed until he'd put most of it down in simple language: TIMES REPORTER THREATENED BY MOB.

A week later, despite being banned from the premises, he was coming out of City Hall, where he'd been eavesdropping on the personal assistant of a certain alderman. The personal assistant liked to get blown in the men's bathroom during his lunch hour and after work, and usually the alderman's pretty receptionist was doing the blowing. Walter didn't mind that. To each his own, right? Everybody in the city knew that alderman liked 'em tall and leggy, which was good news for the alderman's personal assistant. Even better, when this particular pair of legs was done sucking cock, she talked a mile a minute.

Mostly she talked about people in the office—who was banging who, that sort of thing. Now and then she might be encouraged to spill everything she knew about certain business dealings some particular gentlemen had with the city, especially if those gentlemen were good friends of the mayor. The new development down by the waterfront would bring in hundreds of jobs for people, revitalize the whole area— and the Masettis stood to make a goddamn fortune. Too bad that whole area had to be razed to make way for new construction, but what can you do? Walter had captured some absolutely sizzling dialogue between sucker and suckee, enough verbal evidence to send several of the Masettis upstate along with their politician cronies. This was good stuff, and it wasn't even time for dinner yet.

He'd just packed away his digital recorder and stepped out onto the sidewalk when a huge armored truck, the kind used for bank transports, hopped the curb just in front of him. The doors slid open and two men got out, all dressed in black, each carrying an Uzi. Just like the two men who'd shot at him in the store, they were wearing ski masks that left nothing bare except their eyes and mouths. They didn't speak. One of them handcuffed him roughly with a zip tie and slipped a black bag over Walter's head, shutting out the daylight. He was shoved into the truck and the doors slammed shut with a reverberating clang. It was so surreal that for a moment he wondered if some movie company filming in the area had mistaken him for one of their extras.

"You can't do this," he protested. "I'm a member of the working press."

"Shut your trap," one of the men said wearily. "I get sick of listening to you guys."

"Let me out of here," Walter said. "I swear to God—"

"Shut up!"

They drove for some time, circling and doubling back until Walter had no idea where they were. The truck turned onto what felt like a concrete pad or parking lot.

When the doors opened, Walter could smell the putrid stench of the waterfront and hear the harsh cries of circling gulls, overlaid with the repetitive *beep beep beep* of trucks backing and turning. He was grabbed and shoved out, propped on his feet, and frog-marched to where several steel shipping containers were stacked. "You don't have to do this," he said. He hated the way his voice sounded, pleading and shaky, pathetic. "I promise, I won't tell anybody."

He was shoved hard from behind, and as he stumbled, someone ripped the bag off his head. There were more than just the initial two; there were four of them now. Walter had no illusions. They were going to kill him, and not quickly or painlessly. He would suffer.

"I hate having to do this, Walter." The big guy from that day in Divvy's, the one with the shiny shoes and gold cufflinks, the one who'd warned him what would happen if he didn't listen. "But you don't take advice so well, you know what I mean?" His fist moved with preternatural speed, hitting Walter square on the cheek and slamming him backward to the ground. It felt like he'd been run over by a bus with enormous fists.

The four of them all leaped on him at once, kicking him, beating him with baseball bats. Someone held his arm out straight while somebody else stomped on it; the pain was so intense, Walter thought he'd throw up. A pointed shoe rolled him onto his back, and he was staring at a patch of sky while two of them took turns jumping on him. He heard somebody yelling, "Hey!" from what seemed like a long way off, and the goons who'd been beating him scattered like flies.

He lay there for a long time, while day turned into evening and then into night, and a few barely visible stars gleamed above him. Then it started to rain, and the rain seemed to loosen whatever was holding him, and he could sit up.

His head and torso were sticky with his own dried blood. He groped his way to his feet, fumbling for his cell phone. It was unbroken, which was more than Walter could say for himself. His whole body felt like it had been fed through a wood chipper. He dialed the only cab company he could remember, but when the dispatcher asked for his location, Walter didn't know. "I'm on a wharf... concrete wharf. I think it's maybe Brooklyn."

"Wharf, concrete wharf, Brooklyn," the dispatcher said. "I don't know where you are, mister, so you're outta luck."

"Wait!" Walter clung to the phone desperately. "Don't hang up." He looked around him, peering out of eyes almost swollen shut and crusted with his own dried blood. Walter was no freight and shipping expert, but he recognized this place. "Red Hook," he said. He could see the new World Trade Center from where he was standing, the gleaming single column built to replace those destroyed on 9/11. "Definitely Red Hook. Some guys beat me up. I... I need help getting home."

There was a long pause on the other end. "All right," the dispatcher said finally. "I'll send somebody."

Walter sat on a pile of wooden pallets. The rain had slacked off a bit, and here and there the night sky was torn by patches of stars. Normally Walter would have enjoyed the view, but it was raining, he was cold, and he hurt like hell all over. He wrapped his coat around his sore ribs and shivered until a pair of headlights stabbed the darkness at the other end of the pier. A large, dark sedan pulled up in front of him and stopped. *How the hell did they know?* Walter wondered. *The dispatcher... goddamn taxi dispatcher must have told them.* Masetti's goons had come back to finish the job, which meant Walter was definitely dead this time.

The passenger side door opened and a man got out. He was about Walter's height, slender but not skinny, maybe ex-military, wearing a suit and tie. He was so unbelievably neat and looked like he'd been pressed out of plastic. His expression said he didn't put up with any nonsense. Walter remembered him from the mustard incident—Detective something. *Cops.* Walter sagged with relief. *They're cops.*

"You the guy who called for a taxi?"

A second man got out of the car, taller than the first, slightly heavyset, wearing baggy, rumpled clothes that looked like they'd been salvaged from a dumpster. "We came as soon as we could. You okay?"

"We would have been here sooner," the first man said, "but we didn't get the call down at the precinct 'til half an hour ago."

The taxi dispatcher must have alerted them. They were probably wondering what Walter was doing, hanging around the docks at this hour of the night.

The first man approached him, badge in his hand so Walter could see it. "Detective Brian Schrade. You're the guy with the mustard." He nodded at his partner. "Mustard guy," he said. "From the store."

"Right," Walter said. His lips were stiff with his own dried blood.

"This is my partner, Detective Jack Niedermeyer."

"Right," Walter said again. He couldn't think of anything else to say.

"You want to see a doctor?" Niedermeyer asked.

"No, I'm fine."

Schrade peered at him through narrowed eyes. "You don't look fine."

"No, it's…." Walter sighed. "I don't need a doctor. Honest."

They helped him to the car and gave him a blanket, and when they arrived back at the station, Schrade found some dry clothes Walter could wear, and his partner—Niedermeyer—brought him coffee from the machine. It tasted like plastic, but it was hot and that was good enough for Walter. Then they sat down with Walter on the other side of the desk, and Schrade sharpened a pencil and Niedermeyer put his reading glasses on.

"I know you're probably still in shock," Schrade said, "but it would help us a lot if you could tell me the whole thing, from start to finish."

He talked for nearly an hour, while Schrade and Niedermeyer scribbled notes and exchanged cryptic glances with each other. Niedermeyer brought more coffee, and one of the clerks in the administrative office came by with a dozen donuts from a bakery down the street, still warm.

"We have reason to believe you're being targeted by the Masetti crime family," Niedermeyer said. His voice sounded tired, as if merely being awake exhausted him. "They're pissed off because you keep writing stuff about them." He shook his head. "Not a wise thing to do."

Walter was in serious danger, Schrade said. The Masettis were poised to launch a huge new construction project worth literal billions, and Walter's constant scrutiny was pissing them off. If Walter didn't get out of the city, something bad would happen to him, something worse than an impromptu ride to the waterfront and a beating. "We can't guarantee your safety if you stay here," Schrade said. He was about Walter's age, maybe a year or two younger, with an earnest face that probably looked incredible when he smiled. Walter suspected he didn't smile very often, not in his line of work. Schrade ran a hand through his close-cropped hair. Definitely ex-military. "In protective custody cases, we usually put you somewhere the bad guys can't get at you." He frowned. "In this instance I'd have to send you to the moon."

"We figure the best thing to do is maybe hide you in plain sight," Niedermeyer said. "Put you the last place the Masettis would think to look."

"Some big house out on Long Island," Schrade said. "I'll send a guy to keep an eye on you. You'll be safe there."

THE RAIN had come in earnest, streaming down the long french windows of Chase Gordon's private library. He sat and watched as water slid down the glass like tears, forlorn rivulets that trembled into impatient globes and fell apart. It was five past four in the afternoon, but the rain had made things dark, so Juliet had turned on the lights. The library was a warmly lit, cozy cave of a room, lined with polished walnut shelves that boasted every important work of literature ever published—and a lot of what Juliet sniffily called "absolute rubbish." These latter were Chase's hobby and his passion: vintage pulp novels with luridly drawn covers, burly men in fedora hats looming over femme fatales in slinky evening gowns. One of his personal favorites had a woman in full evening dress up a telephone pole, fending off her attacker with one spike-heeled shoe. *Sex Road to Ruin,* it was called. He'd read it so many times, he could practically recite it from memory. Another favorite featured a big-busted blonde in classic Jayne Mansfield fashion, her bosom spilling out of her dress, her mouth open in a parody of preorgasmic bliss. *Don't Say No to a Killer*, the cover read.

He was most proud of his Raymond Chandler collection, first editions of the Marlowe novels: *The Big Sleep*, with the perfidious Sternwood sisters lying in wait for the hapless detective to step into their trap; *Farewell, My Lovely*, the story of beautiful Velma and her black heart; *The Lady in the Lake*, two women, both of them dead and practically carbon copies of each other; and his personal favorite, *The Long Goodbye*, which for him was the story of a doomed romantic friendship. Forget Linda Loring—as far as Chase was concerned, the great love of Marlowe's life was Terry Lennox.

When Chase wasn't reading pulp detective stories, he put his time and education to good use, improving upon a prototype for a bionic exoskeleton that would allow paralyzed people the chance to walk again. In peacetime the exoskeleton had obvious applications, but in wartime, its sophisticated circuitry could be calibrated to allow a fully mobile soldier to carry loads well above his or her usual tolerance. Since battlefields were seldom paved in asphalt, the exoskeleton needed to work under any possible condition. Its design meant it could be configured for any type of terrain.

After several unsuccessful semesters at both Harvard and Yale, he'd dropped out in favor of the prestigious Summerwood School of Engineering at Cumbria. The English academic environment agreed with him, and he'd majored in applied science, finishing his undergraduate degree in three years before completing a master's degree in engineering. Since college, he'd experimented ("fiddled round," Juliet called it) with innovative designs for intuitive prototypes, including a thought-controlled helmet that could greatly enhance communication for persons with neuromuscular diseases, and a thin, breathable membrane that constituted a wearable computer. It would give visually disabled people the opportunity to read.

"Master Chase?" Juliet tapped on the door and stepped in. "That same"—she made a face—"gentleman is on the telephone. He insists he'll keep calling until you consent to speak to him. Shall I ring the police?"

Juliet, Chase knew, was formidable. The fact that she was female in no way hindered her from carrying out her duties, and her fierce devotion to him was unusual to say the least, for a domestic servant. There had been female butlers before, and no doubt there would be later, but Juliet was exceptional. She resembled the acclaimed actress Judi Dench in both looks and carriage, and spoke in a clipped accent that to Chase sounded like the Queen of England. Chase knew very little about her life before she came to work for his parents, but his mother had often hinted that Juliet was very well educated. She obviously came from an upper-class family and knew which utensil was the salad fork at dinner.

"How many times has he called?" Chase wheeled himself around to face her.

"He's been at it since earlier this afternoon. He claims...." Here Juliet raised one impeccable eyebrow. "...he is a school friend of yours."

"Let him keep calling," Chase said. "Just don't answer. I don't know any school friend who'd call me now."

"While I have your attention," Juliet said, "there's a matter of some urgency...."

"Oh?"

She cleared her throat, suddenly unable to meet his gaze. "As you are probably aware, Master Chase, I'm... getting on in years." She held her hands out in front of her, her fingers spread. The joints were swollen, and large red bumps had begun to form at the ends, near the nail. "Arthritis, or so the doctor says. In my legs as well." She clasped her hands behind her back. "I find it more and more difficult to meet my responsibilities here."

A cold chill ran through Chase, and he hunched his shoulders. "What do you mean?" he asked, alarmed. "Are you leaving?"

"Oh good God, no!" She huffed out an irritated breath. "I should like an *assistant*. An underbutler, if you like."

"Underbutler." Chase smirked. "That sounds dirty."

Juliet wasn't laughing. "Seriously, sir. I shall be seventy on my next birthday. If I am to continue here as your butler... I need some help."

"I bet you've already drafted the ad," Chase said, "haven't you?" And, when Juliet admitted this: "Of course. Hire two if you like."

"I only require the one," she said. She couldn't quite manage her usual frosty tone, and Chase thought he detected the hint of a smile lurking at the edges of her lips. "Thank you. Do you require anything else, Master Chase?"

"No thank you, Juliet. I'm... just fine."

He waited till her footsteps had vanished down the corridor before allowing his smile to slide off his face. Hiring someone meant bringing a stranger into the house... a stranger who'd have daily access to him, who would be waiting on him, bringing his meals, and helping him get ready for bed at night... assisting him into and out of the bath when and if he needed it, tying his shoes....

Chase laid his fingers against his temples, then pressed hard. There would be a stranger in the house, a man nobody knew, and he'd be touching Chase, putting his hands on him, looking at him. The looking was the worst of all. He felt the gaze of others as a judgment and a dismissal. He was selective about the people he allowed near him, fearing that casual gaze. He didn't want to be looked at.

Long ago a doctor had told him it had to do with the surgery— Chase had had plastic surgery to repair a cleft lip when he was four— but he couldn't see how something that had occurred so long ago could have any bearing on his life the way it was now. He barely remembered the entire episode beyond waking up in the recovery room of a large children's hospital and being given chocolate milk to drink. Still, the lip had become an obsession, something he touched and stroked when he was deep in thought or nervous. The surgeon had insisted the scars would fade in time, and so Chase endured some amount of playground bullying and cries of *catface, catface!* until the incisions healed. He pretended he didn't care.

He'd failed Juliet by not noticing that she was getting older, that her duties were likely to be more difficult at this stage of her life. He hadn't even bothered to ask her if she needed anything, if she was all right. Christ. His father would be ashamed of him, and he'd have every right to be. Chase had been brought up to respect others, to honor their needs as well as his own, to help them through life. His father would have already made provisions for Juliet's old age, for her possible retirement. He'd have set aside a trust or an annuity payable in her name, and somewhere for her to live, on the estate perhaps.

Chase sighed. Perhaps he could have one of the guest houses renovated and refurbished for her to live in when she was old and no longer able to work. She'd need a vehicle, something sturdy and reliable... perhaps a Land Rover, or maybe one of those Toyota SUVs with the fat wheels, good for any terrain. He wanted to call Juliet back and ask her, but he didn't know how to frame the question without offending her sensibilities....

And as far as an underbutler went, he couldn't imagine what kind of person would willingly shut himself up in this... *mausoleum* in exchange for wages. "This isn't a happy place." He said it aloud, even though there was no one to hear him. It hadn't been a happy place for a long, long time.

CHAPTER TWO

"IT SAYS here you have been educated as a journalist."

Walter Godfrey sat *very* still on the *very* edge of his chair and tried his *very* best to answer the English lady's questions. She was dressed in the sort of uniform Walter thought had died out with the dodo bird: narrow striped trousers, swallowtail coat, starched white shirt, and an actual, honest-to-God silk cravat. His first mistake had been to ask if she was the housekeeper. She looked like she could be James Bond's boss. "Yes, ma'am. That's my formal education. I spent my four years of college working in the hospitality industry."

She peered at him coldly through her half-moon reading glasses. Walter was convinced they were a prop, that she didn't really need them. Those steely-blue eyes could probably see through time and space. "The... hospitality industry." She drew one short, manicured fingernail down the page. Walter imagined it scoring deep grooves in his résumé, peeling off the thin veneer of lies and evasions he'd presented her with. "At the..." She glanced at him. "...Peekaboo Motel. What sort of an establishment is that?"

A hot flush crept up Walter's neck, blooming spectacularly in his ears. He adjusted his collar, which was suddenly too tight. "A hotel, ma'am. It's closed now. It used to cater to businessmen and their... er, lady friends, in a discreet atmosphere." He waited for her expression of disgust, but it never came.

"You can cook?" she asked.

"Of course." An outright lie. Walter's specialty was those ramen noodles you put in boiling water.

"And dishes," she said. "I assume you can wash them without breaking the lot?"

"Yes."

"Are you able to prepare cocktails, mixed drinks, that sort of thing?"

"I am." That was quite true. Walter's experience with bartending at the Peekaboo's in-house "lounge" was significant.

"Are you writing for newspapers now?" Her gaze said she'd tear his flesh off in great bloody chunks if he was. A journalist worming his way into the Gordon household under false pretenses, digging up dirt, and airing the dirty laundry? She'd probably grind his bones to make her bread.

Walter's hands were suddenly sweaty. He pressed them together between his knees. "Well, it's—"

"You are, aren't you?" Her smile was grim as death. "No doubt that's why you're here, to get some exclusive on Master Gordon and the rest of this household. What do they say about him in the city, hmm? Do they say he's lost his mind? What sorts of things does your newspaper print about him, Mr.… Godfrey?"

"We ran the story about a charity auction for his animal farm—"

"Sanctuary," she put in pitilessly. "It is a sanctuary for abused and unwanted animals."

"One of my colleagues wrote it. It was…." He trailed off, not sure what she wanted him to say.

"Never mind." She waved a hand. "I've read it. We keep up on the news around here. Master Chase insists on it." She laid his résumé aside. "As much as it pains me to say this"—*it doesn't*, Walter thought, *appear to pain her one bit*—"Mr. Godfrey, you won't find much of a story here. You are, however, welcome to try."

That was unexpected. *Very* unexpected. "I appreciate it."

"Not for the reasons you think." She smiled archly. "I mean it when I say there is absolutely nothing here to write about. If you are looking for sensation, you've come to the wrong place. I think you'll find us very dull, Mr. Godfrey. Very dull indeed."

His credence as an actual journalist wasn't the point, and Juliet Lavish knew it. Walter wondered how much the NYPD detectives had told her, pending his installation in the household.

Walter clasped his sweating hands together between his knees. "I greatly appreciate the opportunity to—"

"To worm your way in here," Juliet said. "Going to write an exclusive, are you?" Her gaze was like needles. "Show the world the inner workings of the place? Expose Master Chase to the common gaze?" She glanced over his résumé again, with great disdain.

"I'm interested in Mr. Gordon's charities," Walter said. "Really."

There was a significant silence while Juliet's gaze scoured him. "And if I allow you in here," she said, "and you abuse my trust so you can write some filthy article...." She leaned forward and smiled. It was not a pleasant smile. "Do you know what I would do to you, Mr. Godfrey?"

Drawn and quartered. Decapitated... impaled on a wooden stake....

"We have considerable legal resources," Juliet continued. "I would bring every single one of them to bear, Mr. Godfrey. Do we understand each other?"

Walter nodded mutely.

"You are here," Juliet said, "by request of the police, and for no other reason."

"Of course."

"There are certain things you must understand. Master Chase is... indisposed much of the time. He does not care for company. He is a gentleman of very refined tastes, and he has certain inviolable rules that must be followed."

Walter nodded mutely.

"There are no other family members in residence here. I regret to say...." She cleared her throat and continued in a brisk, almost strident tone of voice. "Master Chase's mother and father were killed in a plane crash some years ago, in Honduras. I expect you've heard. Master Chase is the only surviving descendent of his father, Elliott Gordon. As such, he is heir to the entire Gordon estate and is sometimes called upon to manage family interests overseas. Master Chase is an extremely private person. He dislikes scandals and public attention."

Walter blinked rapidly, suddenly very excited. A reclusive billionaire and his overprotective butler. It was journalistic gold. He could write a series of articles highlighting the various facets of the Gordon tragedy. It would sell like toothpaste. "Absolutely," he managed to say. "Naturally." He was beginning to sound like an idiot. No, scratch that. He already sounded like an idiot. *Just go in there and pretend*, Detective Schrade had said. The detective had made it seem like a really good idea. *Do some dusting, sweep the floor—just until we get the Masettis off your tail.*

Juliet pointed over her shoulder at a large portrait done in oils of a saggy-faced man with pronounced jowls, sitting in a wingback chair. His expression said he'd seen much of the world and it had disappointed him to the point of despair. "Sir Gideon, Master Chase's esteemed ancestor," she said. "The family founder, if you like. Came here from Aberdeen when Long Island was merely a provincial backwater." Her tone said Long Island—indeed, much of the country—was still merely a provincial backwater. "Do you have any questions for me, Mr. Godfrey?"

Walter opened his mouth, thought better of it, and shut it again. He shook his head.

"Very well. Now if you'll come with me, I'll introduce you to Master Chase."

He followed her down a wide hallway tiled in white marble, so smooth that he was briefly tempted to take off his shoes and skate across it in his stocking feet. There were niches set into the walls, each containing some ornament or sculpture, and fine art Walter had only ever seen in museums. At the end of the hallway, a grand staircase ascended in a wide, sweeping arc toward a second-story mezzanine carpeted in thick woolen rugs that spread out before him like Ali Baba's treasure cave.

Their footsteps made no sound, and Walter wondered if the thick carpeting was designed to muffle noise. Perhaps his new employer disliked excessive sensory input? From what Walter had heard and read, Chase Gordon was a member of the billionaire boys' club—a shallow, facile playboy who only cared where his next thrill was coming from. As a young boy, he'd been sent to a series of exclusive, private prep schools and was expelled from each of them in turn. He'd gone to college, most notably at Harvard, where, not finding it to his liking, he'd quit in the middle of the winter semester to thumb his way home from Boston to Long Island. The next autumn had seen him enrolled in Yale, which didn't stick either. Walter suspected Gordon's wealth insulated him to the point that nothing in the real world made much of an impression.

It would be a pleasure, Walter thought, *to skewer him in print*. Eleanor might even give him his old job back. At the very least, he'd make enough to pay his rent.

Juliet stopped in front of a thick wooden door some ten feet high and extracted an old-fashioned skeleton key from her waistcoat pocket. She fitted it into the lock and twisted it clockwise. A solid clunking sound resonated from somewhere deep inside the door. "Master Chase inhabits this wing of the house. Unless you are specifically summoned by either Master Chase or myself, you will not enter this area. Is that clear?"

"Whatever you say."

She gestured him through, then locked the door behind them both. "When Master Chase's parents were alive, we kept a full complement of staff. Now that...." She let the rest of it hang there. "I am the only full-time servant, with the exception of George, the gardener. We employ day servants, and there are support staff whom I call in as they are needed. A young woman comes during the day to clean. She always goes home at night."

"What's her name?"

Juliet drew up and looked at him. "What does it matter?" she asked sharply. "You will have no need to speak to her. If I find that you and she have been fraternizing, you will be summarily dismissed and expelled from these premises."

Jeez, lady, take the stick out of your butt. "I'm not interested in the cleaning woman." He offered her a wry smile. "I'm gay."

Juliet looked him up and down, and nodded. "Good. That greatly simplifies matters."

They passed through an arch to what looked like a sort of waiting room, a large antechamber furnished with couches and leather armchairs. At either side of the door, there was a wingback chair, each with its own small table and lamp.

Maybe he was expected to sit out here, polishing the silverware, while he waited for orders from the *Mohstah.*

"—this way, if you *please.*" Juliet stood beside another heavy oak door, waiting for him. "This is the door to Master Chase's private suite. I will introduce you and then you will be alone with him. I'm sure there are some questions he would like to ask you before you begin your employment here."

"You're allowing me to stay?" Walter asked. He wondered, again, how much Detective Schrade had had to tell her, to get her to agree to this. Surely the woman knew the truth, but did she know the whole truth?

"So it would seem," Juliet said dryly. "Since you need sanctuary and we very much need an underbutler."

She pushed open the door to a sumptuous private library, paneled in dark wood. The light was dim, and it took a moment for Walter to see the man sitting by one of the long french windows. "Master Chase, Walter Godfrey, your new underbutler," Juliet said before stepping smoothly backward and leaving him alone in the room—alone with the very rich and very famous Chase Gordon.

"Don't just stand there like an idiot." The man sitting by the window beckoned to him. "Come over where I can see you. It's as dark as Satan's asshole in here."

Walter did as he was told. He almost expected to find Gordon on a velvet throne, sipping champagne, surrounded by piles of money and beautiful, half-naked women. He wasn't prepared to see a pale, angry-looking man wearing a dressing gown over lounge pants and a T-shirt, and sitting slumped in a wheelchair. Too late, Walter hid his expression of surprise. "Oh… I beg your pardon." The figure at the funeral, Walter thought, sitting in the wheelchair, the one everybody had thought was some elderly relative, indisposed… had been Chase himself.

"She didn't tell you. Juliet didn't tell you I'm an invalid… a cripple, as it were."

He was about Walter's own age, dark-haired and dark-eyed, handsome…. *God*, he was handsome. He wore his hair combed straight back over his head, the better to showcase his large brown eyes with their thick lashes. His chin was faintly stubbled with perhaps a day's worth of beard, but it didn't look messy, not on him. His face was lean, with high cheekbones and a certain suppleness around the mouth; Walter had seen his face in so many photographs, splashed on the front pages of newspapers and all over social media, but no photograph did him justice. He was beautiful. He was more beautiful in person than any man had a right to be.

"I… no, she… she didn't." He didn't want to say he wasn't reacting to Chase's disability, but to Chase himself, to his overwhelming physical beauty and the air of utter solitude that wrapped itself around him like a cape.

Gordon held out a hand, and Walter grasped the cool fingers tentatively. "Chase Gordon." His tone was friendly, but he didn't smile, only regarded Walter with his head cocked to the side. Walter could detect the light scarring from a cleft palate repair on Gordon's upper lip. He spoke with a very slight lisp that was absolutely charming. "Did she tell you not to molest the cleaning lady?"

"I'm gay." He was starting to get tired of saying it. "I assure you, sir, your cleaning lady is in no danger from me."

"Gay?"

"Yes, sir." Walter wondered if Gordon would dismiss him on the grounds of his sexuality. He almost hoped he would. It would make one hell of a human rights case, and he'd get to write the exclusive for the paper.

"Good." Gordon seemed unconcerned about Walter's actual qualifications for the job, or maybe that was Juliet's domain. He wheeled himself over to a large upright cabinet set against the wall. "Do you like music?"

"Me, sir?"

"You're the only one here." Gordon lifted the top of the cabinet, revealing an old-style record player. "What kind do you like?"

"Uhh... jazz, I guess. The old standards, you know. Basie and Holiday, Satchmo." He shrugged. "Some of the West Coast stuff is good."

"Anything you don't like?" Gordon drew a record out of its cardboard sleeve.

"Later Sinatra gets on my nerves... that big, brassy Vegas sound, like he's got something to prove. I don't like it. His early stuff's good, though."

"T Bone Burnett?"

"Sure. T Bone's great."

Gordon put the record on the turntable and carefully dropped the needle.

Walter stood awkwardly nearby, wondering if he ought to sit. There were no rules for this sort of thing—at least, no rules he was aware of. Since he was the butler, he figured he'd better stay standing. Anything else could be misconstrued as uninvited familiarity. He waited till the first song was over, then awkwardly asked if Gordon wanted anything.

"Do I want anything?" He reached out one long, slim hand and turned the record player off. "I want a lot of things."

Great. Here's where he gets all high and mighty so he can prove he's the boss. "Of course, sir."

"I want you to sit down and listen to this record with me," Gordon said sulkily. "I want you to have a brandy—you do drink alcohol, don't you? Actually, it's cognac, but who cares?" He wheeled himself over to where a decanter was set on a side table.

"Yes, I drink." A hot flush crept up Walter's neck. "Uh, socially, I mean. Not... you know, I'm not an alcoholic."

"That's too bad." Gordon passed him a glass brimming over with brandy, poured one just like it for himself, and dumped the entire contents down his throat. "Personally, I love my vices, but I suppose you're a good little boy," he said, smirking. "Always does what he's told. Goes to bed early, says his prayers—"

"I'm an agnostic," Walter put in. "Sir." He sipped the cognac, enjoyed its subtle fire sliding down his throat. "Very nice. Cuvee Leonie, isn't it?"

"Eighteen fifty-eight," Gordon replied. "I'm surprised."

Surprised that I can identify the brand, or surprised that I recognize good cognac? Once, the owner of the *Times* had invited some of the reporters to partake in a soiree in the boardroom, after the newspaper had broken a huge story concerning insider trading on Wall Street. It was the one and only time Walter had ever tasted Cuvee Leonie. "Very good, sir." He finished the brandy and laid his empty glass down carefully. The liquor burned a warm streak all the way to his stomach. "Is there anything else, sir?" It appeared the strange ritual was at an end. For a second, no more than that, Walter thought he saw something cross Gordon's handsome face, something sad and remote and terribly lonely. Of course, it could have been his imagination.

"No," Gordon said quietly. "Your presence is no longer required." He turned his back.

Walter had been dismissed.

"So you sat there and listened to his records," Billy Newman said. He shook his head in what he probably thought indicated disbelief. "And that's it."

The reporters' bullpen was oppressively noisy, and Walter had to lean in close to hear what Billy was saying. An argument had broken out at the far end of the room, and one of the more senior journalists was very publicly firing his secretary. *Good old* Times, Walter thought, *and I don't even miss it.* He suspected Brian Schrade wouldn't be too happy that he'd seen fit to show himself at the office this morning, but Schrade didn't need to know everything.

"That's it. We sat there and listened to his records." Walter had stopped in at the paper to see whether anything of interest had developed in his absence. A manhole had exploded near Battery Park, two teenage girls stabbed a third inside a Macy's department store, and someone had tried to blow up a coffee shop in Tribeca. None of it appealed to Walter. He was on his own kind of hunt. The newsroom's usual frenetic activity competed with a cacophony of ringing phones and shouting. "He's not what you'd think." He was reluctant to discuss Gordon casually, even with someone like Billy, who was probably the closest thing to a best friend Walter had. He wasn't boisterously social like most others at the paper, and apart from infrequent forays to a neighborhood bar, he preferred to keep his own company unless his participation was absolutely necessary.

"But there's an old lady, right?" Billy snagged a chair from the empty cubicle and sat next to Walter.

"Do you mind?" Walter elbowed him playfully. "I'm reading my e-mail."

"You don't get e-mail." Billy bumped Walter with his shoulder. "You don't work here, remember?" He lowered his voice and spoke directly into Walter's ear. "What's he like? I've heard he's smokin' hot. Is that true?"

"He's gorgeous," Walter said. Recalling Chase's handsome features sent a titillating little shiver through him. "Seems kind of lonely, though." He suspected Chase could no longer rely on his former playboy image to ward off intrusions into his privacy—he hadn't been seen in public for over a decade, and there were even rumors he'd died. The Chase Gordon of the old days was all flash and glamour, handsome and rich and carefree. The Chase Gordon who Walter had seen was a sad, lonely man too proud to admit he yearned for a little company. It was true what people said: money really didn't buy happiness. If you were lucky, it bought a temporary surcease from the more unpleasant vagaries of life, and nothing more.

"Alec Pratt was here yesterday," Billy said casually. He ran a hand through his sandy hair and squinted like someone in pain. "He was asking where you were. I mean, he was asking *everybody*."

Alarm bells clanged a warning inside Walter's skull. "What did you tell him?"

"I told him you were on assignment." He shrugged. "It sounded better than saying you got fired."

"Fuck." Walter cursed softly. "What the hell does he want with me?"

Alec Pratt was the only son of the paper's current owner, Franklyn Pratt, and the kind of spoiled, privileged young idiot everyone assumed had disappeared with the Jazz Age. He considered the newsroom his personal playground and himself something of a journalist. Mostly he hung around and got in the way. Now and then he'd fixate on a random staff member who appealed to him on some personal level and make the unwary man or woman his new best friend. Alec spent a great deal of time and column inches remarking favorably on the fortunes of certain Manhattan "businessmen," albeit under an alias. Shunned by the other reporters and regarded as a snitch and a nuisance, he nevertheless managed to get hold of some pretty juicy information that he disseminated in shallow, op-ed pieces buried in the back pages of the newspaper. It was almost like Pratt was trying to shield the mob, rather than exposing their nefarious deeds.

"I think he wants to make you his new BFF," Billy said.

"You didn't tell him where I was, did you?" Walter's heart thumped against his ribs. "Please tell me—"

"Relax." Billy held up a hand. "I told him you were covering the by-election at City Hall. He doesn't know they kicked you out. He's been down there every day this week looking for you."

This was bad. Pratt was a pain in the ass, but he wasn't stupid. Eventually he would figure out Walter wasn't at City Hall and would begin his search in earnest. "If he finds out…." Walter forced himself to calm down and breathe. He leaned toward Billy, speaking quietly. "If he finds out I'm chasing down the Gordon story, he'll shit kittens." If he found out Walter had been hired as Chase's butler, he'd shit bricks.

"I'll hold him off," Billy promised. He glanced around the office, checking to see if they'd been overheard. "Trust me."

"You can only hold him off for so long," Walter said. He pressed the heels of his hands into his eyes. Yes, that was a headache starting—right there, behind his left eye. He'd have a screaming migraine before the day was over. "He'll know something is up."

"Then you better hurry and get the dirt on Chase Gordon." Billy got up and slid the borrowed chair back into its cubicle. "Before Alec beats you to it." He cast a quick look around the newsroom. "You ever hear anything about those two guys? The ones who shot at you?"

"No," Walter said. "I guess I'm off their radar." He turned off the computer and stood. "Gordon thinks I'm on an errand." He took his coat from the back of his chair and shrugged into it. "Later."

"On an errand doing what?" Billy called after him—but by then, Walter was at the elevator and he pretended not to hear.

THE RECORD shop Walter had in mind was one he'd frequented himself, all through his adolescence and young manhood. Tucked away on a tiny side street in Greenwich Village, it carried obscure music by even more obscure artists, including jazz greats that hardly anybody remembered anymore.

His father had brought him here when he was almost too young to remember, holding his hand while they made their way through the labyrinth of empty Sunday morning streets. Pop always insisted they get up early on Sundays, and he'd cook a big breakfast and they'd read the paper while they ate. Walter's mother had died when he was just a baby, from an infection caused by a scratched arm—she worked as a seamstress in the garment district—that progressed to septicemia. His father looked after him, brought him up all by himself without advice or help from anybody. He'd made sure Walter was clean and well-fed, that his schoolbag was packed, that he had adequate milk money for lunch and recess times. There were no helpful aunts or hovering grandmas waiting to lend a hand, unless you counted Mrs. Temmolini on the second floor, who owned a fruit shop and whose maternal instincts ran to offering Walter covert sips from the fifth of vodka she carried in her purse.

Before his retirement, Walter's father had been a stevedore, loading and unloading freight at the docks. Two or three evenings a week, he played trumpet in a jazz band, just hanging out with some other guys from work and running through their repertoire of all the old tunes. On Sundays, he and Walter would go to the Village and buy a record. It was a ritual.

The store was called The Aqueduct—the name meant nothing to Walter—and was located below street level, underneath a shop that sold pipes and cigarette makers, rolling papers, glass tubes for smoking crystal meth, and perfidiously large bongs made out of unusual materials. The Aqueduct was owned by two brothers whose names Walter never knew—they mumbled—and whose preferred location throughout all transactions was sitting behind the counter on folding chairs.

"Get me some of that Wynton Marsalis," Walter's dad would say, pointing. He knew where everything was, but one didn't just go into The Aqueduct and help yourself. The brothers regarded themselves as more than mere shopkeepers: they were curators of a vast and varied collection that only they were allowed to handle.

One of the brothers would raise himself from his chair, cough, blow his nose, and say, "Come down here." Walter and his father would follow along behind him until he stopped before a shelf or bin and said, "Right here." It was how Walter learned about music.

The bell over the door still jingled the way it always had when Walter stepped inside. The two brothers—gray-haired now and bent with age—knew him on sight and had long since allowed him the right to pick through the records as he saw fit. It was a privilege granted to few others. Even Walter's dad was still obliged to ask for the things he wanted from the shelves, a fact that galled him to no end.

Walter found an early Art Tatum, but Tatum was sometimes a bit frenetic for Walter's tastes. Influential, yes; technically brilliant, yes—but chaotic. He preferred the slumbering ironies of Freddie Hubbard's laid-back melodies, climbing and retreating slowly and lingering along the way to tease and suggest there was more there than met the ear. Dizzy Gillespie's clean, bright trumpet was always in season, and so was Louis "Satchmo" Armstrong. Walter hesitated to introduce Benny Goodman or Glenn Miller, fearing the big band sound would rattle around disconsolately in the huge, echoing Gordon manor. Perhaps Zoot Sims, smooth and mellow, yet deeply introspective….

He found two records—vinyl records; the brothers didn't allow the blasphemy of CDs—and paid for them and said his good-byes in time to catch the train at Sheridan Square. He was walking with his head down, immersed in his own thoughts, stepping over the various litter on the sidewalk, and evading a fluttering newspaper as it sailed toward him, caught on the wind.

"Hey."

The summons came from somewhere behind him. Walter didn't bother to look around. Most likely it was some down-on-his-luck drunk looking for a donation.

"Hey, you!"

He glanced back as he turned the corner. There was a man behind him—a big man. Walter had never seen him before, and he didn't think it wise to engage in some light chitchat. The guy looked like the stereotypical movie goon: a big gorilla with a small head and no neck, and hands the size of full-grown turkeys. He wasn't the man from Divvy's; this one seemed to have an even keener interest in Walter.

"Don't run away! I wanna talk to ya!"

Walter slipped down a narrow street off Maiden Lane. The henchman—or whatever he was—quickened his pace. Walter dropped any pretense of nonchalance and ran. He ran past the offices of *The Village Sentinel* and a restaurant called Pita Place and a long line of temporary plastic signs advertising HOAGIES HOAGIES HOAGIES. He passed yet another sandwich shop, a toy store, a sex shop with a display of bondage gear in the window, and a combination tailor shop and Laundromat that was probably a front for some mob operation. It took fifteen minutes—he'd often timed himself—to get from The Aqueduct to the Sheridan Street Station, if he was walking fast, and Walter almost always walked fast.

He glanced back. The gorilla with the turkey hands was gone. Maybe he'd mistaken Walter for someone else, some other poor bastard he'd been sent to beat the crap out of. Walter grimaced, yearning for the relative safety of the train station. He turned his head....

...and ran face-first into a torso the approximate size of a traveling snack truck.

"No, don't run," the man said. "I just wanna ax ya a question, that's all." He laid a friendly paw on Walter's shoulder, gripping it. The touch so far was gentle, but Walter knew if he pissed this guy off, he'd end up with a few bruises and broken bones. At least. "Just wanna ax ya."

"So go ahead," Walter snapped, "and ax me."

The gorilla walked him backward until Walter was pressed against the brick wall of an adjacent building. "You the guy that writes for the *Times*?" When Walter didn't answer right away, the man slapped his cheek gently. "I ax ya: are you the guy that writes for the *New York Times*?"

"Y-Yes." Walter despised the quaver in his voice. "I am."

"See?" The goon slapped his face again, a little harder this time. "That wasn't so difficult, was it?" He leaned closer. Walter could feel the man's hot breath on his face. Minty fresh, oddly enough, but he supposed even henchmen had access to good dental care nowadays. "You the guy that wrote about the construction job, ain't ya? You're that guy."

Walter confirmed that yes, he was indeed "that guy."

"So where's a smart guy like you get his information?" The gorilla's hand clutched the front of Walter's shirt, twisting it around his neck. "I'm just axing. Just a civil talk between gentlemen."

"I had sources down at City Hall," Walter whispered. The knotted shirt was cutting off his air. Small black spots had begun to dance in front of his eyes. "An alderman... his secretary."

"This alderman told you some stuff, huh?" He shook Walter gently. "And you just hadta go ahead and print it." He didn't wait for Walter's reply this time. "We heard you was fired from the paper. Does Mr. Masetti know you're back?"

The shirt squeezed tight, cutting off his air. *This is a stupid way to die*, Walter thought. *A really stupid way to die.* He hadn't even listened to his records yet.

"Don't do it no more." The hulking man released his hold on Walter's shirt.

Walter staggered back against the building, gasping for air.

"We're sick and tired of telling you. Mr. Masetti don't wanna see your byline on any story's gotta do with him or his friends." He stepped back and pointed one meaty forefinger at Walter. "You got a pretty face. Be a shame if somebody messed it up for you." He bent and gathered Walter's records. "Here," he said, shoving the paper-wrapped package into Walter's chest. "If you got any brains, you'll get out of the city. Go on home and be a good boy."

THE WESTBOUND train was more or less empty at this hour of the morning, the rush-hour crowd having already been decanted into the offices and mercantile spaces of the city. Come four that afternoon, the entire process would be reversed; the gleaming towers of Manhattan would give forth vast hordes whose only concern was getting home, away from the noise and stench of the metropolis.

Walter found a seat near the back of the car and sank into it gratefully. Someone had left a Batman comic behind, and Walter thumbed through it, but he was more tired than usual and the story couldn't hold his interest. He told himself it was simple fatigue. He was working too hard.

He'd spent the previous day helping Juliet move furniture, put away the summer clothes, and bring out the winter ones. October had given way to November, and already there was a chill in the air and a cold morning mist that portended frost sooner rather than later. Chase Gordon had an astonishing array of clothes, more clothes than Walter had ever seen in his life, outside of the textile display at the Smithsonian in DC. There were the usual suits in summer-weight wool, and silk ties that cost more than Walter made in a month. There were tennis whites and sailing outfits, clothes for fancy dress and clothes for hanging around the house—all with their attendant haberdashery. There was even, for some reason not readily apparent, a full set of cricket whites and a bat. These were packed away in cedar-lined trunks that slid neatly into the closets and held warm-weather clothing for the balance of the year.

The bed linens too had to be changed, silk and cotton switched for flannel and huge feather duvets. Only three bedrooms in the vast house were currently in use: Juliet's room, Walter's small apartment, and Chase's master suite. All the others were vacant, save the servants' quarters at the back of the house, where George the gardener had a flat of his own. The master suite was vast, comprising nearly half of the second floor. It contained not only Chase's enormous bed—a thick slab of memory foam on a custom-designed stainless-steel pedestal imported from Sweden—but a luxurious en suite featuring the largest shower stall Walter had ever seen, with numerous nozzles set into the high ceiling, intended to mimic rainfall. This could be adjusted for anything from a gentle mist to a thundering downpour.

Neither Walter nor Juliet was responsible for heavy cleaning or maintenance. The cleaning lady came in every day to handle light housekeeping, and a full complement of personnel came in three times a week. "I run the household," Juliet had told him. "You run Master Chase."

Walter had hinted around, trying to find out what was wrong with Gordon, but she would say nothing. And yet he hadn't always been disabled. Walter remembered seeing many photographs where he was standing alongside family or friends, seemingly hale and hearty. Obviously his disability was a fairly recent thing—the result of injury or illness, perhaps. It was hard to tell because hardly anyone saw him anymore. Since his parents' death, he'd withdrawn from all society. It was rumored that he'd suffered a mental breakdown, but Walter wasn't willing to believe supposed facts that came from unproven sources.

He leaned back against the headrest and closed his eyes. The motion of the train was hypnotic, rocking him into a state of not-quite sleep. He was hungry too, and his neck hurt from his shirt being twisted tight around it. Maybe Juliet would have something good for lunch, something involving thick sandwiches and hot soup, and pie for afterward.

Now that Walter had come to work for Gordon, Juliet had more time for other duties, and she had taken to the culinary side of things with a vengeance. She knew quite a few fine French recipes, but her specialty was, as she'd put it, "good old English stodge." Walter worried the seemingly endless parade of soups, stews, roasts, and meat pies with thick pastry was wreaking havoc on his physique. Thankfully, the manor house was outfitted with a complete gym, where he spent his off-hours running on the treadmill and lifting weights. Chase, too, made use of the equipment, although never when Walter or Juliet was around. Walter wondered how he managed but didn't have the nerve to ask. Maybe the wheelchair was mere affectation, and Gordon didn't really need it. No, that wasn't true. Walter had seen him trying to stand one day, supporting himself by holding on to a table, and Gordon had nearly fallen flat on his face. His legs were useless. Walter felt embarrassed, watching him, and so he'd turned away before Chase knew he was there.

It must be terrible, he thought, to have everything in the world you wanted, except the use of your legs. Money meant nothing in that situation. He was richer than God but still couldn't walk. Surely Chase had run the gamut of specialists, seeking a cure for his condition. Was that why Juliet Lavish had stayed on so long as his butler? Because he needed to be taken care of? How much, Walter wondered, was he capable of doing on his own?

The train slowed, then bumped to a hissing stop at the platform. Walter stepped out, zipping his jacket against the chill wind. He'd left the station and crossed to the parking lot to pick up his car when he heard someone calling his name. He turned slowly.

"Walt!" A lanky, rawboned young man ran up to him, panting slightly from the exertion. He wasn't quite as tall as Walter's modest five feet ten inches, and his abnormally pale skin lent him an air of fragility. "This is such a pleasure," he said formally. "My dear, old friend. I thought I'd never see you again." He caught Walter's hand and wrung it vigorously before dropping it.

Walter flexed his fingers, uncertain if he retained feeling there or not. "Good to see you, Alec." Alec Pratt. Of all the people he'd rather not meet, today or any day. Walter unlocked his car. "Wish I could stay and chat—"

"I'll ride with you." Pratt went around to the passenger side and tried the handle of the locked door. "How far you going?" He blinked his ice-blue eyes at Walter, confused. "I can't get in."

Walter ignored him and got in. He turned the key in the ignition. "Sorry, Alec. I guess I'll see you around."

Franklyn Pratt, Alec's father, despised the Gordon family and had been trying for ages to get dirt he could print. Obviously Alec had heard about Walter being admitted to the Gordon mansion, which probably irked him, since it was the kind of story Alec liked. Several years ago the *Times* had printed a piece about Chase Gordon's mother, asserting that she'd spent many years in an "insane asylum" before Elliot Gordon had consented to marry her. Whether it was true or not, Walter didn't know. Mrs. Gordon *had* spent some time at a private clinic, but such information nowadays usually meant you were getting work done. Women of a certain age went away for a "rest" and reappeared several months later with new cheekbones, new noses, and new chins. Alec's assertion that Mrs. Gordon was insane saw him on the wrong end of a libel suit. It was unknown how he'd managed to wriggle out of that one.

He put the car in reverse. "See you later, Alec."

"Wait!" Pratt clung to the doorframe like a barnacle. "This is important. You need to listen."

Walter accelerated slowly, making him run alongside the car.

"Drop the Masetti story, Walter. For your own good."

"No comment, Alec." *It's none of your goddamn business*, he thought. If he wanted to write about the Masetti properties, he would. Why would Alec care? The Masettis had nothing to do with him, nor he with them.

"You don't want to do this." Alec was panting, trying to keep up with the car. "I mean it."

"Thanks," Walter replied. He pressed hard on the gas, and Pratt was forced to let go. When Walter glanced in the rearview mirror, he saw Alec was standing in the middle of the road, watching him drive away. He was red-faced and winded, breathing hard.

"Don't be a fool, Walter!" he called.

His insistence that Walter bury the story seemed genuine. Which bothered Walter. Maybe Pratt was on to something. It seemed unlikely, since Pratt's journalistic prowess was nonexistent and he lacked the initiative to track down a story on his own, but he seemed serious enough. He seemed very serious, in fact, almost afraid, like he knew something....

Walter took the long way back to Gordonstoun, on the off chance that Alec might have followed him in another car. He drove the winding back roads, passing through scenic small towns and villages, some of them with historic names, their heritage carefully encapsulated in monuments and mile markers, and painted wooden signs advertising cemeteries where local notables were buried. Walter loved cemeteries—in fact, they were some of his favorite places in the whole world—but he had never gone to Gary's grave. He'd never ventured past the gate, knowing as he did that Gary was gone and what was in the ground with his name over it was nothing but dust and ashes. He knew some people, even people he worked with at the newspaper, made regular visits to the graves of loved ones, leaving offerings of flowers and having conversations. *What was the point?* Walter wondered. There was no one there.

A late-model Jaguar was parked in the circular driveway when Walter drove up to Gordonstoun. This in itself wasn't unusual—it was Long Island, after all. The car was big, shiny, British racing green, and looked as if it had just come out of a very large and very pristine box.

Walter's heart sank. "For fuck's sake." He had an idea who the car's owner might be. He pulled up to the servants' entrance at the back of the house and went inside.

Juliet was in the kitchen, standing over an ironing board on which was positioned a pale ivory tablecloth edged in fancy cutwork embroidery. She nodded as he entered but said nothing. Juliet could be a woman of few words at times, wholly devoted to Chase Gordon and the memory of his parents. She entertained no gossip, indulged in no rumors, and did not countenance such things from others.

Walter had no problem imagining her as a faintly jokey set piece in some Universal monster movie, the butler who sees all and knows all but stays absolutely mum. Juliet Lavish would, Walter thought, know the mad scientist was sewing together a monster in the basement—but as long as the monster was clean and tidy and minded his manners, she would tolerate him. Barely. Walter often felt as if Juliet were looking down her faintly aristocratic nose at him, dismissing him as just another gauche American—a mountebank. A bounder.

"Walter."

He stopped on the verge of stepping out into the corridor, glad to get away from her silent disapproval. "Juliet." *So close*, he thought. *I was almost there.*

"I should like you to prepare luncheon for Master Chase and his guest. He is entertaining a gentleman of the press." She waved a hand in the general direction of the kitchen table. "We are to serve broiled free-range chicken with new potatoes. I've already made the salad. It's in the refrigerator." When he didn't speak, she turned to look at him. "Well?"

There's always one thing, Walter thought, *to trip you up.* "Er… broiled chicken?" Free-range? What "gentleman of the press" was Chase entertaining?

"Broiled chicken. Under the broiler. In the oven." She spoke in short, staccato bursts, as if he were a child, or an idiot. "You do know about the oven, do you not?" The huge, commercial-grade Sub-Zero crouched under an equally massive range hood and seemed to glare at the room like it wanted it to suffer. "Chicken, under the broiler, and don't forget to baste with the drippings throughout, or it will be dry. I'm going into the city for several hours, but I shall be back early this evening."

"Baste with the drippings," he repeated, as if he knew what she was talking about. "Of course." He begged leave to go to his room and change, with the promise he would be right back.

He shut and locked the door behind him and stowed the records he'd bought in the top drawer of his bureau. When "in residence," as Juliet put it, Walter wore the standard servant's outfit for the Gordon manor, a copy of Juliet's own. He wore striped trousers over highly polished black shoes, a starched shirt, a swallowtail coat, and, depending on the time of day, either a silk cravat or a regular tie. He shucked his street clothes and struggled into his uniform, cursing the tie that refused to knot correctly.

Cook… she wanted him to cook. She wanted him to put a dead bird inside the oven and turn on the heat… cookbook… he needed a cookbook. *Why did I ever leave the paper,* he fumed. *I had my own cubicle and everything.* He should have fought harder to keep his job. He'd still be there, writing his little stories about the clogged storm sewers of New York City and the latest political debacle at City Hall. *This is what ambition gets you.* Hell, he'd write obituaries after this. Want ads. The lonely hearts column. Recipes, for chrissake.

Recipes.

He retrieved his laptop from under the bed. Gordon manor had its own dedicated Internet server, and the Wi-Fi was more than adequate. *There are times,* he thought wildly, *when a man needs to save his own life.* Chicken recipes, broiled chicken, roasted chicken… it couldn't be that hard.

Set aside agar-agar jelly pearls... crush juniper berries gently with the back of a spoon, just to the point of bruising... add half a cup of wild mushrooms, freshly picked....

I am so fucked, he thought, panicked.

A chat window popped up from the taskbar—Billy. *Wut up?*

Not now, Walter typed. *Chicken.*

He arrived back in the kitchen to find Juliet gone. Good. At least she wouldn't be standing around and criticizing him. *You can do this. Anybody can do this.* He found the knob for the broiler and turned it on. The chicken was in the fridge, laid out on a clean plate covered with plastic wrap. Was he supposed to rinse it first? Maybe you had to put something on it, salt and pepper? Yes, salt and pepper would be a good place to start. He applied generous amounts of both and patted it into the chicken with his hands. Chicken juice... something about raw chicken juice. He turned on the hot water and scrubbed his hands, then dirtied them again picking up the chicken to put it on a tray. Washed his hands again. Opened the oven door and slid the chicken under the broiler. Was the oven on? How hot was it supposed to be? He turned it to 500 degrees and hoped it would be sufficient.

Salad. Juliet said she'd already made the salad. It was in the fridge. He found it easily, but there was no trace of bottled salad dressing anywhere. Goddammit, the wretched woman probably made her own from scratch.

For one terrible moment, Walter thought he might break down and cry. What went in salad dressing? Did anyone know? He called Billy at the paper and asked.

"I dunno," Billy replied, "vinegar and stuff, I guess." Someone spoke in the background. "Hold up," Billy said, and Walter heard him talking to a woman who was probably Eleanor. "El says lemon juice and olive oil. Throw some herbs and stuff in there."

"Really?" It was that simple?

"And shake it up good." Billy hung up.

Walter had the salad dressing under relative control when a loud, shrieking noise cut through the kitchen. "The smoke alarm. Fuck." Thick clouds of black smoke roiled from the oven, very quickly turning the air a dull, unhealthy gray. He dove for the oven door and let it fall open, reaching for the hot grill pan without thinking; it seared a jagged hole in his palm, the same hand only recently healed from his nasty encounter with a bottle of mustard. He dropped the pan. The chicken—now badly charred—slid off the pan as if in slow motion and fell on the floor. The pain in his hand was so intense, it brought him to the edge of tears.

"Walter?" Chase called from the dining room.

Walter stuck his burned hand into his pants pocket and went to answer the summons. "Sir?"

There was another man with Chase, but he stood in the deep shadow of the massive dining room, and all Walter could make out was dark hair and a pale face atop a bulky frame that seemed vaguely familiar but which excited no true recognition. He fixed his attention on Chase. His burned hand throbbed in time with his pulse. The pain was making him physically sick.

"Would you mix a couple of whiskey sours and bring them to us in the library?" Neither Chase nor his guest said anything about the smoke emanating from the kitchen.

"Of course, sir." Walter returned to the kitchen and hastily dumped a measure of whiskey into a cocktail shaker with sugar and lemon juice. He shook it up as well as he was able with one hand, thankful it was at least something he could do. During his tenure at the Peekaboo Motel, he'd learned how to mix every kind of cocktail there was, and even invented a couple new ones. He placed the drinks carefully on a tray and went down the hall to the library. The door was ajar, but Walter knocked—with his foot. "Your drinks, sir." He laid the drinks on a small side table with a flourish.

"Walter Godfrey. Imagine seeing you so soon again."

Franklyn Pratt. The man standing in the dining room, smirking like a courtesan, was Franklyn fucking Pratt. The same Franklyn Pratt who owned the *New York Times*—the Franklyn Pratt who was Walter's boss. Walter's former boss. This was bad, Walter thought. This was very, very bad.

He straightened, the tray in his one good hand. His suspicion about who owned the Jaguar in the driveway was suddenly confirmed. "Good day, sir. It's nice to see you again."

"Walter," Chase said, "Mr. Pratt here is from the *Times*. We've been talking about Shep's Place."

"It's an animal charity," Pratt said. "Mr. Gordon maintains a number of animal rescue farms, especially for abused and unwanted animals. The *Times* is involved in publicity for the annual ball." In other words,

Pratt had made sure he'd be front and center at what was going to be an important social function. When it came to getting themselves noticed, the Pratts were about as shy as the Kardashian family. "It's a wonderful cause," Pratt said. Walter detected a hint of smugness in his tone.

"I agree." Walter had heard of it. Shep's Place raised astonishing amounts of money—and public and corporate support—for the "rescue ranches," as they were called. The Christmas ball was held every year at the Waldorf ballroom and was The Event of the Season. "That's great," he enthused. "A good cause."

"A wonderful cause," Pratt said. Why the hell did Franklyn Pratt have to drive all the way to Long Island just to pay a visit to Chase Gordon about a charity ball? Wasn't that the sort of thing his toadies usually took care of, over the phone or by e-mail? "Do I smell something burning?" Pratt asked. "I could swear there's something burning in here."

"I had a little accident in the kitchen," Walter replied, with as much dignity as he could muster under the circumstances. "I'm afraid lunch will be rather delayed, Master Chase."

"It's fine, Walter. Just do the best you can."

Walter retreated to the kitchen and began to pick up the burned chicken off the floor. His hand hurt worse than ever, the pain in his palm radiating up his arm and into the center of his chest. Rather than bending to retrieve the burned meat, he knelt on the floor, his right arm cradled against his body. A fluid-filled blister of remarkable size had appeared on his palm. The damned thing would handicap him for the better part of a week—if he managed to stay employed here for a week, which he now seriously doubted. Many of the *Times* staffers ate lunch at Divvy's, a small pub around the corner from Walter's office. Pratt or one of his cronies would make sure Walter's new "employment" at Gordonstoun came up in conversation, and one of the office loudmouths—Alec Pratt, probably—would waste no time alerting his father about Walter's latest project. Pratt the Younger would be sent to Gordonstoun in his place, and Walter would be lucky if he lived past the middle of next week. Where was the "guy" Schrade had promised him, the one who was supposed to keep an eye on him, keep him safe?

The kitchen door swung back and Pratt was there, tugging imperiously at the hem of his Brooks Brothers suit jacket. "I have to talk to you."

"I'm, ah, rather busy at the moment, sir," Walter replied. At the office he did his best to stay out of Franklyn Pratt's way. He was surprised Pratt even knew who he was.

"I am not joking, Walter." Pratt's pale eyes tended to take up the color of his immediate environment. Right now, in the half-lit kitchen, they looked almost silver. "You found your way here. Now stay here."

"What?" Walter asked. Where had Pratt gotten his information? Did he realize Walter was essentially in protective custody? How much did he know?

"Ernesto Masetti," Pratt told him. "He's gunning for you. Everybody knows it." He glanced at his watch. "Don't come back to the city. He's pissed about the stories you wrote. He wants to teach you a lesson. He's been talking, Walter. That's never good." Pratt looked him up and down, an appraising glance. "Believe me, I know these things."

Walter wondered how Franklyn Pratt could know so much about the inner workings of a prominent crime family. He'd heard rumors that some of his son Alec's friends liked to play rough—the cement shoes kind of rough—but he couldn't picture stolid, upper-crust Franklyn cozying up to one of the Five Families. "Respectfully, sir, you've been watching too many mob movies," Walter said. He softened this remark with a smile. "But I admire your imagination."

"Do not come back to New York," Pratt said. "Please. You don't know Masetti. You don't know what he's like."

"And you do?"

Pratt's expression changed so subtly, it was like watching snow melt. "My son went to the same prep school as Mr. Masetti's youngest boy, Nino. Ernesto Masetti and I have had…encounters." He glanced around, as if wary of being overheard. "It's just business, Walter… but business can get dirty and dangerous. Remember what I said." He turned and left without another word.

Walter heard him talking briefly to Chase, and then the kitchen door swung open and Chase wheeled himself through.

"Pratt's gone," he said. "Something about remembering an appointment. Let me see your hand."

Walter dumped the ruined chicken into the sink and ran cold water on it. The kitchen was full of smoke. He remembered Juliet saying something about an extractor fan. He found a switch near the toaster and turned it on. There was a thump and a reassuring whine as the powerful motor began removing the thick pall of smoke. "I'm sorry about lunch," Walter said. "I'll prepare something as soon as I get this mess cleaned up."

"Fuck lunch," Chase said. "I'll drink it like I usually do. Let me see."

Walter went to stand before him, his hand extended like a naughty child. The palm and fingers were burned a deep, raw-looking red that exuded sticky lymphatic fluid. The blister in the center was really—

"Spectacular," Chase said. "Were you trying to burn your hand off?"

"The broiler pan," Walter replied, turning to gesture. "The chicken was burning and I thought—"

"Stay still." Chase wheeled over to the cupboard under the sink and retrieved a first aid kit. It wasn't the usual home safety-type kit Walter was used to seeing. This was the Cadillac of first aid kits, with scissors and tweezers and tape and ointment and all the bandages that had ever existed.

Walter pulled a kitchen chair over to where Chase was and sat.

"So you aren't really a butler," Chase said. He raised an eyebrow. "Like I couldn't have guessed."

"Oh?"

"Detective Schrade seems to think you'll be safer here than in the city." Chase very gently patted antiseptic ointment onto the palm of Walter's hand. "He approached us some weeks ago." He glanced up. "So you're hiding from the mob." It wasn't a question.

"Yes," Walter said.

Chase's soft, dark eyes scrutinized him intensely. "And that doesn't scare you?"

Walter shrugged. "If they get me, they get me." He didn't feel nearly as nonchalant as he sounded.

"Word of advice." Chase draped clean white gauze over Walter's ravaged hand. "Use oven mitts."

"That's three words," Walter said, and Chase smiled. He had, Walter decided, a really nice smile. "You should smile more often."

Chase taped the dressing carefully. "I think you ought to stay out of the kitchen until this heals." And, when Walter protested, he said, "No. Do as I say. Juliet can get along without you for a few days, and we can get some temporary staff to take over your duties." He put the first aid kit back under the kitchen sink. "Come and have a drink and tell me why you decided to do this in the first place."

Walter followed Chase out into the dining room and waited while Chase expertly mixed two whiskey sours from the liquor cabinet in the sideboard and handed him one.

"I thought there might be a story in it," Walter said. "The whole mob thing. I've been writing about the Masetti family for a while."

Chase sipped his drink. "Chasing down the mob? Didn't anybody tell you that was dangerous?"

"My editor thinks I'm here doing a profile on you for the *Times*," Walter said. He was briefly ashamed of himself. "Nobody's even seen you since... in a while. I mean, you're the head of Gordon Industries, which comprises over fifty companies in seventeen different countries." He gazed down into his glass, unable to meet Chase's eyes. "Everybody assumed you'd take over as CEO, but...." He couldn't finish the sentence. He didn't want to hurt Chase's feelings. Even though he barely knew him, Walter sensed there were unsounded depths in the man, a hidden network of psychic wounds.

"Except my parents were killed in a plane crash," Chase said quietly, "and I—for lack of a better term—took a ride on the crazy train."

"I'm sorry," Walter said helplessly. "I shouldn't have said anything at all." There was a long silence, and then he asked, "Were you close? With your family."

Chase drew a slow breath. "There was never any family as such. My parents married late in life and I was an only child." He laid his half-empty glass on a small side table and moved to one of the large windows overlooking the garden. "My mother often said they waited a long time for me. I got the impression my conception required some medical intervention. They were both well over forty when I was born."

Walter went and sat at the dining table, where he could see Chase more clearly. He hoped Chase wouldn't misconstrue the gesture. "I've heard it's harder to conceive as you get older."

Chase nodded. "Yes."

He'd grown up an uncommonly serious boy, he told Walter, perpetually in the company of adults. His father had suggested boarding school, but Chase's mother wasn't keen on sending him away for ten months of the year, and so at first they'd engaged a tutor. He could, his mother reasoned, always go to boarding school some other time, and he did, jetting off to the exclusive Institut Le Rosey in Switzerland, to associate and mingle with others of his social class. Chase read a lot, in French and German or Italian, as well as English, and his written compositions reflected a quiet, studious nature. He wasn't shy or self-effacing—he was a Gordon, after all—but neither did he care to put himself forward unduly. He was more comfortable in the shadows, perhaps, keeping his own counsel and thinking his own thoughts, without being forced to defend his opinions to others.

"It sounds idyllic," Chase said, "doesn't it?"

Walter lifted his shoulders and let them drop. "I was going to say it sounds lonely." He offered an apologetic smile. "I hope that doesn't offend you."

Chase didn't answer. Instead, he asked, "How's your hand?"

"It hurts like a son of a bitch." Walter regarded the bandage. "You know, if this billionaire thing doesn't work out for you, you'd make one hell of a nurse."

ELEANOR RIGBY wasn't in her office when Walter disregarded Franklyn Pratt's advice and showed up at the paper a week later. She wasn't in the conference room, or the ladies' room—he didn't actually check in there personally, but had one of the girls do it—or the break room. At ten minutes past eleven, he found her outside on the sidewalk smoking a cigarette.

It was mid-November and an unseasonably cold day, and the wind held the promise of a hard winter to come, but Eleanor wasn't wearing a coat. She looked angrier than Walter had ever seen her. "Why are you here?" she snapped. "Tell me something good or I'll break your nuts." She stalked back and forth, her Manolo Blahnik heels—fire-engine red with a diamante buckle near the toe—clacking like an angry typewriter. "Do you know who was in my office this morning?" She stabbed the air with her cigarette. "That little suck-up, Alec Pratt."

"Sorry," Walter said. He didn't really know what he was apologizing for.

"Alec Pratt thinks he ought to be covering the Chase Gordon story," she said. "Alec goddamn Pratt thinks I should send him to the Gordon mansion for a little visit. Like he needs to ask *my* permission, when his old man owns the fucking paper."

Fuck Pratt and his big fucking mouth. "There is no Chase Gordon story," Walter said, "not really—and if there was, I'd be covering it."

He wondered if that was the reason for Pratt's sudden and unheralded appearance at Gordonstoun. "Gordon suffered some kind of… traumatic injury, and he can't walk. That's why he never goes out. It's common knowledge."

None of this mattered, however. He knew what was going to happen next: Pratt the elder had found out Walter was working at the manor. He'd call the paper and demand to have Walter removed from the story and Alec put in his place. Alec was a star reporter—at least in dear old Dad's mind—while Walter was nobody. Old Pratt would pull whatever strings were necessary with his rich pals to get Alec inside Chase Gordon's house, and he'd make sure Alec had free rein while he was there. Pratt Senior would find some way to make it happen. Walter would be captured by the Masetti family and carved into tiny little pieces.

"What happened to your hand?" Eleanor pointed to the bandages. Walter told her. "Have you seen a doctor?"

"It doesn't need a doctor. He put some ointment on it, this disinfectant stuff." He lifted his hand and turned it at the wrist, experimentally. The joint felt stiff, not easily articulated, probably because he'd been favoring it ever since.

"*He*?" She tried unsuccessfully to suppress a smirk. "The great and powerful Chase Gordon bandaged your boo-boo?"

"He's hardly great and powerful," Walter asserted. "He's actually really nice."

Eleanor shrugged. "Whatever."

"Why are you smoking on the sidewalk?"

"Building manager threw a hissy fit. Don't get me started." She took a final drag on her cigarette and tossed the butt into the gutter. "Come on. Let's get inside before I catch goddamn pneumonia."

Chase followed her into the elevator and up to her office. The two small tables just inside her door were cluttered with piles of miscellaneous paper—clippings, editorial dummies, copies of upcoming heads and subheads printed out larger than normal—and her huge glass-topped desk featured the same. Eleanor was efficient, but these days there was more work than ever, thanks to cutbacks and the general downturn of the industry.

"They all want to read the goddamn paper on their goddamn smart phones," she said, waving at the piles. "No goddamn time to read the goddamn thing otherwise." She huffed out a sigh. "Walter, sit down."

Walter sat. "I know what you're thinking."

"No. You don't." She started to light a cigarette, cursed, and put it away. "Pratt wants me to assign his crotch spawn to the Gordon story. He thinks Alec should be chasing the Gordon story, especially the 'dying recluse' angle."

"I told you. There *is* no Gordon story." Walter's heart sped up to an unpleasant degree, and he felt cold all over. "Remember the story we did on him a few years ago? He lost his parents just before 9/11, and he can't walk. That's it. If you're gonna turn it into tabloid fodder, you can count me out."

Eleanor speared him with a look. "I don't print anything that isn't news." She leaned over the desk. "I don't print hearsay, I don't print gossip. I don't print bullshit. Do you feel me, Walter?"

Walter mumbled that yes, he was in fact "feeling" her.

Eleanor put on her most likable expression. "Look, you don't have to be best friends with Alec Pratt."

Walter snorted.

"Give him something to do around the house… something to keep him busy." She nodded at his hand. "You can't work with that burn, anyway."

"You want me to turn Alec Pratt into a servant?" Obviously Pratt knew the real reason Walter was at Gordonstoun. God only knew how he found out. "I don't know if Chase—Mr. Gordon—will go for that."

Eleanor got up, walked over to the window, and stood for a moment looking down at the street. "Christ. Look at them all down there. Sometimes I just want a flamethrower." She turned, her arms crossed in front of her. "Look, Walter, it's like this: old man Pratt owns this paper, which means I do what he wants. What he wants is for his son to have a real journalistic career. He was pretty insistent on that point. I got the feeling somebody was leaning on him, if that's even possible."

"What's that got to do with me?" His head was aching. He massaged his temples gently, in small circles, trying to coax the pain away. He always seemed to have a headache lately.

"You were fired," Eleanor said, "but I like you, Walter, so I'm going to overlook that simple fact. If Franklyn Pratt thinks there's a story, then there's a story. End of convo." She leaned over and peered at him. "Help me get Alec Pratt in there and you can have your job back."

"How can I help get him in?" Walter asked. "I've got no pull in that direction." The pounding in his head was like the marching of a Roman legion. He felt vaguely nauseated.

"Are you all right?" Eleanor asked.

"Headache," Walter mumbled as he got up.

"You'll do it?" she pressed. "You'll help me out?"

"Yeah, I'll help." He wrapped his arms around himself, trying in vain to stem the sudden wracking shudders. "And turn up the heat. It's like a meat locker in here."

"You help me out, Walter, and I'll help you. That's the way it works, huh?"

"Send him out to the house," Walter said, heading for the elevator. "I'll see what I can do."

He caught the LIRR back to Long Island, sleeping most of the way. He woke as the train pulled into the station, feeling groggy and out of sorts. The wind seemed to cut right through his clothes when he stepped onto the platform, so he hurried to get to his car and turn the heat on. He was shivering so hard he could hardly fit the key into the lock. He fumbled twice, dropping his keys on the ground and nearly falling when he bent to retrieve them.

I'm not usually like this, he thought. *I'm better than this. I handle things.* He was sitting on the ground; it didn't make any sense. Why was he sitting on the ground?

"Sir? Are you all right?"

A huge head loomed over him, blocking out the light. He tried to tell the head to go away, that he was just fine, he was looking for his keys. Then there were hands under his arms, lifting him up. He tried to get away from them, but the giant head wouldn't let him. There were feet running underneath him and he was lying on a flat thing with wheels. A squat white vehicle, its back doors yawning open, waited for him.

"I must be sick," he murmured.

Then he was in the ambulance and they were driving fast, the siren shrieking. A young woman, her blonde hair tied back in a ponytail, bared his arm and stuck a needle in him.

I'm gonna throw up, Walter thought. *I'm gonna throw up.*

"Getting a line in him now," she said. She smiled and patted Walter's other shoulder. "You're gonna be okay there, bud. Close call, huh?"

"Yeah," Walter slurred as the sedative coursed through his veins, "ssshumthing like zzzat."

"You got anybody you want to call?" she asked. "Who's your next of kin?"

"Shase Gorbom," Walter said. There were definitely drugs in the IV. "Risssh guy. Big housh."

"Chase Gordon, huh?" She drew a blanket over him. "You're hanging with the big boys now."

"Shure am." Walter sighed and closed his eyes. The ambulance was going really fast and he was going with it, and the inside of the vehicle had things hanging on the walls, and they were going too. *Better if I go to sleep*, he thought, so he did.

A BEEPING noise woke him. It went on and on. He turned his head to the side and saw a blinking box on a pole. *IV pump*, his mind supplied. He was lying in bed and someone had put a tube in his mouth. He tried to speak and couldn't.

A young man came and looked at him. He was the same height as the bed. He was sitting in a wheelchair. "Juliet, I think he's coming around."

An older woman, stern and steely-eyed, leaned over him. "You've got some nerve," she said. "Do you know you've got a serious infection?" She then proceeded to tell him he was in the hospital, being pumped full of broad-spectrum antibiotics to counter the sepsis in his hand. The makeshift bandage Chase had put there had been replaced by a thick hospital dressing that went from his elbow to the tips of his fingers. "Why didn't you come and tell me?" she asked. "You know I am responsible for the household. If you'd told me as soon as you burned yourself, all this could have been avoided." She pressed her lips into a straight line. "Don't ever neglect to tell me about an injury. The Gordon household is my responsibility—*you* are my responsibility. Do you understand me, boy?"

Walter nodded. He was more tired than he could ever remember being. He wondered if they were pumping drugs into him along with the antibiotics. Probably a sedative to keep him quiet, to make sure he stayed in bed. He tried to keep his eyes open, but they were suddenly heavier than garage doors. *Alec Pratt*, he thought. *I'm supposed to be training Alec Pratt... under-underbutler....*

When Walter opened his eyes again, he was alone. Just beyond the open door of his room, he could hear people talking, shoes squeaking on the tile floors, and intercom announcements advising Doctor Whoever to get to the operating room. He turned his head on the pillow. The window was dark, the outside world submerged in a heavy pall of fog. He wondered what time it was. All he remembered was being at the paper and then lying on the ground. What else had happened?

The small table to the right of his bed held a jug of water and a plastic tumbler, a copy of some newspaper—not the *Times*—and a thermometer in a clear case.

He fumbled for the call button and pressed it.

A very young nurse stopped at his door and looked in. "Do you need something, Mr. Godfrey?"

"Can I have a drink?" The jug was out of his reach, and he didn't feel much like getting out of bed.

The nurse filled a glass and handed it to him.

"Thanks," Walter said. The water was ice cold, delicious. "How long have I been here?" It seemed a logical thing to ask.

"You were brought in yesterday. Gina told me, because Gina worked yesterday and I didn't—I switched shifts with Jacinda, because she had to go to a baby shower—and it was sometime in the afternoon." A series of bongs sounded outside in the corridor, and the intercom murmured some broad, distorted syllables. *Definitely sedated*, Walter thought. *Whole goddamn place is starting to feel like Disneyland.* "You okay, Mr. Godfrey?"

"Sure," Walter said. "Thanks for the water." He fumbled for the TV remote and turned it on, but there was nothing he was interested in, merely some reality show with one of the Kardashians—he couldn't tell which one. He wondered what had happened to his laptop. He usually left it in his car. If he had it, he could at least surf the Internet and send e-mails.

A movement in the corridor alerted him to the presence of a newcomer, and he tensed. There was no need for such hypervigilance, not here, but he couldn't help it. Ever since the two masked men had shot him in the mustard, he'd been jumpier than usual.

"Hey, you." Billy Newman appeared in the doorway, bearing a huge bouquet of flowers. "You sure like making people worry." He laid the flowers on the bedside table and leaned down to hug Walter very gently. "How are you feeling?"

"Crappy," Walter admitted. "I'm surprised they let you in." He patted the side of the bed. "Come on, sit down. How did you know I was here?"

"Three guesses," Billy said. "Pratt was spreading it all around the office, how you were drunk in public and had to be taken to the hospital." The hospital bed compressed under his weight as he sat. "Everybody thinks you're a lush."

"Alec Pratt?" That didn't make any sense. "How did Alec Pratt know?"

"Beats me," Billy shrugged. "Maybe he's psychic."

"Or psychotic," Walter said.

They were both silent for a moment. "Do you think he's stalking me?" Walter asked.

"Maybe," Billy said. "He's crazy enough to do anything, and I wouldn't put it past him." He glanced around the room. "Got it really comfortable here, huh?" He rubbed the edge of the blanket between his fingers. "Nice. Almost luxurious."

"Don't remind me," Walter said. "I'm not looking forward to the hospital bill." He had a little money stashed in the bank, and despite the mundane nature of his job playing at being a butler, he did receive a modest salary. He had no medical insurance, and every day he spent in the hospital meant added costs.

"You could always come back to your old job at the *Times*," Billy said. He picked up the remote and began flicking rapidly through the television channels. "So, how are things at the McMansion?"

Walter shrugged.

"But you are going back there," Billy said. "For the story, I mean."

"Why do you think I wouldn't go back?" Walter asked.

"Nothing," Billy replied. He glanced at his watch and stood. "Shit, I gotta go. Lance will think I'm dead in the gutter somewhere." He hugged Walter. "Take care of yourself, huh?" With a grin and a wave, he was gone.

Well, that was the shortest visit in the history of everything, Walter thought. He reached for the remote, clicked off the television, and turned to replace it on the nightstand. Footsteps paused in the doorway. He turned around. "What are you doing here?" His pulse throbbed almost painfully in his wrists, his ears. It was the guy from Divvy's, the big guy in the expensive suit, the one who'd warned Walter to keep his nose out of Masetti business.

"Came to pay my respects," the big man said.

Walter felt like he was choking. "That's something you do at funerals."

"Exactly." The big man smiled. "That's exactly right, my friend." He came and sat on the side of Walter's bed. "You don't look so good. Maybe you ought to take better care of yourself, huh?" He gazed at Walter in silence. "You're a handsome guy. Why don't you get a decent job? It ain't healthy, making up lies about people you don't even know."

"Are you threatening me?" Walter asked. "Because if you are, I wish you'd hurry up. This is starting to feel like a farce."

"A farce, huh?" He smiled. "Excuse my manners. I neglected to introduce myself." He held out his hand, realized too late that Walter's was in bandages, and withdrew it, smirking. "Vincent Barone, at your service."

"You're almost civilized," Walter said. "Imagine that."

"Listen, Walter." Barone laid a hand on his forearm, the good one. "I don't mean nothing by it, but you gotta bad habit of sticking your nose in." His fingers tightened, squeezing. "You put your nose into the wrong places, bad things happen." He loosened his grip and stroked Walter's skin. "I'd hate to see you get into trouble like that." He slid his hand down and brushed the back of Walter's knuckles with his thumb. "It don't gotta be that way."

His eyes were a curious blue-gray color, his hair dark blond. He obviously cared about his appearance, for he was meticulous in his dress, clean-shaven, and his nails appeared to be manicured. He smelled really good, like pine needles and citrus, and his stocky figure filled his suit quite nicely. He reminded Walter of a long-ago boyfriend who'd worked at an Italian restaurant and who always wanted to have sex in the backseat of Walter's car, a 1983 Ford Fairmont sedan held together with rust and wire. For a fleeting instant, Walter wondered if Barone was anywhere near as sexually adept as his old boyfriend had been. Those big hands could probably work wonders....

"Are you threatening me?" Walter asked, "or trying to seduce me?"

Barone's round face was suddenly suffused with hot color. "We're having a little discussion, okay? Just you and me. I'm telling you to take better care of yourself. Something might happen." He leaned in, so close that Walter could see the darker ring of blue around his pupils. "Consider it some friendly advice." He cupped Walter's cheek in his palm, caressing gently. "See you around."

Walter waited for five minutes, forcing himself to breathe deeply and calmly. Then he picked up the phone and called Detective Schrade. "He was here. Vinnie Barone, one of Masetti's boys. You'd better get me out of here."

"HE IS a stupid young bugger," Juliet said. She lifted one of Walter's wrists, taking his pulse. "Stupid young bugger." She turned to Chase, sitting quietly by the window. They were at home in Gordonstoun, and upon Detective Schrade's advice, Walter had been moved into one of the big rooms on the ground floor. "And you. You should have notified me immediately, as soon as he'd burned himself."

"You weren't here," Chase said unhelpfully. "I suppose he's lucky."

"Lucky." She snorted. "Lucky I'm still in possession of my wits, you mean. Not to mention my professional qualifications."

The hospital had agreed to release Walter into Juliet's custody after she'd presented proof of her medical degree. The British army had furnished a very young Juliet Lavish with her doctorate, in exchange for several years of her life. She had extensive experience in just about any kind of wound or condition, and a good many that were so rare, they might have existed only in medical textbooks. Nothing fazed her; no wound was too terrible for her to look upon. Blood, guts, snot, ordure, feces—she had seen it all. Her time in the army was followed by a stint in MI6, doing things Chase would never know and Juliet would never tell—even though he knew MI6 was British intelligence, which made Juliet essentially a spy.

For the next several days, Chase sat vigil at Walter's bedside. Walter was unconscious for most of it, surfacing only briefly to sip some water before sinking back into his pillows. Juliet changed the bedding every day and kept a close eye on his wound. Five days after he'd collapsed at the LIRR station, Walter was awake and able to take small amounts of liquid, things like Popsicles and soup, which Chase helped him with. Chase spent time with him, watching movies or television or reading aloud. It seemed to cheer Chase up, as if he'd been waiting for just this sort of task.

"Tell me why," Walter said, one morning. It was a chilly day, overcast and with a cold wind from the northeast blowing the leaves around, occasionally dashing them against the bedroom window.

"Why what?" Chase asked.

"Your legs." Walter's gaze remained fixed on the window. Sometimes the best way to get information was to ask the inconvenient questions.

"I don't know," Chase replied. He waited till Walter turned his gaze away from the window. "I woke up like this one morning, after…." He drew a deep breath and hurried to tell the rest of it. "After my parents died."

"Couldn't Juliet…?"

"Fix me?" Chase shook his head. "No. The psychiatrist thinks it's psychosomatic—you know, in my mind. He's tried several ways around it, but I'm afraid it's a no go."

"I'm sorry," Walter said.

"So am I." Chase forced himself to smile. "So am I."

CHAPTER THREE

HE'D BEEN out running, training for a half marathon he and some other friends were interested in. It was an unusually hot mid-September day, and he really shouldn't have been running in the heat, but he was young and stupid and not inclined to muse on his own mortality.

He called for Juliet as soon as he came in, but there was no answer. He thought he could detect the faint murmur of her voice from somewhere else in the house… talking on the telephone, probably. She did all the ordering for the house: groceries and booze and filtered water. The well on the estate was no longer any good; a stubborn bacterial overgrowth had fouled the water, so Elliott Gordon had invested in an artesian well, which produced water suitable for washing but with a distinct sulfur odor that made it impossible to drink.

Chase took a cold bottle of spring water out of the fridge and tossed it down his throat, then immediately opened and drank another one.

Master Chase. Juliet had come into the kitchen so quietly, he hadn't heard her. *You might wish to sit down.* Their normally very stoic butler was emotionally shaken and fighting to keep her composure. *I had a visit from the chief of police when you were out.*

His thoughts immediately went to the raucous party he'd attended at a friend's house the previous night. There had been booze and music, cocaine, and lots of pretty young things male and female, and they must have upset at least some of the neighbors. Chase wasn't bothered about that part of it. Fuck the neighbors. You were only young once, and it was too bad if you couldn't have a good time. One of his friends had accidentally driven his father's Porsche into the swimming pool, and they'd all screamed with laughter, especially since the man was on vacation in Bermuda and not expected back for weeks.

It's about your parents.

The National Transportation Safety Board had contacted the local police detachment several hours ago. A small plane—a Beechcraft—had crashed in Honduras, somewhere on the aptly named Mosquito Coast that ran from Honduras to Nicaragua.

He asked the obvious question: *Are they all right?*

There were no survivors. Juliet drew a slow, meditative breath. *I'm afraid your parents are dead.*

He groped for the counter behind him, his legs suddenly unsteady.

Their private jet had disappeared from radar an hour into its flight. *They were going to see about the church.* His parents had invested their own money in revitalizing a small village in Honduras, including a new nondenominational church and community center. They had set up a library and a school, bought books and supplies—even school uniforms. His mother had made the rounds of their family church back home in Long Island, soliciting clothes and toys for the village children and monetary donations for their parents. They had obtained the necessary permits and licenses to begin construction of new housing after wrangling for months with Honduran authorities for permission. They had even set up an annuity, an amount of money earmarked for humanitarian aid, which would pay the yearly operating expenses. His parents loved doing things like that.

"I can't—" Chase started back toward the fridge but changed his mind halfway there and moved to the kitchen window instead. "The grass back here is terrible. It looks like it hasn't been mowed in years. Didn't we hire somebody to do that? Why isn't he here? Surely we aren't paying the man for nothing."

"Chase." Juliet indicated one of the kitchen chairs. "Please, sit down."

"I'd rather not. The hedges on this side of the house look like they've been gnawed by a goat—" He stuttered into silence, drew a breath to say something, but seemed unable to. He kept his gaze on the window. "I was supposed to—Dad asked me to call about that leaking well pump, the one in the basement." He nodded. "I should do that."

"Their remains are being flown home from Honduras," Juliet said quietly. "You will be expected to take possession."

"Well, I can't!" he snapped. "I have my own things to do. I can't just—" His forehead was itchy. He couldn't stop scratching it. "Juliet, what am I going to do?" He turned to her. "I'm all alone now... I'm alone."

Juliet went to him, pulled his hand away from his forehead. "You've never been alone, and you aren't now."

She offered to go with him to take possession of the remains, but he insisted on going by himself. A mortuary assistant from a Long Island funeral home met him at the cargo area and accepted the two coffin-sized cardboard boxes labeled HUMAN REMAINS: HANDLE WITH CARE, which contained all that was left of Chase's father and mother. The entire episode was bizarre and dreamlike: Chase standing in the crowded, noisy cargo area, listening to the oblivious chatter of other people. Once or twice someone had pointed in his direction, nudged somebody else: *That's Chase Gordon. He's got more money than God.* No one realized why Chase was there, and no one asked. For them, the world went on as it always had—as it always would.

The morning of his parents' funeral, Chase Gordon woke, tried to get out of bed, and couldn't. His legs from the hips down were completely and entirely useless. A wheelchair was brought in for him, and one of the gardener's assistants helped him dress in the black suit and tie he wore to the funeral. His parents were buried on the grounds of Gordonstoun in the small family plot that held several generations of Gordon ancestors. As if in defiance of the day's somber mood, the sun shone brightly throughout. The small group of mourners—friends of his father's, mostly—were invited into the house for drinks or tea, and there were trays of dainty finger sandwiches and tiny cookies, and after a tense half hour, they all went away.

Chase couldn't get up the stairs, so Juliet moved him to one of the guest rooms on the first floor. It was just as well. He wanted to be alone, to get out of the suit he was wearing, to listen to his records—he was an avid collector of antique vinyl—and try to forget.

He would never forget. Everything had collapsed around him. Later, he watched the news, horrified as jet planes ploughed into the World Trade Center and the Pentagon. The whole world had gone to hell.

JULIET, HAVING been duly warned of Alec Pratt's arrival, took control of him the first morning he set foot in the door.

He was in his mid to late thirties, a sleekly self-absorbed, spoiled rotten rich man's son. He was not tall, and he was quite slender, with hair of the blackest black cut short in some impossible style that seemed to defy gravity. His face was unremarkable, pleasant enough in a classical sense, but when he smiled, he was beautiful. His eyes were his best feature was: ice-blue and with thick, black lashes. They looked everywhere and saw everything, yet there was something off about him, something humbled and afraid. He carried himself with the dubious aplomb of a beaten man—beaten by professionals, Juliet thought, hired thugs who knew how to do the job properly, with a minimum of fuss. He inserted himself into rooms apologetically, as nervous as a virgin bride. Juliet suspected there was something going on there, just below the surface. Alec Pratt wasn't what he seemed to be, not entirely—either that or he was a bloody good actor, and the whole nervous virgin thing was a ploy.

Long before Walter's arrival at Gordonstoun, a detective from the NYPD had contacted Juliet, explaining Walter Godfrey was in protective custody because of some unpleasantness with the mafia. *I just need somewhere safe to stash him,* Detective Schrade said, *until we get a handle on this thing with the Masettis.* Apparently the Gordon mansion offered safety sufficiently far from the city, at least for now. It didn't hurt that the huge mansion had an exceptional security system. The Gordons had always kept close ties with the police, and Schrade had often traded on this familiarity. Juliet wondered if Alec Pratt was part of the package deal.

"No doubt you know my father," Alec said.

Juliet looked him up and down. "No doubt I do," she said dryly. She led him into the kitchen and handed him an apron, a spray bottle of all-purpose cleaner, and a fistful of clean rags.

"I believe you misunderstand," he said archly. "Now see here, my father—"

"Your father asked that you be embedded within the Gordon household, to gain inside information for a profile you intend to do for the paper." It was, Juliet thought, becoming increasingly difficult to remember who was working for whom in this tangled affair. "This is as embedded as it gets."

"My good woman." Alec spoke with a fussy, old-fashioned diction that did absolutely nothing for his essential strangeness. "I hardly know where to begin," he said, finishing with a self-deprecating laugh.

"I want to see this kitchen spotless. And the stair balusters could do with a thorough dusting."

"What do you think I am?" he sputtered, hot color mounting into his cheeks. "Are you under the impression that I'm—"

"A household servant?" Juliet said, with some relish. "Yes, as a matter of fact, that is precisely my impression. I suggest you snap to it."

She went down the hall and into Chase's section of the house, carefully locking the door behind her. Young Pratt made her very uneasy; in the midst of Juliet's well-ordered world, he was an unknown. Schrade had sent him to keep an eye on Walter, a notion Juliet found laughable.

His old man thinks he's here chasing down a story, Schrade said. He seemed to think this made it all right. Schrade didn't actually say the Gordon family owed the NYPD, but the inference was there when Juliet spoke to him. *I know you'll want to help*, he said, *considering.*

It seemed to Juliet that Schrade's control of the entire case was slipping fast.

Walter was asleep under the thrall of heavy sedation when she looked in. Chase was sitting beside the bed, reading a book. She tiptoed in and tugged the curtains, shielding Walter from the early sunlight. "How is he?"

"He's been sleeping, mostly," Chase said. "I suppose that's a good thing. He woke up around two this morning and asked for water. Other than that he's been quiet." He held Juliet in his level gaze. "Don't start," he warned.

"Have you been sitting here all night?" Juliet moved about the room, gathering stray newspapers, discarded candy papers, and empty soda tins.

"I didn't mind," Chase said. "I slept while he was sleeping."

"Sitting up in that chair? Well, Armand will be here in half an hour, so I suggest you shower and change."

Armand was Chase's personal masseur and physiotherapist, brought in from some very chi-chi clinic in the city for an astronomical amount of money. It was Armand's job to make sure Chase's muscles didn't seize up from lack of use, so three times a week, he put Chase through a series of punishing exercises that left him sore and winded.

"Juliet," Chase said, just as she was leaving, "have we heard anything from Gardiner Frey this week? He was supposed to send me the fundraising report."

"Not a peep, sir." She tucked the sheaf of discarded newspapers under her arm and gathered up a half-eaten donut wrapped in a paper napkin.

"He's supposed to report to me every week, at least once...." Chase tapped his upper lip with his index finger, something he claimed helped him think. "What's he doing? Where is he? Why haven't I heard from him?"

"Do you want me to get him on the telephone?"

"Could you?" Chase shook his head. "It's probably nothing, but I get the feeling something's not right over there. He's always at the ranch."

"The ranch" was short for Shep's Place, an animal rescue and sanctuary that took in all the abused and unwanted pets unable to find homes through conventional means. Out of all the Gordon charities, it was Chase's favorite, a cause to which he'd always donated his time and a significant share of his personal fortune. The plight of unwanted animals tore at Chase's heart. A solitary child, he'd found great solace in the company of animals, especially dogs. Shep's Place was named after a sweet-faced, chubby mixed breed Chase had adopted from the local pound. Shep was a mixture of just about every kind of dog there was and some Chase had never heard of. He was fat, with wavy black fur and a curly tail, and a body the approximate shape of a shoebox. He was utterly devoted to Chase.

When Shep got old and developed canine dementia, Dad and Chase had a long, tearful discussion. *You aren't doing him any favors, son, keeping him alive.*

I don't know if I can do it, Dad. I don't know if I'm strong enough.

Anything but that, he'd thought. *Let him pass peacefully in his sleep. Don't make me kill my dog.*

I promise I'll go with you, Dad had said. *I'll stay with you and with him the entire time.*

I don't know if I can.

He'd never forgotten what Dad had said: *Chase, sometimes the right thing isn't the easy thing.*

It was hard, the hardest thing Chase had ever had to do, but when it was over, he was glad he'd done it, glad his sweet old dog was without pain and safe—Chase believed this absolutely—safe at home now, safer than he had ever been.

A week afterward, Dad had invited Chase to ride out to the old Thompson dairy farm with him. Dad had something to show him, something he hoped would interest his son. At first Chase was utterly confused.

What am I going to do with a farm, Dad? He was seventeen, on the threshold of his adult life, planning for high school graduation and then college after that. *What do I do with it?*

Anything you want. Dad had gambled on not only his son's ingenuity and cleverness, but also on his deep humanity, the love Chase had always demonstrated for every living thing. He didn't push, didn't suggest or hint or try to guide Chase's decision in any way.

A week afterward, Chase came to him and said he wanted to use the land for an animal sanctuary, a home where rejected and abused pets, animals nobody wanted, could live the rest of their lives in peace and safety. They'd found a willing and competent staff in the new graduates from the state veterinary college, young women and men who believed in the things Chase did. They hired a caretaker, a kind of general manager who would be in charge of the sanctuary's daily running, but ultimately answerable to Chase and his father. Gardiner Frey had come all the way from Australia, where he'd managed a small rural zoo dedicated to the Outback's most unusual inhabitants. He'd come highly recommended, with a long list of qualifications and references from some of the most prominent names in the animal rights movement.

It was highly unusual not to hear from him; at least once a week, he contacted Chase to give him a report.

"I'll have him call you," Juliet said. "Now you'd best run along and ready yourself for Armand."

Chase left Walter sleeping and went into his personal suite to shower and change. The bathroom had been adapted for him, with nonslip floor mats, grab bars, and water taps positioned at just the correct height. Everything he might need was readily to hand, including shampoo, soap, and stacks of fluffy towels heated to the perfect temperature. He showered quickly, dressed in the loose cotton pants and T-shirt Armand insisted were necessary, and wheeled himself out into the hallway.

A young man was standing by a window, wearing a butler's uniform and holding a dust rag in his hand. The bulk of his attention seemed centered on something happening outdoors, while he made half-hearted passes at a small, round table—Chippendale, if Chase remembered correctly. It had belonged to his grandfather. The stranger turned, saw Chase, and grinned. He was not unhandsome, but there was something sly about him, something that suggested an unusual attachment to luxury and an inbred love of leisure that bordered on indolence.

The sort of person, Chase thought, *you didn't turn your back on.*

"Who are you?" the young man asked pompously. "Do you have permission to be here?"

Chase's eyebrows threatened to climb into his hairline. "I happen to own this house. Who the hell are you? You have until the count of three and then I call security."

"Alec Pratt." He dropped the dust rag and extended a slender, nervous hand. "I'm—"

"Not supposed to be in this section of the house," Chase snapped. "Which you doubtless know."

"Of course, sir," he said, averting his eyes. "I must have wandered in here by mistake."

"Make sure it doesn't happen again." Chase watched him leave and locked the door behind him. He made a mental note to ask Juliet about him as soon as Armand finished his therapy.

ALEC PRATT'S impression of the Gordon mansion had thus far been disappointing. He'd expected a great behemoth of a house, a Gothic monster, with the bones of the Gordon ancestors resting uneasily in the attic and Chase Gordon a debauched ruin along the lines of Dorian Gray.

Gordon couldn't walk, it was true—Alec made a mental note to find out what that was all about—but otherwise he was his father's son in every way that mattered. He had the classic Gordon good looks, brought to the States many years ago by wealthy Scottish ancestors, landowners who'd strenuously resisted the oncoming wave of Highland clearances, to no avail. The very first Gordon had set himself up in business, managing trade between Britain and the new world via a fleet of ships that by the end of the nineteenth century had grown exponentially. He had married the daughter of a local land baron, one of the Astors, and the rest, Pratt thought sourly, was history.

It was all right for someone like Chase Gordon, he supposed, accustomed to a life of wealth and ease. *His* ancestors had all worked for a living, and while it was true that Franklyn Pratt owned several newspapers, a racehorse named Simple Plan, and numerous lucrative real-estate developments, Alec felt he personally had gotten the fuzzy end of the lollipop. Fortunately, he was the type of young man who instinctively made the most of all available resources. He'd watched his father for years, taking careful note of Pratt Senior's talent for influence and power. Alec's intelligence was applied more stealthily than the old man's, but Alec was confident in his interests and determined to get where he thought he should be. He'd been that way since college, when the first of many appealing opportunities had come along.

Just now he was involved in polishing the enormous stained-glass windows that lined the upstairs hallway, wiping the intricate patterns carefully with a soft cloth. The old woman had given him the work to do, as well as a long list of other things for which he was responsible— washing, dusting, vacuuming, and cleaning.

His father assumed Alec was here to spy, and not merely spy, but to bring back useful intelligence about the Gordon household that he could then spin into a sensational story. He'd told the old man he wanted something fantastic and improbable, something that would blow the doors off every other newspaper in town. It was exactly what Pratt Senior had wanted to hear. Lately Franklyn was up to his ears in financing Alec's sister Cecily's upcoming wedding. Every time Alec tried to speak with him, the old man sent him away, angrily declaring that whatever it was, Alec couldn't have it, and did he think his father was made of money? *Find something useful to do*, Pratt elder had told him. *Go out into the world and look around a bit.*

Of course, Alec had already looked around, and as far as the world was concerned, he'd found something useful to do, something he liked—and it wasn't butlering or journalism. But he'd only hinted at his particular vocation, especially where his parents were concerned, preferring to keep the details to himself. He was careful to play both ends against a tenuous middle, allowing Franklyn Pratt to think he did freelance work for the more esoteric members of the Manhattan business community while feeding information to the police. That was the part Alec's father didn't know about.

Despite his many business interests, Franklyn Pratt was up to his neck in debt. Cecily's wedding was to be the social event of the season— never mind that she was marrying "Hardy" Henry Ashbottom, one of the country's youngest millionaires. Alec's mother hadn't stopped talking about it ever since the engagement last Christmas, declaring it to be "absolutely true love, the very best kind!" It was, Alec knew, nothing of the sort. Ashbottom was a business failure and a roaring drunk who loved his string of polo ponies far more passionately than he did Cecily. It was rumored he was marrying for money, which seemed to slip through his fingers all too easily these days.

True love. His mouth twisted. *What a joke.*

He sprayed a dab of glass cleaner onto his cloth and applied it to the window, spreading it carefully over a very detailed image of Saint Fiacre, who was extending a finger toward a woman kneeling on the ground. Saint Fiacre's expression said he'd rather be anywhere else, and the finger he extended toward his supplicant was disturbingly long, with several unnecessary joints. The woman's bright, unnaturally red hair was spread around her, hiding her naked body from Fiacre's less-than-interested gaze. Alec polished Fiacre and the woman until they shone. He didn't mind this sort of work, but he wasn't about to tell Juliet Lavish. It was all he could do to keep away from her. Wherever he turned, she seemed to be there with some new task he was obliged to perform. She worked him like a farm animal, and by the time Pratt made it into bed at night, he was exhausted, bone-weary, and aching in several places where it should have been impossible to ache.

He was also proud of himself—proud he could do the often-arduous work required of him; proud Juliet only needed to show him how to do something once; proud he was engaged in honest toil—unlike his sister's fiancé, whose idea of work involved the newspaper and a bottle of Glenfiddich. Yet Cecily insisted she was deeply in love.

True love, Alec thought, was only for certain people. The rest had to make do. Anyway, he wasn't here for love. There was lots of that around for others. He had work to do.

He finished the windows and stood back for a moment to admire them. It was a dull day outside, but they seemed to glow with their own inner fire, casting jeweled shadows onto the paler floor. It was a lovely effect. Whoever the Gordons had decorating the place knew his stuff. Except....

There was a sculpture on a small table in the corner. Immediately Alec disliked it. It was a Picasso as far as he could tell and ugly as sin: the head and neck of an elderly woman whose face seemed to be collapsing inward. Christ. He remembered seeing his parents *oohing* and *aahing* over something similar in one of the private galleries downtown: a misshapen man with what appeared to be a horn growing out of his forehead.

"The Picasso bothers you?" Juliet stepped into the hallway. "Or are you perhaps secretly in love with it?"

Alec glanced up and nodded. "I understand the desire to introduce a note of modernity into what is obviously a very old part of the house, but that... *thing*... is all wrong for this space."

Juliet said nothing.

"Sorry." Alec was suddenly contrite. "I'm probably not supposed to say that." He offered one of his nervous laughs. "I apologize."

"On the contrary," Juliet replied, "you are absolutely right." She regarded the piece for a moment. "What else bothers you about it?"

"I always feel there's a monstrousness inherent in his work," Alec said. "He attempts restraint, but fails to pull it off completely. Eventually he doesn't care, and gives into his animal instincts." *Animal instincts?* He cringed. He'd taken that directly from his undergraduate thesis.

"Go on," Juliet urged him.

He gestured at the windows. "This piece inserts a jarring note into what otherwise would be a sanctuary. The space, the beautiful windows…?" He shook his head. "It doesn't work."

"You know about art." Juliet studied him for a moment. "And you understand interior design."

Alec shrugged. "It's a hobby, really." He glanced down at the dustrag he'd been unconsciously twisting in his fingers. "I studied art history in college."

"What else do you do?" Juliet asked quietly. Her eyes bored into him like lasers.

Alec froze. His mouth worked soundlessly for a moment. "Well, I, ah, read a lot. N-Newspapers and magazines." He wondered what else she wanted him to say. The woman made him extremely nervous. "Is that wh-what you meant?" He uttered a wobbly little laugh. "I'm sure you have some work for me," he said finally.

Juliet fixed him with her icy stare. "Who are you? Really?" She moved closer. She and Alec were of a height, and at this proximity, her scrutiny was not something he could easily avoid.

"I'm Alec P-Pratt," he stammered. "My father wants me to write—"

"Your father wants you to write nothing," Juliet snapped. "And I have no bloody idea what that policeman"—she meant Detective Schrade—"intends by sending you here."

Alec swallowed hard and looked away. He tossed the dustrag onto the nearby tabletop and turned back to Juliet. "Look." He smiled. "This is going to sound… well, ridiculous, but it's the truth—my father thinks I'm here to write a story for his newspaper." He arched an eyebrow. "It's easier than telling him why I'm really here. Believe me, it wouldn't be healthy for either of us."

"You're talking," Juliet said, "like a mafia movie."

"Mmm." Alec leaned toward her. "Let's not get into that." He waved a hand. "It's way too complicated—" He caught Juliet's sour expression and rushed to redeem himself. "Not that you're unintelligent or that you couldn't understand if I were to tell you, give you all the details, fill you in on—"

"Are you working for the police or not?" Juliet asked. She seemed to be losing patience with him. "If you are, tell me, instead of talking round and round in these bloody riddles!"

"Yes and no," Alec said. "Like I said, it's complicated." Her expression goaded him, and he hurried to finish what he meant to say. "My father thinks I'm here as a journalist. You're supposed to think I'm here as a butler or footman or whatever. Chase—Mr. Gordon—thinks I'm a butler. Walter thinks I'm a butler. You think I'm—"

"A pain in the arse."

"Schrade wants me to keep Walter well within my sights. He's not safe, but you already know that. He's safer here than he is in the city, but not entirely safe."

"And they sent you… to protect him." Juliet narrowed her eyes at him. "Just what the devil are you going to do?"

"My good woman." Alec smirked. "I am rather more competent than I appear. Detective Schrade wouldn't have sent me otherwise." He hoped this explanation would suffice. He didn't feel like getting into a protracted discussion about his personal history or his fitness for this particular assignment. "Really, there's no need to worry." He took up his dusting cloth and prepared to continue where he'd left off.

Juliet regarded him narrowly. "You've got a hell of a lot of nerve."

Alec gave her his brightest, winningest smile. "So I've been told."

CHAPTER FOUR

CHASE HAD the gardener, George, drive him over to the animal ranch to check on things since he hadn't heard from Frey in several days. The ranch, a former dairy farm, was situated some miles out, on a piece of Long Island that all the land development companies had somehow missed, surrounded by native woodlands. In the summertime the pastureland would be full of cows, horses, donkeys, and even a disenfranchised zebra named Jeb. There were fields of wildflowers left to grow as they pleased, and a small apiary at the rear of the horse barn, where industrious bees hummed clandestine messages to each other all day long.

The main office was at the end of a long drive, a small white clapboard building that looked like a fairy tale cottage. It had old-fashioned mullioned windows and a huge door that folded back on itself, taking it neatly out of the way should any of the farm's nonhuman inhabitants wish to pay a visit. The sign over the door read: SHEP'S PLACE.

George pulled the car up in front of the office and went to get Chase's wheelchair out of the trunk. He unfolded it and set it to one side of the car door; he knew Chase could do the rest himself.

It was a beautiful day, the sort of day that remains almost forever in the memory. The sun was shining but the air had a delicious autumn nip to it, and many of the deciduous trees around the property had finished dropping their leaves.

Lucy Benjamin looked up and smiled when she saw Chase. She came out from behind the reception desk and bent to give him a hug. "You look better than you did last time," she said. Lucy was twenty-two and had just been accepted to the prestigious veterinary program at the University of Wisconsin. She was one of a dozen volunteers working at the farm.

"Well, thank you," Chase replied with a grin. "I think."

A large yellow Labrador with perhaps ten extra pounds ambled in from outside. He went to Chase and nuzzled his arm, gently nudging him.

"Baron," Lucy said. "You're such an attention whore."

Baron was old, his muzzle nearly pure white and his eyes filmed with cataracts. He laid his head in Chase's lap and sighed, as if he'd just then released the weight of the world. Chase stroked his ears.

"You're probably looking for Frey," Lucy said.

"How'd you know?" Chase asked.

She laughed, a humorless sound. "We're all looking for him." She went back to the desk. A large gray tabby cat with three legs jumped off the filing cabinet and onto her shoulder, rubbing her head against Lucy's cheek. "He hasn't been to work all week. We can't get him on the phone. I've sent numerous e-mails, but he doesn't reply." She stroked the cat absentmindedly. "Joel and Bethany have taken over his job in the meantime, but that's on top of their other chores."

"I don't understand it," Chase said. "He had excellent references. I'd never have hired him otherwise. Everything checked out."

Frey had locked his office before he left, so Chase got the key from Lucy and went down there. Frey's office was a small white shed roughly the size of a single-car garage. It had originally been a tack house and had only one window that let in a disconcerting lack of sun. Chase found the light switch just inside the door and turned on the overheads. The office was completely empty of human presence. He rifled through the papers on Frey's desk and opened all the drawers, but found nothing at all amiss—until he booted up Frey's computer and had a look at his accounting program.

Up until six months previous, Frey's accounting had been a model of efficiency as well as honesty. Then the entries became more erratic, as if Frey wasn't keeping track of smaller expenditures. There was no discernible pattern, almost like Frey had deliberately blurred his tracks to avoid detection for as long as possible. Paging through the entries, Chase noted accounting discrepancies dating back nearly a year. Obviously Frey had given some thought to the process: the missing entries all occurred on or around the times when Shep's Place—and its parent foundation, Canis Noir—would take in the most money.

Chase didn't need it spelled out for him. He shut down the computer, the knot in his gut torquing even tighter. Frey had done a runner, taking all the money he could get his hands on. He could be anywhere by now, Chase thought, living off his ill-gotten gains and thinking nobody knew anything about his crimes. *That son of a bitch.* It would have been bad enough if Frey had stolen from some other Gordon property, but that would have been a lesser blow than this. Shep's Place wasn't meant to turn a profit, had no external holdings outside of its investments, most of which created a large part of its sustainable funding. Frey hadn't just stolen from Gordon Industries. He'd stolen from abused and needy animals, creatures who had no one to speak for them, no one to care if they lived or died. He'd carelessly disregarded their housing and their sustenance for his own gain.

Chase pulled out his cell and dialed Ben Higdon, one of his personal bankers. Higdon's firm had been safeguarding Gordon wealth since the beginning, and Chase trusted him implicitly. He had only to wait a moment or two before Higdon came on the line.

"What can I do for you, Chase?"

"I need you to transfer some money for me." Chase gave him a figure, three times the usual operating budget for Shep's Place. It wasn't excessive generosity or carelessness: Frey had been secretly siphoning money for a while, and the finances had suffered because of it. Chase's cursory glance at Frey's accounting had revealed that the ranch was seriously overdue on some of its bills. "If you could get that to the Canis Noir Foundation as soon as possible, I'd be grateful." He briefly explained the situation, leaving out the nitty-gritty details.

Higdon was appalled. "Sounds like Frey has been busy," he said. "Any idea where he went?"

"None," Chase said. "But I have someone who can find out for me." He hung up, then immediately keyed in the number for Sam Jessup's office. Jessup was a laconic private investigator with a dingy little office in the Bronx and a fortysomething secretary who snapped gum and called everybody "sweetheart." Jessup favored rumpled Columbo-style raincoats and the occasional thin cigar. He'd been Elliott Gordon's go-to guy whenever situations precluded involving the police, and Chase knew he could rely utterly on Jessup's discretion. "Sam, I have a problem."

"Yep. Tell me what it is."

Chase outlined the situation for him, stressing that Frey could be anywhere. "I'd rather not get the police on this if I can help it."

"I'll get him," Jessup said. "Phone you back later."

Chase left Frey's office—his *former* office, he amended silently—just the way it was and locked the door behind him. He had all the information he needed for now, and he was ready to leave. He found George talking to Yancy, the bison, near the main office.

"All set, Mr. Gordon?"

"I think so." Chase reached up to tangle his fingers in Yancy's woolly mane. "You are a beautiful boy," he murmured quietly. The big animal ducked his head and gently bumped Chase's shoulder. "You beautiful boy."

Yancy had come to them from a squalid little circus out of Kansas, run by two drunken brothers who shuttled their animals from town to town without regard for exercise or proper shelter. When Yancy first came to Shep's Place, he was dangerously underweight, his great shaggy mane matted beyond all hope. He feared and hated humans—with reason, Chase thought—and it took a year and a half of gentle coaxing before he would even come out of his enclosure. Madison, a recent veterinary graduate, had worked exclusively with Yancy, soothing and gentling him, teaching him the sound of her voice. She even slept on a cot next to Yancy's enclosure, within a hand's reach of him, and fed him carrots. When Yancy finally consented to step foot through the gate, it was with Madison at his side. He kept company now with several other large ruminants, including an orphaned deer, a llama named Jorge, and a moose who'd been hit by a car and had miraculously survived, but walked with a limp.

Chase said good-bye to Lucy and the others, and started back to Gordonstoun. "What would make someone do such a thing?" Chase asked when he and George were in the car.

George turned to glance at him. "Some people are just rotten on the inside."

Chapter Five

ALEC WAITED till Walter went to sleep before venturing into any of the manor's bedrooms. He needed some scrap of something to build a story on, something that would convince the old man he was a "serious" reporter. It was important that Pratt Senior believe this, so Alec could get on with what he'd really come to do. Franklyn Pratt was the type to demand physical proof, and Alec intended to give it to him. It was the only way to keep the old man off his back.

So far, his search had proven disappointingly futile. The Gordon mansion was empty of anything scandalous, dirty, or even slightly newsworthy. He'd even gone through Juliet's room and found nothing more exciting than some cooking magazines and a copper arthritis bracelet. He found nothing of interest in Walter's bedroom, so he left the sleeping underbutler and took the lift up to the second floor. Here was where Chase Gordon's parents had slept and conducted their private matters. Most of the rooms were uninhabited and had been that way for a long time.

The Gordons' master suite was colossal, beautifully decorated and somehow still cozy, even though it hadn't seen human habitation for a while. Alec let himself in with the passkey he'd taken from Juliet's room and shut the door quietly, even though there was no one to hear. The entryway opened onto a lavishly decorated sitting room, complete with fireplace and a view of the Sound. The bed was enormous, perhaps two feet off the floor, and with a set of tiny stairs to one side, presumably for getting in at night and out again in the morning. There were two wingback chairs upholstered in cream silk, and a small sofa of the same, set around a low coffee table in front of the fireplace. Of course, Alec had seen luxury before, but this was rather beyond the pale. Did anyone actually *need* a four-person Jacuzzi tub in the en suite?

He found the drawers of the massive bureau unlocked and wasted no time going through them. Juliet had evidently seen no need to pack the Gordons' things away, for everything was just as they'd presumably left it. He found no old love letters, no secret plans to destabilize the dollar, only a photo album. He took it out and sat on the floor with it resting on his bent knees. It was the usual sort of thing: birthdays and family trips; vacations in Europe or China or Tahoe, or their private lakeside retreat in northern California. They seemed incredibly close, Chase and his parents, and apparently spent much of their time quite happily together.

Alec felt a stab of envy at pictures of Chase being hoisted in his father's arms or hugging his mother around the waist. There were photos of young Chase on a bicycle, riding a pony, chasing a soccer ball, or sitting in front of a birthday cake ablaze with brightly colored candles. The pictures documented each stage of Chase Gordon's life, from early childhood through boarding school, high school graduation, and his first day of college. *Such a happy, happy life*, Alec thought sourly. *Look at all those happy, happy smiles.*

But there were other photographs as well. A thin, almost emaciated Chase in pajamas and a dressing gown, pale and sick-looking, like he'd been recovering from some catastrophic illness. He squinted into the camera with an expression of distrust and suspicion, his arms held stiffly at his sides as if pinioned there. Another picture showed Chase sitting in a rocking chair on some anonymous porch, wearing jeans and a sweatshirt, hands clamped onto the arms of the chair, knuckles bulging against the skin. What the hell happened? Had Chase been in some terrible accident? Was there some suppurating psychic ulcer that finally burst, flaying him open like a butcher shop carcass?

Several newspaper clippings were appended to the album, not sealed under plastic as the photos were, but tucked between pages at the back. Alec remembered seeing the headlines: POLICE CAPTAIN DIES IN FIERY CRASH.

Captain Aaron Damon had been driving with someone else, but whoever had been in the car—a late-model BMW—with him was unknown. Alec suspected this nameless someone preferred it that way. He wasn't unfamiliar with the media's ability to turn even the most innocent events into a veritable circus, so it interested him that whoever had been in the car with Damon had had their identity carefully concealed. *You had to have money*, Alec thought, *for that kind of influence*. The kind of money Chase Gordon had. It was an intriguing thought.

He suddenly lost interest in the photos and returned the book to its drawer. *Come on, gimme something for the old man. Something to keep the old bastard quiet.*

There had been rumors that Chase had been involved with Aaron Damon; some people even suggested Chase had been in the car the night Damon was killed.

"What are you doing?" Juliet stood in the open door. She was, as far as Alec could tell, furious. "You have no cause to be on this floor. I should toss you out of the house on your backside." She hustled him down to the broom closet, where she loaded him up with mops and buckets and a pair of rubber gloves. "You have work to do. I suggest you get to it, if you want to keep your position in this house."

He attempted to protest: "Yes, but Dadders—"

"I don't give a rat's behind for Dadders," Juliet hissed. "I work for Master Chase, not your father. Now get going."

As the afternoon wore away, Alec busied himself with housework and eventually found himself sitting by Walter's bed. The small table next to him was crowded with bottles of pills and other medical paraphernalia. His bandaged right hand rested on his chest; an IV line ran from the back of his left, while a pulse oximeter on the tip of his index finger dutifully counted his heartbeats. Apparently Walter had burned his hand so badly that serious infection set in, and he required massive doses of antibiotics to bring it under control. Alec supposed that butlering was more dangerous than he'd previously thought.

Walter was deeply asleep and obviously dreaming, now and then murmuring something unintelligible. Alec wanted to touch him, wanted to reach out and press the tip of his finger against Walter's smooth cheek, but he didn't dare.

Walter captivated and interested him as no one ever had. It was something Alec wouldn't dare confess aloud. If his father suspected for a second that Alec was... inclined *that way*, Alec could kiss his inheritance good-bye. It was for that reason he kept his assignations on the down-low, his sexuality a carefully guarded secret. It galled him that, in this day and age, he was forced to pretend—escort some pimple-faced debutante to the New Years' Ball, her ugly sister to the spring cotillion, pretend to fall immediately in love with the season's latest beauty queen—all because his old man was a raging homophobe. He'd almost been caught once, during a student trip to Amsterdam, when he and another boy from his sophomore class had exchanged caresses in the privacy of his hotel room—but Walter.... Walter was beautiful.

He laid his hand over Walter's, fingers resting gently on his skin, not quite a caress.... His heart hammered in his chest. If this were one of his daydreams, Walter would awaken quietly, would smile at him, would reach to kiss him—

"Are you holding my hand?"

WALTER OFTEN dreamed about Gary's death, even now, so many years after the fact. The dreams were all alike: he and Gary were standing in a stairwell, talking, then the top half of the building was gone and Gary was gone, and Walter stood alone, bent double in the screaming, dust-filled wind. He no longer bolted awake, gasping for breath, but the dream still had its claws in him.

Alec Pratt was sitting beside his bed.

Walter blinked, trying to orient himself in reality. "Are you holding my hand?"

Pratt snatched his hand away. "I was adjusting your blankets." He peered at Walter as if seeing him for the first time. "Do you want a drink of water? Juliet left a jug here for you." At Walter's nod, he poured and helped him hold the water. "Do you want anything else?"

Walter glanced up over the rim of his glass. "Pratt, why are you here?"

Alec's cheeks turned a dull red. "I was in this part of the house and I thought I should look in and see if you were okay."

"I'm fine."

Alec nodded at Walter's bandaged hand. "Does it hurt?"

Walter turned the affected arm and looked at it. "Not really. When I burned it, it was really painful, but it's not so bad now." He tilted his head to the side. "Considering how you and I have never exchanged more than a handful of civil words in our lives, I have to ask...."

"I told you," Alec said peevishly. "I was working in this wing of the house."

"Ah," Walter said. "Is that why you kept coming by my desk at the paper?" *I think he wants to make you his new BFF*, Billy had said. "Or, wait... maybe you're here to make sure nothing bad happens to me." The idea that Alec—slender, nervous little Alec—was standing between Walter and the mob was hilarious.

Alec's cell phone chimed; he ignored it. It chimed again, a little more insistently this time.

"Your pants are ringing," Walter said.

Alec swiped the phone's small screen. "Alec Pratt."

As Walter watched, Alec's face paled through several shades until he was bone white. It was like some heavy invisible structure had been lowered over him and tightened until the constriction was painful. "Of course," Alec said to whoever was on the phone. "I'll do that right away. No, trust me, this time will be different. Entirely." A pause, while Alec licked his lips nervously. "I understand." He ended the call, smiling sheepishly at Walter. "My uncle," he said. "Always so demanding." Alec had a naturally husky voice, which most of the time was rather charming—right now it sounded like his vocal cords were being crushed. "I… gotta go."

"Alec, is something wrong?" Walter's intuition pinged loudly. "Are you in some kind of trouble?"

"I really do have to go." He bolted for the door like a rabbit somebody had flushed out of the undergrowth. "I'll see you later."

ARMAND HAD positioned Chase facedown on a large foam mat, his arms by his sides. "Lift your head," he said, "and now lift your arms." It wasn't unpleasant—rather like a yoga posture—but Chase could feel the strain in the curve of his back. Armand saw that immediately. "You can feel that, huh? Come up a little bit higher for me."

Chase did, holding the position until Armand indicated he could relax.

"How'd that feel?"

Chase shrugged. "I can definitely feel the muscles in my lower back engage." He rolled onto his side. "Maybe it doesn't mean anything."

"I think it means quite a bit," Armand replied. He was a young man around Chase's own age, and despite his somewhat exotic name, had been born and raised in Jersey City. "When we started, you couldn't feel anything past your breastbone." Armand had always hesitated to say the paralysis was all in Chase's head. He often said he believed Chase could regain his entire mobility, but only if he wanted to. That wasn't, in Armand's opinion, something Armand could help him with. It was something Chase had to do on his own. He'd hoped Chase would demonstrate an interest in pursuing his recovery from that angle. Chase had been angry when Armand suggested that Chase *needed* his debility.

"You know, there's some people say that sex is a great motivator." Armand grinned. "Maybe you should look into that."

Chase laughed. "Are you propositioning me?"

"Not me, man." Armand raised his hands in mock surrender. "I got Gina waiting for me at home."

"You're breaking my heart," Chase said. He rolled into a sitting position and supported himself with both hands.

"I'm serious." Armand bent to fasten a wide nylon belt around Chase's waist, used to help lever him back into his chair. Getting out of chairs and beds Chase could manage, but the mat was too low for him to easily transfer himself from it to his wheelchair. "You need to meet somebody."

"Can I try it myself?" Chase nodded at his chair. "I think I might be able to do it on my own now."

"Sure thing, man." Armand brought the wheelchair close and locked the wheels. "Go for it."

Chase laid his left elbow on the seat of the chair, his right hand by his side. Uncertainty flickered on his features for a moment, but he steeled himself.

"That's good," Armand encouraged. "Do it like we practiced."

By pressing down on his elbow and pushing up with his other arm, Chase was able to lever himself off the floor, but just as he twisted to sit in the chair, his feet became entangled in the footrests and he fell facedown, smashing his nose and upper lip into the hardwood floor. Armand raced to help him, but Chase waved him off. "I'm okay." He swiped at his bleeding nose with his sleeve. "I want to try it again." He checked that the wheels were locked and pulled the chair a little closer. This time, he slid his elbow farther in on the seat and tried again. He was able to twist his body, but before he could complete the motion, his strength gave out and he sat down hard on the mat.

"Try again next week," Armand said. "You're wearing yourself out."

"I can do it," Chase insisted.

"Chase, I understand this is important to you—"

"Goddammit," Chase roared, "will you leave me alone?"

There was a long space of silence while the two men stared each other down. "I can't just leave you here," Armand said quietly. "If something happened to you, I'd be responsible. I can't take that chance."

"I will assume all responsibility for myself," Chase gritted out. "Now go."

Armand picked up his bag and started for the door. Halfway there, he stopped and looked back. "Is there somebody I can call?"

"No." Chase didn't turn to look at him. "I can do this on my own."

He waited until Armand's footsteps had receded before trying again. Getting into his chair wasn't vital by any means, but Chase refused to give in to his frustration. If he could do it—and he felt certain he could— it would be one more hurdle he'd cleared.

He tried positioning his hands different ways. He tried putting the wheelchair on the other side. He rested, panting, while sweat pooled under him on the mat and his nose obligingly started bleeding again. *I can do this, goddammit. It's a chair. I can get up and sit in a goddamn chair.* He swiped his hair out of his eyes and positioned his hands. Pushing hard, he concentrated on lifting himself. Chase grunted and sweated and swore, but finally found the right combination of physics and strength that landed him in his chair. He sat for a while, eyes closed, panting, trying to squeeze some feeling back into his tortured hands and wrists.

"I didn't realize you were in here." Walter started backing away. "Sorry about that."

"You're out of bed," Chase said. "Does Juliet know?"

Walter shrugged, one corner of his mouth lifted in a half smile. "I'll give you my chocolate milk if you promise not to tell her. Are you okay?"

"I'm fine," Chase assured him. "I was just…." He gestured at the chair. "Trying to get back into this thing."

"You're bleeding." Walter stepped into the adjoining bathroom and came back with a wet cloth. He crouched beside Chase and gently sponged the blood off his face in a concentrated silence. "Much better," he said quietly when he was done. He fetched Chase and himself a cold bottle of water and sat on the floor mat.

"Thank you," Chase murmured. "Is this part of your butler's duties?" He smiled. "You're supposed to be recuperating."

"I got lonely," Walter said. His eyes were very blue, his lashes long and thick and black. Anyone seeing him for the first time would think him happy and carefree, almost reckless. Chase had thought that, too, until he saw Walter's eyes. They were the eyes of a man who no longer trusted the world.

Chase understood that level of mistrust.

He nodded at Walter's bandages. "How's your hand?"

"Juliet has been giving it round-the-clock surveillance," Walter said, laughing. "She's taking good care of me." He fell silent. "I understand she's been taking good care of you for a while."

"Since I was very young," Chase said, "and especially since my parents—" He stumbled over it, recovered, and carried on. "Since my parents died."

"I'm sorry," Walter said. There was an awkward silence. "I got a new record. Billie Holiday. It's a bit of a cliché, I know, but she's great. I just love that voice."

"'Good Morning Heartache,' that's my favorite," Chase said. "The inevitability of sadness, the sweetness of unrequited love. It's all there." He cringed, listening to himself. Good Christ—could he be more pretentious?

"Do you want to hear it?" Walter asked. "Maybe later?"

Walter's lips curved up at the sides, giving him a perpetually amused look, matched by the slightly upward tilt of his eyebrows. *He would be serious in bed, though*, Chase thought, *serious and highly focused and—goddammit why am I thinking this?* His nose was still bleeding; he dabbed at it with his sleeve.

"You're going to ruin that shirt," Walter observed mildly. "Give it here. I'll soak the blood out in some cold water." He held his hand out for the shirt.

Chase lifted it over his head and pulled it off. He dropped the shirt into Walter's outstretched hand.

"Thanks," Walter said. He sighed and stood. "So I'll see you later?"

"I'd like that," Chase replied, suddenly breathless. "I'd like that very much." He wanted to lean forward and lick a slow trail up the side of Walter's neck, then turn his face and kiss him, a deep, heartfelt kiss he'd feel for days. It had been a long time since he'd felt physical attraction to anyone, but something about Walter made his libido sit up and take notice.

It wasn't like Alec had never seen the room before. In the years since graduating college, he'd spent more time in this particular building than he had in his own bedroom. And it wasn't like the men arrayed around him were strangers. He knew them as well as his own family—which was to say, well enough to be scared spitless of them. They were men who held grudges like nobody's business; it was a bad idea to get on the wrong side of such people. It wasn't an exaggeration. Alec knew it for a fact.

"So, Alec, you been busy? You working for a living these days?" A tall man emerged from the shadows, smoking a cigar. He was at least six and a half feet tall and probably weighed little more than 120 pounds. He was known around the premises as Boney Joe, but his real name was Joseph Giambino. He was the youngest son of Sal Giambino, one of the lower-ranking mugs with tenuous attachments to a Napoli crime family, who nowadays confined itself to money laundering, prostitution, and underworld banking. He'd formed an attachment to Alec for reasons unknown and liked to show up whenever Alec was summoned to a meeting.

"That's right." Alec tried to swallow and couldn't. "I've been busy." He glanced around the room. "I like what you've done with the place."

Boney Joe pulled up a chair and sat. They were now sitting practically nose-to-nose. It wasn't a position Alec particularly enjoyed, especially since Joe liked to chew garlic. "Tell me something," Joe said conversationally. "Just what the hell are you doing on Long Island?"

Alec adjusted the knot of his tie. "Working?" His habitual nervous laugh dropped into dead air.

"We're concerned about you." The man who'd spoken shrugged. Alec didn't remember his name and didn't want to ask. He wasn't anybody important. "The boys tell me you been kind of hard to reach lately. They got no phones out there on Long Island?"

Alec uttered a nervous sound that wasn't quite laughter. "Of course they do."

Boney Joe reached out and smoothed the lapels of Alec's jacket. "It's important that you keep in touch with us, Alec. It hurts my feelings when I don't hear from you."

Alec cringed from Boney Joe's touch. "I'll be sure to remember that."

"See, there's something you can do for us," Joe said. "It's easy. A bright young man like you? Should be no problem."

Alec had an idea where this was heading, and he didn't like it. "Well, you see, fellas, I'm pretty busy these days, what with my new job and—"

Boney Joe shut him up by the simple act of slapping him—so hard Alec tasted blood. "You aren't hearing me, Alec. We need you to do this." He reached into his coat pocket and took out a switchblade. "I'm sure you know what this is."

"Yes." Alec's face burned where Joe had slapped him. He'd have a bruise later—something to try to explain away when he got back to Gordonstoun.

"It's easy. He did some work for me, made a delivery, you might say." Joe handed him a folded slip of paper to go with the knife. "Unfortunately he kept the proceeds of this enterprise to himself."

"That's terrible," Alec said. "After all, trust is the cornerstone of business—"

"His name and address are on there. Look him up after four o'clock. And try not to make too much noise. His mother's sick."

"Okay." Alec tried for a smile, but his face felt like cement. "I'll get right on it." He stood, but Joe's hard hand slammed him back into the chair.

"Make sure you do," Joe said. "I'm trying to send a message here. Fuck this up and I'll cut your goddamn ears off and feed 'em to ya."

As soon as he was able, Alec fled. He went through the kitchen, out the back door, and traversed a narrow, foul-smelling alley until he finally emerged on 9th street. Anyone who saw him would surmise—incorrectly—that he was afraid and walking fast to get away from whomever or whatever was pursuing him. They would be wrong. Alec was furious. He tossed the switchblade down the first storm drain he saw, then hailed a cab to take him to the address on the slip of paper: 247 Mulberry Street, in Little Italy.

The apartment was a fourth-floor walk-up with stairs that looked as if they hadn't been cleaned since Jesus was a cowboy. Alec found apartment nine and rapped on the door. He hoped this wouldn't take long. He had no other reason to be here apart from the slip of paper Joe had given him; the quicker he could get this over with, the better. For everybody.

The door opened a crack, the chain still fastened. An old woman's face peered out of the gap. "Yes?"

"I'd like to speak to your son, Mrs. Martel." Alec was polite. He found civility got him things that a lack of manners never did, and Alec was always exquisitely well-mannered. "Is he in at present?"

"He's not here." She made to close the door, but Alec wedged an arm in the opening.

"I'm an old friend of his." Alec offered her a beatific smile. "I'm leaving town tomorrow and I'd love to speak with him before I go."

"I told you, young man, he's not—"

"Who's at the door, Ma?"

The old woman threw up her hands and backed away. The gap was filled with a puffy red face surmounted by greasy black hair.

"Who the fuck are you?"

"I need to talk to you."

"Fuck off," Red Face said. "I don't know you."

"Boney Joe sent me to talk to you," Alec said. "Actually he sent me to kill you," he continued conversationally, "but since you've been so accommodating, I think we'll let that slide."

The expression of hostility slid off the man's face.

Alec stepped back to let him unhook the chain, then the door opened to its full extension.

"Joe sent you, huh?" He took a swing at Alec, but Alec caught his arm and twisted it behind him, bending his fingers back painfully.

When he was certain the man was subdued, he leaned down to whisper into his ear. "Boney Joe sent me here with a knife so I could slice you up," Alec said pleasantly, "but I talked myself out of it. He says you have something that belongs to him, and he wants it back." He twisted the man's arm for emphasis. "Joe is going to be pretty peeved with me if he finds out I didn't kill you. So my advice is this: send him back his money and then disappear." Alec released him so suddenly, the man fell forward, catching himself on his hands. "If I find you're still here after... oh, let's say three days, I'll be back. And then I will kill you."

The man roared, swiping at Alec's legs with one huge fist, but Alec had always been blessed with quick reflexes. He dodged the intended blow and kicked the man viciously in the face, laying him out prone on the dirty floor.

"Three days," Alec said. "And Joe still wants his money. Don't make me come back." He stepped past the fallen man and went downstairs. By the time he reached the street, he was sweating, trembling, and nausea was rising in his stomach. He wasn't good at confrontation, despite how it seemed. He needed to breathe. If he didn't breathe, he was going to be sick. He passed a man with a hotdog cart, the smell making him retch painfully. He bent at the waist and swiftly vomited everything he'd eaten and drunk that day. The crowd on the sidewalk parted around him, several of them exclaiming in disgust. Alec wiped his mouth in his sleeve just as a hand came down on his shoulder. He froze.

"Next time I'll bring a barf bag." The man the voice belonged to was taller than Alec, handsome in a quiet sort of way, an unassuming brunet with clear gray eyes. Detective Brian Schrade.

"Don't you know not to sneak up on people like that?" Alec tugged his handkerchief out of his pocket and wiped his mouth with it. "What are you doing here? Don't you have somewhere else to be?"

"I could ask you the same thing," Schrade said mildly.

"Do you know what I really hate?"

"Puking your guts up in the street?"

Alec glared at him. "You, checking up on me."

Schrade squeezed his shoulder, turned him around. "There's a diner just down the street a ways. Let's get some hot coffee."

"I don't want any coffee," Alec spat. "I just want to go home. When Joe finds out—"

"He won't. My guys will have Martel in custody inside of an hour. He'll be relocated upstate, where he can't give anybody any trouble."

They reached the diner—Minnie's—went inside, and took a booth near the back. Detective Schrade stood to remove his coat, the badge at his waist winking in the light.

Never leave home without it, Alec thought sourly.

Schrade opened a menu on the sticky tabletop and glanced up at Alec. "I wonder what's good here."

"Try the botulism," Alec snapped. "Fresh every day." He stopped talking as the waitress arrived with a jug of ice water to fill their glasses.

"Give me the thing with the eggs," Schrade told her, "and some hot toast for my friend here and maybe some coffee."

"Tea," Alec said. He shrugged. "The English woman makes a lot of it. I got used to it." He was starting to feel better, the nausea receding gradually and with it a little of his habitual edginess. He sipped some water and took a quick, nervous glance around the diner. Besides the two of them and an old man at the counter, the place was empty.

"You were never in any danger, you know," Schrade said as soon as the woman had gone. "I had five guys on you." He tilted his head sideways into the palm of his hand and scratched his short-cropped hair.

"How comforting," Alec said—but the sneer had left his voice. "I'll remember that when Joe's boys chop me into fish food."

"Hey." Schrade reached across the table and caught hold of Alec's wrist. This was new, as far as friendly gestures went. Alec had known Schrade for years, but up until today, Schrade had never touched him. Schrade's hand was warm, and his touch was comforting. This was unusual. People didn't usually try to offer Alec comfort. "Nobody is chopping you up." His eyes were dark gray, slate-colored, his gaze penetrating. "What did Joe say?"

"After the 'kill him' part?" Alec asked. He looked up as the waitress appeared with a pot of tea and a cup.

"Just be a minute for the food," she said, and went away.

"He's been pretty tight-lipped lately." Alec lifted the lid of the teapot, inhaling the warm steam. "I don't know why. I still get called to meetings, but it's never anything big, just housekeeping. He gives me anything to do, it's crap like Martel, busy work. It's like he doesn't trust me." He poured some milk into his teacup and added a measure of hot tea. "They know I'm on Long Island these days, and they've figured out why."

"Do you think that's what it is?" Schrade asked. There was a small cut in his lower lip, a split in the tender flesh. Alec wanted to reach across the table and touch it gently, smooth the hurt away. "They don't trust you?"

Alec shook his head. "I don't know. They don't talk around me anymore. It's like they send me off to bed when the grownups are in the room." He frowned. "In a manner of speaking."

"So you think Joe suspects something?"

Alec shrugged. "I don't know," he said again. He tasted his tea, grunted, added sugar. "They seem to be a lot more cautious. I'm not comfortable. Something's going on."

"And how is dear old dad?" Schrade asked.

The waitress appeared and laid down two plates of food.

"Any luck there?"

"He got me into the Gordon estate when I told him I wanted to do a story," Alec said. "If I back off a little, he might feel comfortable enough to let his guard down. I'm supposed to be the underbutler. The old man wants me to think he's sent me to Gordonstoun because there's a big story there, something that will make my journalistic 'career.'" He made air quotes around the word "career."

"Being on Long Island keeps you from getting under his feet," Schrade said. "He's keeping you out of the way." The police had long suspected Franklyn Pratt was into something more than newspaper ink. As soon as Alec displayed an interest in his father's business dealings, various improbable stories appeared, seemingly out of nowhere. Each was the perfect opportunity, Pratt Senior said, for Alec to develop his journalistic skills. Putting him in the Gordon household would allow Alec to dig up as much dirt as he could carry. Alec knew that if Franklyn Pratt had to generate some leads for Alec to follow, he would. Anything to keep his son busy and out of his hair. He needed to keep Alec close at hand, relatively speaking, to know where he was at all times.

"I don't think this is working out so well," Alec said. "Everybody on Joe's end seems to be shutting me out. I can't get any information." He spread marmalade on a piece of toast. "I went home last weekend and the old man stayed in his office almost the entire time. I think he's even got a slop bucket in there for when it's necessary."

"He's avoiding you?" Schrade asked. "Deliberately?"

Alec traced the rim of his saucer with his index finger. "I think he knows something's going on, something out of the ordinary." He flickered a glance at Schrade, then away.

"Your father's business interests in Honduras," Schrade said quietly. "We may have a lead." He swallowed some coffee, wincing, and Alec was suddenly glad he had ordered tea instead. "A small lead," Schrade amended.

Alec, busy with his toast, raised his eyebrows in query.

"Some money went missing from a bank account in Honduras," he said. "The money was held in trust for a small church the Gordon family had sponsored, some kind of village revitalization thing."

Alec nodded. "I heard about that. Wait… it's been what? Thirteen years since the Gordons' plane went down?"

Schrade smiled, but it was an ironic smile. "Small amounts have been siphoned off gradually, over a period of years. Never so much that it would be noticed."

"Skimming the till?" Alec asked, buttering another piece of toast.

"Skimming *all* the tills," Schrade said. "They've been stealing from just about every subsidiary and division of Gordon Industries, even pissy little ones so far off the beaten path they don't even register. And they were really good at covering their own tracks."

His gaze lingered as Alec licked butter off his fingers. Just for the hell of it, Alec licked them again, more slowly this time. Schrade's eyes darkened, his pupils blown wide with what Alec recognized as emerging desire. *Gotcha.*

"At first we couldn't figure out where the money was going," Schrade said. "It just disappeared. So we did some more digging. Looks like your old man's set up a dummy corporation in Honduras, something called Nuevo Dia."

"New day," Alec said. "It's Spanish for 'new day.'"

"It's supposed to be part of a corporate plan to inject some cash into the really poor areas of Honduras and Venezuela." Schrade helped himself to a piece of toast from Alec's plate. "They intend to set up factories, turn the smaller villages into manufacturing centers that will employ the local people."

Alec didn't see how this was a bad thing. "So?"

"They're modeling the factories after Valentin Sabino's maquiladora. He's the capo of the Mencia drug cartel operating around Juarez. On the surface, the factories produce cell phones for export. They're cheap, easy to make, and the labor costs are miniscule."

Alec smirked. "Miniscule."

"Will you shut up and listen?" Schrade huffed out a breath. "The phones are dummies, completely empty inside. They're being used to smuggle samples—cocaine, heroin, ecstasy. These bastards are flooding the market with it, and this isn't your grandmother's ecstasy. They're cutting it with ketamine—Special K—and bath salts."

Alec winced. "Wait, that stuff that makes you eat people's faces? Those bath salts?"

"Bath salts are designer drugs," Schrade replied. "They're incredibly dangerous—and incredibly difficult to detect. They aren't covered by any of the laws meant to keep a lid on illegal substances, because technically they aren't drugs, as such." He sipped his coffee thoughtfully. "We think Sabino is involved with human trafficking, mostly migrants."

"Smuggling them across the border?" Alec tore a piece of toast in half and bit into it. "I can't see how that would benefit him; people in that situation are hardly flush with ready cash."

Schrade pushed his eggs around his plate. "Slavery, sex trafficking, forced labor… the really nasty stuff." He glanced around the restaurant. "Some of these people make it out alive. A lot of them don't." He studied

Alec's face for a moment. "I'm sorry I'm the one telling you that your father is a scumbag."

"Don't be." Alec gazed at him, unblinking. "You think this is news to me?"

An awkward silence fell between them.

Alec searched in vain for something to say. He felt like he had inadvertently exposed some deep and faintly shameful part of himself, something Schrade didn't know about, didn't need to know about. He cleared his throat. "But why would my father need to siphon Gordon Industries funds?" he asked. "He has more than enough wealth to finance such an enterprise."

"He does," Schrade agreed, "but this is better. The Gordons were always considered ultralegitimate, at least in these parts. Your old man approached Elliott Gordon years ago, but Gordon wouldn't do business with him. I think he knew Franklyn Pratt was dirty." Schrade paused to take a sip of coffee. "Somehow your father got his hands on Gordon's money, money that was set aside for humanitarian projects like the factories. It's *Gordon* money that's paying for all of this, money Nuevo Whatsis—"

"Dia."

"It's Gordon money paying for these factories and all the rest of it, and it's set up to look like Gordon Industries is funding Nuevo Dia." Schrade sat back. "Do you see what I mean?"

"You lost me somewhere around Venezuela," Alec confessed.

"It will look like someone with a grudge against the Gordons is siphoning the money. But why steal money you don't actually need? Your old man would never be suspect. Isn't he wealthier than Croesus?"

"He's a bastard," Alec said.

Schrade ignored the comment. "Instead of having to spend his own money, he steals and spends theirs. Somebody discovers the missing funds and immediately assumes it's someone inside Gordon Industries. By then, Franklyn Pratt has made his money, nobody suspects his involvement, and as far as he's concerned, it's all good. Once the money is traced back to its source, everybody thinks Gordon is dirty."

"That is… diabolical," Alec said. "But brilliant." He picked a discarded toast crust from his plate and squeezed it, then licked the butter off his fingers.

"Will you stop that?" Schrade clenched his fists. "For Christ's sake." He swiped a hand across his brow. "I'm trying to do something here."

"Sorry," Alec said. He wasn't. "You call this a small lead? It sounds to me like it's all tied up."

Schrade raised his hand for the check as the waitress went by. "I wish."

The waitress came back with the check, and Alec took out his wallet.

"No, I got it," Schrade said. He laid some bills and change on the table. "Oh, there's one more thing." He leaned across the table, his dark gray gaze boring into Alec. "Stop being such a fucking cocktease," he murmured, "or the next time I see you, I'll throw you down and fuck your brains out."

He retrieved his coat from the hook and left without as much as a backward glance.

ALEC HAD never intended to become a snitch. It just happened.

Like every other phone call with his father, this one ended in a screaming match. No matter what Alec did, no matter how hard he tried, no matter how good his grades were—and they were outstanding—it was never good enough. Franklyn Pratt fully expected Alec to follow him into the family occupation as soon as he finished college. He thought Alec should major in business, perhaps earn an MBA, and for a while, Alec played along. He borrowed textbooks from friends and copied out pertinent passages regarding business and finance, banking, and international trade. Whenever he went home, he'd engage his father in conversations featuring the bits and pieces he'd managed to procure. For two years he was able to convince the old man that he was nose to the grindstone, working his ass off for a business degree, when in fact he'd been studying art history since the beginning. The old man would yank every cent of Alec's allowance if he knew, so Alec was very careful to keep this knowledge hidden.

He was successful until the day he and his father were in the city and ran into a classmate of Alec's making the rounds of the Soho galleries. The conversation covered many topics, but most especially the midterm examinations, and had Alec ever managed to locate any common design element between Art Nouveau, Moderne, and Deco?

His father waited till they were in the car on their way back to Long Island before he broached the subject. *I hadn't realized midcentury design was part of the curriculum.* Alec tried to change the subject, with no success. *Tell me, Alexander, how it is that you are studying Art Nouveau when I know for certain you are earning a degree in business?*

It's an elective, Dad. Honestly.

Franklyn Pratt didn't believe him and pulled Alec's funding, including his tuition, books, and all living expenses. *If you want to study art, you can damn well do it on your own dime.*

Alec was packing to leave one night when somebody knocked at his dorm room door. He opened it to find Lazlo, a former roommate who'd moved to his own room farther down the hall. "Heard your old man fixed it so you have to go home."

"You heard right," Alec said. He carried on folding shirts, assuming Lazlo would leave, but he didn't.

"Guess you're looking for a way to make some money," Lazlo said.

Alec looked at him sharply.

"Legitimately, I mean. Totally legit. One hundred percent."

Alec stopped folding. "Like how?"

Lazlo ignored the question. "You could stay in school if you had money, right?"

Alec asserted that, yes, that was right.

"Well, I know a couple of guys who can make that happen."

"I am not selling drugs," Alec said, suppressing a shudder. He'd heard the horror stories of couriers who made the fatal mistake of trying to outsmart their bosses—heard how they ended up in the river or tossed out of a speeding car. He could just imagine what the old man would say when *that* happened.

"Nobody said anything about drugs." Lazlo made a "calm down" motion with his hand. "These guys are pro all the way. Listen, come down there with me, meet the guys, and if you don't like it, no harm done."

So that was how Alec found himself in the passenger side of a brand-new SUV that Lazlo couldn't possibly afford on the allowance his stepfather sent for his books and tuition. Lazlo drove fast, faster than was safe, and Alec spent much of the ride clutching the door handle. They slipped through the lighted canyons of Manhattan, headed for West 44th Street in the theater district, and Porque, an upscale restaurant run by two brothers, twins with matching shoes and haircuts and an eerie resemblance to Tweedledum and Tweedledee. On any given night, the brothers could be seen in quiet circulation around the main dining room, checking to see that water goblets and coffee cups were being appropriately replenished and nobody was misbehaving. They were very hands-on when it came to business.

Lazlo parked in an alley behind the restaurant. "Come on. You want to meet these guys. These guys are a riot."

Instead of entering through the main door, Lazlo led Alec from the alley entrance into the kitchen, a long room with a lot of people in it. "This here's Barry," Lazlo said, introducing Alec to the dishwasher. He was so nondescript a person that he seemed to blend into the background. Seeing him elsewhere on the streets, Alec was certain he wouldn't even recognize the man.

The other was Pietro, one of the line cooks, familiarly known as PoPo. He had flashing dark eyes and a voluminous cloud of black hair, and his expression implied he didn't suffer fools—gladly or otherwise. Alec was a little afraid of him.

The dishwasher removed his hands from the water and dried them on his apron. He took a small, brown paper parcel from the huge walk-in fridge and handed it to Lazlo with a smirk.

"For Frankie?" Lazlo asked.

"Yeah, that one's for Frankie," Barry replied.

Lazlo handed the parcel to Alec. "Here you go. You might as well learn how it's done."

"So that's it?" Alec was incredulous. "That's all I have to do? Knock on the door and give this to Frankie?" The box was perhaps eight inches long by four inches wide. Its depth could hold a couple packs of cigarettes, laid on top of each other.

"You're a friend of our boy here." Barry wrapped a hand around the nape of Lazlo's neck and shook him gently. "You been real good to our boy. He'd like to help you out."

"Thanks for giving us a hand," PoPo said. "I gotta hand it to you, you're doing us a solid here, boys."

"It's nice to know you're handy," Barry said. He grinned at them, the loose-lipped grin of the village idiot. "You're our guy, hands down."

Alec blinked, not sure if he should laugh. Was he included in the joke? Maybe he was the joke. "Well, thank you, gentlemen. I'm sure we'll be seeing a lot of each other."

When they were back in the car, Alec found himself annoyed by Lazlo's pervasive smirk. "So what's in the box?" he asked. "Given the frequency of the puerile puns, I'm going to assume it's some body part."

Lazlo's grin disappeared. "How'd the hell you know that?"

"I'm not an idiot," Alec hissed. "The place practically reeks of the mob—and I know damn well it's not apple pie we're delivering." He fell silent, seething. "Start the goddamn car," he said, "and let's get this over with."

They drove for a while in silence, the radio a quiet murmur between them, faces illuminated by the near-constant wash of neon. Alec drummed his fingers on the armrest and tried to swallow down the fear crawling up his throat. "Where does he live?" he asked.

"Look, don't be mad at me," Lazlo said when they had stopped for a red light. "You needed money. This is what friends do."

For fuck's sake, Alec thought, *you could have warned me.*

They eventually ended up in the Bronx, in front of a shabby walk-up with too many garbage cans and a hand-lettered sign that read: No Parking. "Let me do the talking," Lazlo said. They went upstairs to a dark, narrow hallway that smelled of urine, and stopped in front of number fourteen. Lazlo rapped smartly on the door. "This guy's real strange," he said, sotto voce. "Don't take too seriously anything he says."

The man who opened the door was skinny, with a prominent nose and front teeth to match. His face was pockmarked with old acne scars and scabs he'd obviously been picking. His jeans hung low on his hips in the current fashion—although Alec couldn't figure out how anybody could walk like that—and a dirty wifebeater. "Yo wan?"

Lazlo smiled. "We brought you something. PoPo says he wants to talk. He knows where Papa Gee's keeping the bitch." He handed over the parcel. "She sent something to remember her by."

The door slammed shut. Lazlo gestured to Alec, and they went down over the stairs and back out to the car.

"What was in the box?" Alec asked. The whole experience was utterly surreal. "What was it—drugs, money?"

Lazlo glanced across at him. "Papa Gee loaned Frankie some money for Frankie's girl to get herself fixed up. Only Frankie's not so good about paying back what he owes, so Papa had to step up his game."

The hair on Alec's scalp prickled. "What does that mean?"

Lazlo reached over and patted him roughly on the knee. "Don't overthink this, Alec. Trust me. You don't want to go there."

PoPo met them in the kitchen, just like before, only this time he gave Lazlo a fat envelope full of crackling paper bills.

Lazlo drove Alec back to his dorm room and split the money with him, handing him a stack of bills. "So can I call on you again?" he asked, as he was leaving.

"What was in the box?" Alec persisted.

Lazlo shrugged. "Not for me to say."

As soon as Lazlo left, Alec took the money out of his coat pocket and counted it. It contained a thousand dollars in nonsequential bills. *Thousand dollars for an hour's work*, he thought. *What would dear old Dad say?*

Later, he lay in bed with the lights off and told himself it was okay, he could do this. He fell asleep sometime around 4:00 a.m. and dreamed he was sifting through a mountain of brittle leaves, looking for somebody's severed hand.

FROM THEN on, Alec could expect a tap on his dorm room door about once or twice a week; Lazlo would be there, car keys in hand. "You feel up for some Italian?" he'd ask—it was the same thing he said every time. Lazlo thought this was very funny, but it mostly annoyed Alec.

It's a stupid thing to say. He snapped at Lazlo once as they were getting into the car. *Why do you always say it?*

Every instance saw them repeat the same procedure: park in the alley around back, go in the kitchen entrance, talk to the cook or the dishwasher. Sometimes they'd have to deliver a parcel; sometimes it was an envelope. The deliveries gradually escalated in importance, from carrying a nondescript cardboard box to some crappy neighborhood, to attending the governor's ball and passing off an envelope full of bribe money to Governor White's personal assistant.

Alec went home for Christmas the same year he'd started doing deliveries for PoPo. He'd moved out of the dorm and into a chic little apartment in Midtown, a refurbished bedsit carefully renovated to preserve its original charm. It had pressed tin ceilings and a panoramic view. The previous owner had been a woman in her nineties who had filled it with furniture from the 1930s and 1940s, and hung gossamer window sheers that diffused all available light. It was a beautiful apartment.

Alec hadn't bothered with a car because it was pointless, especially in Midtown, given he had nowhere to park it and wasn't about to pay exorbitant fees at any of the commercial garages nearby. He took the train home whenever he went, which wasn't as often as it had been. Now that he was financially and personally independent, he didn't feel the need to put up with his father's ranting about how he was absolutely negligible and a nobody, how he had no ambition, would amount to nothing.

His mother and sister met him at the train station as he arrived home for the Christmas holidays. As soon as Alec stepped out onto the platform, he was enfolded in his mother's perfumed embrace.

"Mom, don't crack my ribs."

"I'm just so glad to see you." She cupped his face in her hands and squeezed his cheeks. She'd been doing it since Alec was a toddler. "Look at that face. What a gorgeous face."

Alec's sister, Cecily, allowed him to kiss her cheek, but unlike Mother, wasn't particularly interested in Alec's conversation. When they arrived at the house, Cecily disappeared somewhere.

Marcus, their butler, showed Alec into his old room. The housekeeper had aired it and changed the bed linens, and it smelled like lemon oil, just like always, but it was no longer home. Alec felt like a trespasser, unpacking his suitcase and putting his things away. He caught sight of himself in the bureau's antique mirror: a pale young man, his dark hair in artful disarray—Alec paid a stylist in the Village a king's ransom every six weeks to keep it looking like he'd just rolled out of bed—his lips compressed into a line, his ice-blue eyes remote, colder than they'd ever been.

Between his late-afternoon arrival and dinner, his father called him into his study for a "little chat." Alec was used to these little chats. They usually indicated he'd done something wrong, failed his father in some way.

"Hello, Dad." Alec slipped into the sumptuously decorated room and shut the door quietly behind him. "It's good to see you."

His father's study hadn't changed at all. Even after all these years, it still resembled Alec's earliest memories: mahogany desk, leather chair, walls lined with rare books. His father liked to sit behind the desk and make business calls, issuing his vituperative diktats in his resonant voice that drilled through Alec's skull like a lobotomy cannula.

"Alexander." His father came out from behind the desk and nodded coldly at him, as if they were business acquaintances rather than blood. "It would appear you have resolved your financial difficulties by other means."

"I have a job, if that's what you mean." It came out far more petulant than he would have liked; he sounded like an irate child.

His father took two steps forward and backhanded him savagely, the ring on his hand scoring a deep channel in Alec's face. "Do you think I'm stupid?" Franklyn Pratt roared. "I know what you've been up to. I know all about you."

Alec dabbed at the cut on his face with shaking fingers. "I'm sure we can—"

"Shut your goddamn mouth! Don't you talk back to me, you little bitch. I know all about your *job*. You've been doing deliveries for Fatty Veranda, haven't you?"

Alec gazed at him, saying nothing. There was nothing to say.

"It's going to stop," Pratt said, "supposing I have to drag you back here and lock you in the basement."

During his youth, Franklyn Pratt had been a formidable force in the international business community. His empire stretched across several continents and included such diverse concerns as a fish cannery in Maine and a sweatshop in Bangladesh that made cheap clothing for a national chain of stores. As his business acumen grew, so did his fortune, and now at the age of sixty-four, Pratt had amassed a personal fortune of some four billion dollars. The years had not been kind to him, however, and with his sagging middle and general air of dissolution, he looked like a much older man, one who had been ridden hard by the vicissitudes of life.

As a young boy, Alec had been terrified of him, terrified of the elder Pratt's physical presence and his constant loud harangue. As he grew older, however, Alec began to see the old man as he was, without the gloss of wealth and presence. At some point it occurred to him that his father was scarcely the invulnerable gorgon he'd been made out to be, but rather a ridiculous figure, a diminished lesser god whose power was all but vanished.

"No, you won't." Alec's heart thudded painfully. He drew a deep breath. "You're not going to do anything to me. Those days are over."

He took his handkerchief out of his inside pocket and dabbed at the cut on his cheek. "I don't work for you anymore, Dad. I've found something of my own."

The weeks and months working with Lazlo had taught him many things. He now understood something of the way the world worked— understood, too, his part in it. He'd done things that strained credulity, or would have, if the old Alec had done them. The old Alec would never become a runner for the mob, never carry the kinds of messages guys like Fatty sent. He liked the new Alec much better.

Franklyn started forward, fists balled at his sides.

"By all means, Dad," Alec said quietly. "See what happens." A pearl-handled switchblade had materialized in his hand. Alec was smiling. His cheeks ached with the strain of smiling.

"You're a thug." Pratt seemed horrified, confronted with this new Alec, this cold-eyed man he didn't know. "You're nothing but a common criminal."

Alec shrugged. "I'm well paid. I have a beautiful apartment in Midtown. I'm quite comfortable." He folded the knife and put it away. "You always told me I needed a career. Like yours."

Besides his interest in South American drug cartels, Franklyn Pratt had strong connections with organized crime via his newspaper empire. Alec had discovered this through a series of intimate conversations with one of the underbosses, a man who went by the name of Stitch. Stitch, Alec discovered, loved being humiliated and cursed, especially when the swearing came from someone with as agile a tongue as Alec. He'd taken to picking Alec up whenever he felt the need for some one-on-one. Stitch was always talkative both during and after; Alec found Stitch's pillow talk yielded valuable information, information he could use, and all it cost him was a sore whip-hand afterward.

"I feel so much better now that we've had this little talk," Alec said. He tucked away his bloodied handkerchief. "It's nice to clear the air, don't you think?"

Franklyn Pratt avoided Alec for the rest of his visit, hiding in his study and only emerging on Christmas Eve, when the family exchanged gifts in front of the tree. He was visibly relieved when Alec packed up his things and returned to the city.

Alec was only too glad to be leaving, but felt it important to settle things with the old man before he left. "Thank you," he said, standing with Franklyn at the door. "This has meant a lot to me." He drew his father into an awkward hug and kissed him on both cheeks. The message was unmistakable. "I'll see you, Dad. Maybe we can do… business some time."

THE NEWS of Alec's confrontation with his father made it to the city before he did.

He stopped by the restaurant to pick up a delivery from PoPo, a pink bakery box tied with string.

"Hey, kid."

Alec turned and went cold all over. "Good afternoon, Mr. Veranda." He must have done something really, really wrong. The thought made him queasy. "So nice to see you, sir."

Fatty Veranda was six feet tall and easily 350 pounds. He had an affinity for diamond jewelry and wore a lot of it, mostly rings. His nose had been broken sometime in his youth and had never set properly, and its presence in the middle of his face resembled a fingerling potato. He had bad teeth and the small, sharp eyes of barnyard swine.

"Come into the back, kid." Veranda waved an impatient hand. "Come on, I don't have all day."

Veranda maintained offices at each one of his properties, which made it convenient to meet with his lieutenants and give such orders as were necessary. This particular office was a clone of all the others he'd been in, on various business for Fatty: paneled in dark wood with a big desk and a cigar cutter sitting on the coffee table. Alec, like the other men in Veranda's organization, had heard stories about Veranda's love of fine cigars, and fine cigar cutters, which he kept razor sharp. Veranda liked to use a cigar cutter to send a message, when such a message was needed, and there were several of his goons walking around with missing fingers.

"Sit down," Veranda said. "Take the comfortable chair." He offered Alec a cigar from a custom wood humidor, but Alec declined.

"Thank you, sir, but I don't smoke."

"Yes, you do, because that's what you are, kid, you're smokin' hot. You got everybody in town eating your dust." Veranda carefully cut the end off of his cigar and lit it. "I want to give you a promotion."

Oh God, Alec thought, *I'm a dead man.*

Veranda laughed heartily. "Don't look so worried, kid. Did you think I was gonna bump you off?"

Relief flooded through Alec so strongly that he nearly wet his pants. "Of course not, sir."

"Good, because I got a job for you."

Alec was to deliver a gift-wrapped parcel to a man at the airport who would be waiting in the departures lounge for an outbound flight to Barcelona.

"Sir, with all due respect, I can't simply stroll into the departures lounge." Alec tried to laugh, but it came out sounding like a wheeze. He choked on his own saliva and fell into a coughing fit that wouldn't stop.

"Relax," Veranda said. He poured a glass of water from a carafe and slid it across to Alec. "Have a sip of that and take a look at this." He handed Alec an envelope.

When Alec opened it, he saw it was a ticket to Barcelona, first class. "I-I don't know what to say," Alec stammered. "Thank you, sir. This is very generous."

Alec was to approach the man waiting for him the departures lounge, sit beside him, and say "Melvin says you like this kind of cake." He wasn't to hand the box over until they were in the air.

Veranda summoned one of his lieutenants. "Jimmy, get the box we've got for Gerry's boy."

Jimmy returned with a box and put it on Veranda's desk, then disappeared again.

"Go ahead," Veranda said. "Open it."

"I don't know if I should," Alec demurred.

Something sparked in Veranda's eyes, a brittle warmth Alec knew was entirely for show. "I feel disrespected when you say things like that," Veranda said. "It hurts me when you disrespect me. I feel that, Alec."

Alec opened the box. A pair of severed hands—man's hands, judging by the look of them—lay on a bed of frothy pink tissue paper. The hands had begun to turn black at the nails; the odor was absolutely vile. Alec swallowed hard against the sudden rise of bile in his throat. There was a very real possibility he might faint. If he fainted, he'd embarrass himself in front of Veranda, something he absolutely wanted to avoid. *Don't get sick, don't get sick.*

"Hey, what's the big deal?" Veranda asked. "You done this before. That night you went out with what's his name, Lazlo, to deliver that parcel to Frankie, what did you think was in it?" He shrugged. "It's my trademark. It's why they call me 'The Handyman.'" He gestured at the box. "Take it home with you, put it in the fridge. It'll keep till you get to Spain, huh? You're doing good, kid."

Alec caught a taxi back to his apartment and put the box in the refrigerator, next to some leftover carrot cake.

ALEC ARRIVED at the airport the next morning, groggy, wearing sunglasses, and clutching a cardboard container of black coffee. He'd hardly slept the night before, getting up several times to check that the box was where he'd left it. When he did sleep, his dreams were riddled with horrible images. His muscles pained him and the light hurt his eyes. He didn't want to do this, but he knew what Veranda would say if he didn't. Worse, he knew what Veranda would do.

The man he was supposed to meet was sitting in the departures lounge, wearing a beige topcoat and reading a copy of *National Geographic*. He didn't look up as Alec sat, preferring his magazine.

"Melvin sends his regards," Alec said. He pasted what he hoped was a smile on his face. "You know, Melvin."

The man ignored him.

Alec remembered what Veranda had said and kept the box on his lap until the flight was called. Alec lined up to board with everybody else, but when he presented his passport, the attendant merely glanced at it and waved him through. Veranda's influence, again, he supposed. The man to whom Alec was supposed to give the box boarded immediately ahead of him. Alec wasn't surprised to discover they were seated together in first class. Alec had the window seat, something he disliked. The sight of the ground falling away beneath him made him break out in a cold sweat, and the nausea of the night before pressed at the back of his throat. He leaned over to speak to his seatmate. "Melvin says you like this kind of cake." He handed over the box with what he hoped was an engaging smile.

The man didn't smile back. He set the box on his knees and untied the knot in the string. "I hope I like this kind of cake," he said quietly.

Now he'll open it and see what's inside and my part of this is done, Alec thought. His pulse throbbed in his throat, and he could hear the rush of blood inside his ears. The lid of the box caught for a moment on some internal obstacle, and Alec braced himself to look away. He didn't think he could stand to see the severed hands lying in their grotesque nest of tissue paper like a pair of blackened gloves.

"What the fuck…?" His seatmate stared down into the box and then at Alec, his mouth hanging open comically. "What the hell is this?"

The hands Alec was supposed to bring to Spain were nowhere to be seen. The only thing inside the box was three pieces of leftover carrot cake.

There's a box of severed hands in my refrigerator, he thought. *In my apartment… severed hands….*

He broke into a sweat, fumbling for the airsickness bag, and emptied his stomach somewhere over New Jersey.

WHEN THE plane landed in Barcelona, Alec's nausea had passed and he exited down the Jetway with the rest of the passengers, eager to get a cab and see something of the city before returning to New York where don Veranda would kill him.

He had stepped off an escalator and was on his way to the Customs area when something jammed into his back. *Already?*

A warm breath brushed his ear and a man's voice said, "Drop the box."

Alec froze. "It's carrot cake, swear to God."

"I said—" A hand reached around and slapped the box to the floor. "—drop it." The voice the hand belonged to was American, without any particular regional inflection. It sounded brisk, business-like. The man grasped the back of Alec's collar and walked him to the nearest wall. "Hands flat on the wall, feet spread." Alec did as he was told, enduring a thorough pat-down in silence. "Turn around. And take off the sunglasses."

Alec did as he was told, sliding the glasses off his nose. "I have a headache," he explained. "The light was hurting my eyes."

A badge passed briefly in front of him. "Detective Brian Schrade, NYPD."

Fuck.

"Nice sunglasses," Schrade said. He looked Alec over. "You're a lot younger than I thought you'd be."

"You can't know how that comforts me," Alec retorted. Under other circumstances, he'd have been pleased to talk to someone like Schrade—someone with his light brown hair cut short, and deep gray eyes, and a body Alec suspected was hard and tight under his navy blue suit. Schrade was like a walking wet dream.

"Smart mouth, huh?" Schrade said. He unhooked a pair of handcuffs from his belt and deftly fastened Alec's hands behind his back.

"Which one are you?" Alec asked. "Good cop or bad cop?" He smirked. "I can play it either way."

Schrade didn't answer. He walked Alec through the airport and outside to where a sleek, black car was waiting, its engine already running.

"What about my carrot cake?" Alec asked.

Schrade pushed Alec into the backseat and got in beside him. A second man was already seated on the other side, possibly to prevent Alec from making a sudden exodus. Schrade signaled the driver, and they pulled away from the curb.

The highway wasn't particularly crowded, and what scenery they passed was more or less the same: open fields, trees, crops, the sky. Alec closed his eyes and slipped into a strange state between sleeping and waking, roused occasionally when the car went over a bump in the road. They stopped briefly at a service station, and Schrade went inside and came back with an armload of cold sodas in various flavors, none of which Alec wanted. He dozed fitfully, waking occasionally to look around. There were more houses and less open space the closer they got to Barcelona, and blocks with nothing but apartment buildings and smaller streets that reminded him of a school trip to New Orleans when he was seventeen.

The car stopped in front of an unremarkable hotel one step above a fleabag; Schrade registered the both of them, then escorted Alec to their room via the elevator. The door opened onto a barely furnished closet with narrow twin beds, a mirror set above a small rickety table, and one straight-backed chair.

"Don't get too comfortable," Schrade said. "You're being extradited back to the States in the morning."

"You'll never keep me alive till trial." Alec heard the tremor in his own voice and despised himself for it. "As soon as Veranda—"

"I don't give a rat's ass for Veranda. You're going back to the States, with me, tomorrow." He sighed. "Are you hungry? You don't look so good."

Alec had eaten nothing since the previous night, a scanty supper of leftover Chinese food, some of it stuck to its original carton. "I get sick when I fly. Yes, I am hungry."

Schrade took off the handcuffs and called room service while Alec sat on the bed, massaging his sore wrists. Alec noticed Schrade was always careful to stay between Alec and the door. There was no sign of the third man, the one who'd sat next to Alec in the car. *Maybe*, Alec thought, *Schrade rented him for the day*. The thought made him laugh out loud, which earned him a strange look.

Schrade talked to Alec while they were eating, making the kind of general conversation people usually did at dinner tables. "We were watching you," he said. "The whole time we were watching you. Did you know that?"

Alec put back the tapas he'd just picked up. "Should I be flattered?"

Schrade ignored the dig. "It was pretty damn strange that a college kid all of a sudden moves out of the dorm and into a fancy apartment in Midtown, even if his old man has more money than God." He refilled their coffee cups from the carafe on the table. "We put a man on you as soon as we found out who you were."

A hard little ball of anger formed in Alec's chest. "Who I was? What does that mean?"

"Franklyn Pratt's son. Your old man has been on our radar for a long time."

Alec made a face. "Here I was thinking I'd been the soul of discretion."

"Why do you talk like that?" Schrade asked.

Alec blinked. "Talk like what?"

"Like an English teacher from the 1920s." Schrade's gaze played over him. "*Are* you an English teacher from the 1920s?" The question made it seem like Schrade was interested, but Alec knew better.

He laughed dismissively and glanced away. When he looked back, Schrade was still waiting for an answer. "Of course not."

Schrade's forthright, unwavering gaze made him nervous. Alec couldn't figure out what he wanted, and it bothered him. He was good at reading people, teasing out the truth about them from the warp and weft of their habitual lies. Schrade was uncomfortably opaque.

"Wait, I know." Schrade took a mouthful of coffee, swallowed it, and grinned. "You're that kid everybody picks on, the one with funny clothes. I bet your mother dressed you in short pants and a bowtie, didn't she?"

Alec wanted to grab Schrade by the back of his cheap haircut and slam him face-first into the table. "Mmm." It wasn't quite a laugh. "Something like that."

He'd gone to an exclusive boarding school, where all the other boys came from old money and he was the only one whose father worked for a living… a scholarship kid, too smart for his own good, prone to correcting the other boys because he knew better than they how to conjugate French verbs or write long essays on the fragile state of Balkan politics. Franklyn Pratt's money could have sent Alec to a thousand schools as good or better, but he believed in taking advantage of something when it was offered for free.

"We thought you might be working for your father." Schrade lifted the lid off a bowl of poached fruit and forked a selection of pears onto his plate. "Keeping a hand in the family business."

The food stuck in Alec's throat. He grabbed his water glass and swallowed violently, forcing it down.

"I surprised you," Schrade said quietly. "You didn't know we were gunning for your old man." He laid his fork down and dabbed at his lips with a napkin. He had, Alec thought sourly, exceedingly fine manners for a cop.

"Why would you be investigating my father?" he rasped. The tapas had scraped his throat.

"Your father is being investigated for possible racketeering and fraud." Schrade refilled Alec's water glass. "He's played it close to the vest so far. We haven't been able to get anything on him. That's where you come in."

It took a moment for the implication to sink in. "Really?"

"We have quite the list of charges against you. We're willing to make that go away."

"My father must be a pretty big deal," Alec snapped, "if the NYPD chases me all the way to Spain. What's he into? Purloined ink? Wait, I know: the newsprint he uses isn't Fair Trade."

Schrade didn't say anything at first. When he spoke, his voice was quiet, contemplative. "He is part of a corrupt media cartel that's involved in drug smuggling and human trafficking between South America and the US." He pushed away the plate of uneaten pears. "Last month he helped 'relocate'"—Schrade made air quotes with his fingers—"over seven thousand women and girls from Central America to border towns in the southwestern US." Schrade got up from the table and went to lock the door. It locked with a key on both sides, Alec saw—Schrade's way of telling him he wasn't getting out. "They were told it would be an opportunity to immigrate to America." He paused. "You mean your old man never let you in on his secrets?"

Alec couldn't see Schrade's face—the detective stood with his back to the room—but the stiff spine and shoulders, the taut muscles straining against the thin cotton of his shirt, betrayed him. "No," Alec said. "My father and I don't share things." His voice sounded unnaturally loud in the otherwise silent room.

"But you might say something like that if you thought it'd make me go easy on you," Schrade said, turning around. "Wouldn't you?"

He looks tired, Alec thought. *He looks like nobody loves him.* He wondered if someone was waiting up for Brian Schrade, back in New York. Was some man or woman pacing before a window, wondering and worrying, checking for messages, trying not to call?

"Do I actually have anything to bargain with?" Alec dropped his head and pressed the heels of his hands against his tired eyes. This was starting to feel like an absurdist comedy, and he was the hapless rube in the middle. "Or is this already a done deal?" It occurred to him that Schrade might want something besides information. He looked up; Schrade was standing in front of him.

"Will you help us?" Schrade asked. "It'll save you a lengthy prison sentence."

Schrade wanted him to spy on the old man, to keep track of Franklyn Pratt's business dealings and report what he knew. Occasionally he might be called upon to liaise with others, to act as guide and lookout for other informants in the area. It was really very simple: if Alec agreed, he could walk out of the room and there would be no charges laid against him. If Alec refused, he was going to prison for a very, very long time.

"You'd like that," Alec retorted. "It would make your month if I went to prison."

"No," Schrade replied, "I wouldn't."

They were interrupted by a knock at the door: a waiter from downstairs come to pick up the room service tray. Schrade locked the door behind him when he left.

"Fine," Alec said. "I'll do it." He told himself it wasn't to get back at Franklyn Pratt. The idea that his father willingly traded people across international borders for God knew what reason sat at the back of his throat like a bad taste.

Later, he lay on his narrow bed, gazing across the room at a sleeping Brian Schrade. Looking at Schrade tormented him, put all sorts of ideas in his head, ideas that had no business being there. Men like Schrade were never interested in Alec. A man like Schrade would never let Alec touch him, would never let Alec kiss him. The only thing he'd feel for somebody like Alec was contempt.

CHASE CONCEALED himself in the library with Walter, sequestered behind a locked door and a large stack of vintage jazz recordings. They listened to Billie Holiday and drank cold beer and talked about music and movies and books. Walter fell asleep in the middle of a Wynton Marsalis album, and Chase covered him with a blanket. He liked watching Walter sleep; he'd found this out during Walter's lengthy convalescence. Chase had spent hours sitting at his side, sometimes reading or dozing himself, but often watching the play of emotions, thoughts, and dreams across Walter's sleeping face.

What's happening to me? He wheeled himself over to the fireplace and laid another log on the fire. It was a cold night, and the fire was a comfort to him, as fire usually was. There was, he thought, something primeval about it, about sitting close to the flames and warming oneself; in spite of cold or other privations—

Here Chase stopped, smiling to himself. *What privation have you ever endured?* He reached out with the poker and shifted a half-burned log to the back of the pile. Years ago, when he was a boy, he and his father would go on camping trips to the Poconos and pretend they were fearless explorers chasing some mythical monster. Once it was the elusive Sasquatch, but they also tracked Champ, the legendary lake monster and, some said, cousin to Scotland's Loch Ness monster. He and

Dad lay awake under the stars for ages, picking out the constellations and making up ridiculous stories about the monsters that lived in the sky.

As Chase got older, of course, the camping trips became less frequent, as he and his dad turned to sports events, football, and ice hockey. When Dad died, Chase's interest in spectator sports vanished, and people who had known him and his dad began to drift away. Some of his old friends kept in touch, or tried to, but it was hard to socialize with someone who refused to leave his house. Chase Gordon was alone, and that was fine by him—rather, it always had been, until now.

He glanced back at Walter Godfrey, sleeping peacefully on the sofa. He was attracted to Walter; he knew this, and it frightened him. He couldn't afford another heartbreak like he'd had with Aaron. That had very nearly killed him.

He'd fallen hard for the warm, handsome police captain, friend of his parents and frequent attendee at various charity functions. He didn't care that Aaron was twenty years his senior. Chase loved him and wanted him, and when Aaron died, Chase thought he'd lose his mind. He very nearly had: an eight-month stint in an exclusive upstate psychiatric clinic had set him back on his feet, but only that.

He'd never been identified as the passenger in the car crash that killed Aaron. He'd always wondered about that. After the initial announcement, the story had died away, more quickly than was usual. Chase's family was well-known. There were a lot of people who could identify him on sight. Surely the firemen and other first responders had recognized him. He'd been taken unconscious from the wreck, had spent nearly two weeks in the hospital. When he was well enough to go home, he scoured the media for news of his involvement, but there was nothing. As far as everyone was concerned, Aaron had been alone in the car, alone and driving drunk, something Chase knew wasn't true. Aaron hardly ever drank, and never if he intended to get behind the wheel. It was, Chase had thought at the time, like Raoul Whitfield's novel *Green Ice*, where Mal Ourney was convicted for drunk driving, only he hadn't done it. Of course, Ourney hadn't died in the story. Aaron had, and Chase had woken up in a private hospital room surrounded by people telling him not to worry, everything was all right. It had all the elements of a 1940s noir film, *I Wake Up Screaming*.

The door opened and clicked softly shut. Juliet, in pajamas and a dressing gown and wearing slippers. She wore reading glasses and carried a newspaper under her arm. "Just came to ask if you needed anything," she said quietly. She nodded at Walter, still sleeping. "I see you have some company this evening."

Chase raised a warning hand. "You promised."

"What on earth are you talking about?" She tried unsuccessfully to hide her smile. "I'm glad. It's high time you started living again."

"What have I been doing all this time?"

Juliet opted not to answer that. "Want me to wake him up and send him to bed?"

Chase shook his head. "No. I'll do it." He squeezed her hand. "Good night, Juliet. Sleep well."

She paused where she was for a minute, her hand still joined with his. "If he's bothering you, I can get rid of him."

Chase glanced at Walter's sleeping form. "He isn't bothering me... he isn't bothering me at all." He gave her hand one final squeeze and let go. "You should go to bed... woman your age...."

Juliet pretended to be affronted. "You saucy little bugger." She tapped him on the head with her newspaper. "Chase...." She sighed. "This is probably none of my bloody business, but... don't feel you have to always be alone." She nodded at Walter. "Sometimes it's worth the risk to let someone in." She let the door close quietly behind her as she left.

Chase went to where Walter was and levered himself carefully out of his chair onto the floor. He rested his elbow on the edge of the couch and laid his cheek on it.

Sometimes it's worth the risk.

As much as he respected Juliet's opinion in just about everything that mattered, he wasn't convinced. He'd taken that risk with Aaron Damon. He wasn't likely to take it again. Still....

Walter stirred and opened his eyes. He saw Chase sitting on the floor beside him and smiled. "Sorry. I didn't mean to conk out on you." The firelight picked out red highlights in Walter's dark hair and cast half of his face in shadow. "Was I asleep for long?"

Chase leaned closer. "Long enough," he murmured. His heartbeat thundered in his chest as he reached out and laid a hand against Walter's cheek. His every instinct screamed against this. *What the hell are you doing?*

Walter didn't move, but his eyes darkened with emotion. "Long enough for what?"

"For this." Chase kissed him—a soft, gentle brushing of lips at first, then deepening into something more erotic, more profound.

WALTER, VERY gently and very carefully, levered himself off the sofa and on top of him, covering his body, pressing them down on the floor together. Chase slid a hand between their bodies, fingers stuttering on Walter's buttons, baring the smooth skin of his chest.

Walter sat back on his heels, pulled his shirt off, and tossed it away. He gasped when Chase reached to tag one of his nipples, teasing the tiny bud to an almost painful hardness. "Keep that up," Walter said, "and I'm not going to last." He leaned forward and kissed him again, a slow and lingering caress that spoke to Chase more deeply than words.

Chase's cock was hard, throbbing with his pulse, exquisitely sensitive to even the slightest touch, almost painful. He moaned when Walter reached to tug his pants down to his knees.

"Beautiful." Walter dragged his fingers down Chase's belly, the short nails biting deliciously into Chase's skin, leaving a trail of fire behind. He stood long enough to discard his own pants and underwear, and then he was back, lying with Chase in front of the fire, their naked skins pressed together. *Careful*, he thought. *I gotta be careful*. He didn't know the physical extent of Chase's disability, and he didn't want their first time to end in pain. Walter considered himself a man of the world, and his sexual conquests since Gary's death had been many and various, but he had never felt like this before, like he and Chase were melting together, immersed in each other.

Chase cried out when Walter leaned down and took his cock into his mouth, tongue swirling over the swollen head. "Yes," he murmured. "Do it like that. Just like that." He held Walter's head in his hands, his fingers sliding through Walter's hair, clasping the back of his neck, reaching down to caress his shoulders in an incoherent fever of arousal.

Walter released his cock and slid up to lie on top of him, the long bone of his erection pressing into Chase's stomach. He grunted softly when Chase angled his hips, his pelvis rising off the carpet, grinding into Walter almost desperately. *I like it that way*, he thought. *Do it that way*. He wanted more: he wanted Chase to roll him over onto his back, spread his legs, and drive himself into him; he wanted to feel Chase's long fingers, slick with lube, sliding into him, making him open and wet and ready.

The floor swung wildly away from him as he was grasped and held, his body rolling through an arc. He was suddenly lying on his back, staring up at the ceiling, and Chase was on top of him, Chase's weight pressing him down, holding him in place. There was a small jar of hand cream on a nearby table. Walter reached for it, opened it, scooped some out, and warmed it between his hands. He pushed a hand between their mated bodies, taking hold of Chase's swollen cock. "Can you...?"

"Can I...?" Chase was momentarily confused. "Oh. Yes. Yes, I can." He blinked. "Are you sure that's what you want?"

Walter's entire body trembled. "Yes." His cock jumped, spilling a trickle of precome. "That's exactly what I want."

Walter held out the opened jar of cream, and Chase plunged his fingers into it. He rolled his body to one side and reached to spread the slippery balm around Walter's opening, briefly dipping inside. Chase worked his fingers in and out, pressing the tight ring of muscle at Walter's entrance, smoothing and gentling him. He pushed in deep, hitting Walter's prostate and making him groan and curse, his desire hovering just out of reach, implacable.

When Chase entered him, time stopped. He welcomed the intrusion of Chase's swollen, blood-hot cock, opened his legs to him, wrapped himself around Chase, and rocked with the rhythm of their moving bodies. His pulse beat in his ears, and every muscle in his body was taut with expectation. He wanted to spin it out, take this first time slowly, savor it, but his desire was too great. Chase slid a greased hand around Walter's cock, and he was gone. His back arched, nearly throwing Chase off him, and he came so hard his vision and his other senses went. He could see and hear absolutely nothing; he could feel absolutely nothing except the shattering climax as it tore through him, leaving him breathless and spent.

CHAPTER SIX

"NOW, JUST like we practiced, okay?" Armand stood close behind him, a hand lightly on his waist, the other holding a push-button device attached to the complex bionic exoskeleton Chase was wearing. "On three."

Chase reached out to brace himself on the walker in front of him. He drew a deep breath, perhaps a little unsure, and glanced at Armand. "Let's hope this is going to work."

"I'm sure it will." Armand smiled. "One."

"Two," Chase replied.

"And three."

Holding tight to the walker's handgrips, he stood. He stood and didn't fall, didn't sway or feel weak. He didn't feel afraid. "Wow.... I just—"

Juliet stood silent nearby, with Walter just behind her, his expression somber, intense. He was trembling.

"Now walk," Armand said. "Just like we practiced."

Chase did. He walked to where Juliet and Walter were, then back to Armand. The bionic exoskeleton—Chase had designed the prototype—was held to his body by a series of clasps and buckles. The machine automatically adjusted to Chase's movements, augmenting his strength but allowing him to self-direct the motion. Chase had tested the technology at every stage of its development, working with a team of skilled engineers to hone and perfect it until it was ready to be produced for the general market. Gordon Industries had contracted a Honduran company to make 3D-printed versions of the exoskeleton, for use in poorer areas and those hard-hit by disease and malnutrition. Chase intended to go down there as soon as the prototype was ready, to show them how it worked and to devise a strategy to bring the technology to some of the more remote towns and villages.

"It's really astonishing what they can do these days," Juliet said, crossing the room to where Chase was. "Really amazing." She hugged him hard, kissed his cheek soundly. "I am so proud of you." She reached out and gave Armand a one-armed hug. "And you."

WALTER MOVED closer to examine the exoskeleton's construction. "Now I know what Gordon Industries spends its R & D money on," he said, grinning. "Good God, you look like Iron Man." He was genuinely happy for Chase, and the emotion lit up his face. He waited until Juliet and Armand had gone before speaking privately. "Do you realize how incredible this is?" He allowed Chase to pull him into a hug. "You can walk again. Imagine how many people you can inspire to do the same." He pulled back to look at him. "I'll pitch the idea to Eleanor. Maybe we'll do a big spread. Show you using it, and have some experts weigh in on the technology. We might get some of the bigwigs to come onboard and help out."

The silence that fell between them was hollow, cold, and weighed a thousand pounds. Walter was sure the room's internal temperature had dropped a good ten degrees.

"I know about the technology," Chase said quietly. "I helped invent it."

"Even better," Walter enthused. He looked down between their bodies, at the marvelous machine. "Holy melted codpiece, Batman, this is amazing."

Chase slipped out of his embrace and went to sit in his chair. He unbuckled the straps holding the suit to his legs. "And you would write this story?" His tone, cool to begin with, verged on Antarctic. What the hell was going on?

"Well… yes, I thought I might," Walter said. "It's the feel-good story of the year, and just in time for Christmas. Imagine how much good this invention could do."

Chase unbuckled a few more straps and looked up at him. "No."

Walter bristled. "What do you mean, no?"

"I don't want you to write the story." Chase set the suit aside. "I don't think the media needs to be involved in something as private as this. It's nobody's business."

"Are you telling me what to write?" Walter stared at him incredulously. "Really?" His pulse throbbed in his wrists and in his neck.

"I don't care what you write," Chase said, a bit more gently. "I just don't want you writing about me. Considering that you live and work in my house, it's not too much to ask."

Walter flushed a deep red. His fists clenched. His right hand, finally free of its heavier bandages, still felt unpleasantly tight. "I'll write about whatever I damn well please."

"Not if it involves me," Chase said stubbornly.

"What the hell do you think I'm gonna do—libel you?" Walter laughed sarcastically. "Besmirch the glorious Gordon name? Christ, you really are full of yourself, aren't you?" It occurred to him that he just might be overreacting, but he couldn't seem to stop talking. In a minute he'd say something he couldn't take back, something that would shatter the fragile trust between them forever.

He turned on his heel and left.

He was in Eleanor Rigby's office before noon, still fuming. He told her a condensed version of Chase's paralysis and the exoskeleton. She listened with interest, then sat back in her chair and bit down hard on her pencil.

"He probably prides himself on the eccentricity of being a recluse," she said. "The untouchable Chase Gordon."

"It's not like that," Walter said. "He's really very sweet." Chase had been anything but sweet while he was bitching Walter out about the story.

Eleanor raised a cynical eyebrow. "Did you fuck him?"

"No!" It was the truth.

"Did he fuck you?" When Walter didn't answer, Eleanor leaned forward, her chair creaking violently with the sudden change of position. "What was that like?" When Walter still didn't answer, she said, "Come on. You know it's been ages since I got laid. What's he like in bed?"

Walter couldn't help but laugh. "I think I know why you went into the newspaper business."

"Why? Because I'm a nosy bitch?" She scoffed. "Or because I wanted the honor and prestige that only a serious journalistic career could give me?" She turned the pencil in her mouth and bit it again. Obviously she missed smoking, Walter thought. His surmise was confirmed when she reached into her desk drawer and took out a package of nicotine gum. She popped one of the small brown pellets into her mouth.

"He's really sweet," Walter said lamely.

"Hmph." Eleanor chomped hard on her gum. "And he's using this exoskeleton thing to walk again… after the paralysis… psychosomatic, of course, caused by the shock of his parents' sudden death several years ago." Her gaze unfocused and faraway. "So what does he do for fun, this guy, besides mope around his great big house feeling sorry for himself?"

"He doesn't—" Walter huffed out a frustrated breath. "He's not like that."

"You fucked him." Eleanor smirked. "I can always tell. You've got that freshly fucked look." She picked up the pencil, forgetting she had gum in her mouth, and bit down on it. The gum was quickly shifted to the other cheek. "What's he like? I bet he's an animal in the sack."

Walter ignored the question. "Look, Eleanor, this is the story of the year: Paralyzed Billionaire Walks Again."

"Nah, I don't like the billionaire angle. Makes it sound like his money paid for the whole thing. I mean, it did, but this would work better if he was a Brazilian orphan or a street kid or something. I don't want people to think this is something only the one-percenters can afford." She tapped the pencil against her top teeth; it made a hollow clacking noise, like high-heeled shoes walking on a concrete floor. "How about 'The Bionic Man: Long Island's Own Chase Gordon....'" She trailed off. "Nah, I don't like that either."

"I want to do a serious piece on this," Walter said. "Not front-page stuff, not the kind of sensationalistic garbage these other guys are doing. I'm not interested in putting him on display. I want this to be respectful, upbeat." He was suddenly reminded of the first time he saw Chase, sitting alone in the shadows. "I don't want to play up the pity angle either. He doesn't want pity, and I don't blame him." He spoke excitedly, warming to the subject. "El, you should see him. He's amazing. He's smart and gorgeous and kind. He doesn't care about money. He's—"

"Yeah, yeah, yeah," Eleanor said irritably. "Sing me his praises after you get the story." She tapped the top of her desk with one long red fingernail. "I want a copy on my desk, Walter. No more fucking around. I've given you more than enough rope. You're straining my credibility with the big boys." She nodded at the ceiling.

"I promise, El, it'll be an incredible story. You'll love it."

Eleanor drew a slow breath, then nodded. "I'd better love it. And you're still fired."

Walter left Eleanor's office and took the elevator down to the newsroom. Billy and several others were hanging around what used to be Walter's cubicle, staring intently at the computer screen while Billy industriously pressed keys. They looked up as Walter approached and scattered, all except Billy, who stayed right where he was. "Well?" Walter asked. "Enjoying yourself?"

Billy smirked. "I heard you've been busy." He nodded at Walter's right hand, which was much improved and wrapped in a smaller bandage. "How's the burn?"

"Better," Walter said. He leaned in over Billy's shoulder to read what was on the screen—a tabloid puff piece about some beach vacation Chase Gordon had taken some years before. Gordon frolicked obligingly in front of the cameras, wearing swim trunks and a smile.

"Damn," Billy said. "That is niiiice."

"Gordon Heir Shows the Waves Who's Boss," Walter read aloud. "Why do you read this garbage?"

Billy closed out the browser window and spun around in the chair to face Walter. "Sore spot for you?" He leaned forward, elbows on his knees. "How's that working out, by the way? You must enjoy the housework, huh?" He grinned. "Are there any particular benefits I should know about?"

"Billy, can you keep a secret?"

Billy laughed. "I sense a heartfelt confession."

"This is serious." Walter's brows furrowed. "I could use your advice, in fact."

Billy stood and took Walter's elbow. "Come on. Too many eyes and ears in here." They took the elevator up to the building's roof and stepped out into the cool fall air. Billy turned to Walter, entirely serious now, no longer the joker. "So what's up?" he asked. "You know you can trust me." He held out his fist and Walter obligingly bumped it, like they were teenage boys instead of grown men.

"I'm kind of in trouble," Walter said. He went to the parapet and leaned on it, palms resting against the rough stone. From here it felt like the entire city was spread out at his feet, a sea of steel and glass. It looked cleaner from up here, Walter thought, and the air was fresher, as if by rising some fifty-two stories into the air they could escape the filth and savagery that was New York.

Billy appeared at his elbow. "What kind of trouble?"

"The worst kind."

"Why?" Billy asked. "Who'd you kill?"

"It's nothing like that. I'm in the other kind of trouble."

"There's another kind?"

"The one where you meet a guy, and—" Walter shook his head. Two window washers dressed like Spider-Man and Batman clung to the side of the building opposite, methodically spreading suds and wiping them off. "I told myself it was just going to be a job, an assignment for the paper."

Billy leaned his back against the parapet. "I hear he's a really nice guy," he said noncommittally. He bent his head and peered into Walter's face. "Is it that kind of trouble?"

Walter laughed humorlessly. "I should just back away, right now."

Billy nodded. "Sleep with him yet?"

"Mmm." For some inexplicable reason, Walter felt like crying. "It's not like it was with Gary. It's different." He shook his head. "Sometimes I feel like he's the only person in the world who even comes close to understanding me… and sometimes I want to kick his ass." He looked out over New York. Batman was slightly ahead of Spider-Man with the window cleaning. Clearly Spidey wasn't up to scratch when it came to washing windows. The building housed a specialist's clinic for burned children. Obviously Spidey and Bats were for their benefit. "He likes the same things I like… books, music…." He glanced at Billy. "Ever try to have a conversation about Dashiell Hammett with most people?"

Billy affected a Bogart-esque snarl. "Put the pot on, schweetheart. S'gonna be a long night." He leaned closer. "Think you might stay there? At his place, I mean. If the story's worthwhile, you might as well take your time getting it, right?" He squeezed Walter's shoulder. "Mr. Chase Gordon doesn't seem to mind your being there."

"When it comes to potential boyfriends, he's perfect," Walter said. "That's what scares me. If I let myself, I could—"

"So why don't you?" Billy asked quietly. "Walter, Gary is dead. He's been gone since 9/11. It's 2014. That's…." He pretended to count on his fingers.

"Thirteen years," Walter said. "I dunno, it feels like… I'm cheating. Me and Gary, we were as good as married. He died and I buried him." In actual fact, there had been no identifiable remains to bury. The FDNY supplied Walter with a box of ashes from the scene, but only because he was one of them. There was no way of knowing if the ashes Walter buried were Gary's remains or the remains of a thousand other people killed that day. He waited for Billy to say something like, "You have to get on with your life," or "Gary wouldn't want you to be lonely."

"What do you want to do?" Billy asked instead.

Walter shrugged wordlessly.

"What's your gut telling you?" Billy asked.

"If I let myself," Walter said quietly, "I could fall hard for this guy. I mean, the whole thing, all the way to the altar."

"Or the City Clerk's office," Billy put in.

They both laughed, and Walter checked his watch. "Anyway," he said, "I should get back." He reached to shake Billy's hand but was pulled instead into a tight embrace.

"You're my friend," Billy said, suddenly serious, "and I love you. So don't be stupid."

WALTER STOPPED at a florist's shop before catching the LIRR back to Long Island. It was early afternoon, but most of the cars were nearly full with officious-looking types in business suits and tan raincoats.

A burly man with a lot of camera cases strung across his torso took the empty seat next to Walter. "Goddamn lunatics," he panted. "There's plenty to go around. Why the hell they gotta act like animals?" He nodded at the bouquet of long-stemmed yellow roses Walter carried. "Little present for the missus?"

"My boyfriend." Walter spoke unthinkingly, and as soon as it was out of his mouth, he could have bitten off his tongue. "Well, he's n-not really m-my boyfriend," he stammered. "He's just a guy I know, and we—"

Walter's seating companion flailed a hand in the air between them. "Spare me the details, kid. That whole gay thing's yesterday's news. Unless he's some big celebrity…." He leaned closer to Walter and peered at him. "Is he?"

Walter was silent.

The burly man took the hint. "Well," he said, "whatever way it shakes out, he can't possibly be bigger than this Chase Gordon guy. Half of New York is on its way out there, hoping for an interview."

The tiny hairs on the nape of Walter's neck prickled. "An interview about what?"

The fat man leaned forward. "Somebody who works at the Gordon estate found some dirt. Real personal stuff."

"I get it," Walter snapped, annoyed. "Like what?"

"Hey, follow your own leads. When this thing breaks," he said, chuckling, "it's gonna be the biggest story since King Kong."

"King Kong was fictional," Walter said. His heartbeat thudded in his chest. "What's the story?"

The fat man spread a hand in front of him, unrolling an invisible headline. "'Gordon Heir a Dying Lunatic'—it'll play, my friend. Believe you me, it'll play. I heard he's got twenty-four hours at most."

Walter's lips felt numb with shock. "You can't do that to him."

Something in the way he said it must have alerted his traveling companion. "Why do you care?" He turned in his seat and stared at Walter. "You know him?"

"I… I've heard of him."

"Hey!" His seatmate stood and addressed the entire train car. "This guy here knows Chase Gordon!" He pointed to Walter, who tried to disappear by pressing himself against the window. "He knows Chase Gordon. He just said so!" He pushed his face into Walter's, so close Walter could smell the onions from the pastrami sandwich the man had had for lunch. "Is he your boyfriend?" He turned to the rest of the car. "This guy—"

"Please." Walter appealed to his sense of decency. He hoped the guy had one. "Your source got it all wrong."

The fat man stepped into the aisle and pointed at Walter with a flourish: *"This guy is Chase Gordon's boy toy!"*

BY THE time the train pulled into the station, Walter felt like he'd been trampled by a herd of elephants. His clothing was disheveled and torn, his bouquet of roses shredded beyond recognition. Almost before the train stopped moving, he was out the door, leaping from the carriage to the platform like a man possessed. *Exit, pursued by a bear*, he thought wildly, remembering something of his college Shakespeare. The journalists and camera operators were piling into vans and waiting buses, and Walter knew he had to get ahead of them if he had a chance in hell of making it to Gordonstoun before they did. He ran for his car, jumped in, and started the motor. He gunned it a couple times and pulled out of the parking lot at approximately the speed of sound. Fumbling for his cell phone, he managed to swipe the lock screen while keeping his car on a mostly even keel. "Goddammit." The phone's battery was as dead as the proverbial doornail. He tossed it onto the passenger seat.

The road to Gordonstoun was mostly clear of traffic, but Walter had to pass two buses full of journalists on the way. Doubtless more were coming. He floored his ancient Volvo and ignored the posted speed limits, hoping beyond hope that no cop was waiting by the side of the road with a radar gun. A TV van with a satellite dish tried to speed past him on a straightaway, but Walter stomped on the gas, putting himself once again out in front. *It's like goddamn NASCAR*, he thought. His hands were sweaty, white-knuckled on the wheel, his heart slamming into his ribs like flying kicks from some invisible ninja.

When he spotted the house just ahead of him, he put the gas pedal to the floor and drove through the main gates in a state of flat panic. A broadcast truck was setting up near one of the big oaks on the front lawn, while men with the name of a prominent television network printed across their backs were busily unrolling spools of thick black cable.

He pulled his car around the back and ran into the house. "Juliet! Chase!" He skidded to a stop in the kitchen and looked around him wildly. "Are you here?"

The opposite door swung open and Juliet was there, framed in the doorway. "I've been on the telephone ever since you left. Do you know it's been ringing off the hook?" She came toward him, brandishing a sheaf of pink message slips. "That Pratt boy took fifteen calls in the last twenty minutes, all of them from reporters."

Walter had never seen Juliet this angry. Usually she was the very model of the modern English butler, a pillar of decorum. Now she looked like she'd cheerfully strip the skin from anyone who crossed her path. "I don't understand," Walter said. "I saw them all coming here from the station. Has something happened?"

"Someone got the idea that Master Chase is no longer fit to head the consortium of family companies." Juliet pawed at a newspaper lying on the kitchen counter and held it up in front of him.

Gordon Heir a Dying Recluse?

Walter felt like he'd swallowed a quantity of lead shot. "I don't understand. Who'd print something like this, especially without proof?"

"It gets considerably better," Juliet said. "I've had practically all the television networks in the country looking for him. They're convinced he's on his deathbed, and there's talk he's dying of—" She broke off.

"Wait for it: tertiary syphilis." She looked at the bundle of sticks in Walter's hand, all that was left of his bouquet. "What the devil have you got there?"

Walter mumbled something about "…used to be roses" and dumped the whole thing in the trash. "Where's Alec now?"

"In the west wing, reshelving the library contents after Master Chase's latest foray into research. Why?"

Pratt. It had to be him. That whole business about taking care of Walter was bullshit. He'd wanted the assignment from the very beginning, wanted to impress dear old Dad with his journalistic prowess. Most likely he'd assumed the mansion was little better than a dusty mausoleum and Chase a drooling and prostrate shell of the man he'd been. What a disappointment it must have been to find out the truth.

"He did this. You can bet on it." He turned on his heel and headed for the west wing.

Walter didn't find Alec Pratt anywhere in the house—but he did find Chase packing a suitcase in his bedroom. Rather, the suitcase was open on his bed and he was tossing things into it. His wheelchair sat near the door, and Chase was standing, wearing the exoskeleton. His expression was grim. Walter approached cautiously. "Going somewhere?"

Chase didn't look at him. "Did you see them out there?"

"There were a lot of them on the train," Walter replied. "I knew they were coming here. Some guy was kicking up a racket, trying to get everybody stirred up. I don't get it. Where'd this come from?" He watched Chase toss in several pairs of lightweight pants and some short-sleeved shirts. "I'm guessing you're heading somewhere warm."

"Honduras," Chase said. "There's a situation."

"You mean the one outside on the lawn?" Walter asked. "Did they stumble upon some big story out here?" The rest of what Chase had said clicked into place. "Wh—Honduras? Why?"

"Somebody gave them a lead." Chase slapped the lid of the suitcase closed and locked it. His movements were short, deft—and angry. "Someone went running to the press and told them how I'm a useless cripple who's not fit to run my father's companies." He laid the suitcase on the floor and took his passport out of a drawer in the bureau. "Was it you?"

It was like a slap in the face.

"What?"

"Did you tell them about me?"

"Chase, I would never do that." Walter sat on the bed, legs suddenly weak. "Why would you even think that?"

Chase stuffed the passport in an inside pocket of his jacket. "I know what reporters are like. I know how you'd trample each other for a story. You're like whores," he said bitterly, "scratching each other's eyes out for the next big score." He pulled out his wallet, counted several hundred dollars in bills, and tossed them into Walter's lap with an expression of disdain. "Consider the tip included."

Walter stood, angry. "Let me give *you* a tip." He caught hold of Chase's arms, levering Chase around to face him, the bionic suit between them. "I didn't come here because I wanted your money. I didn't come here to spill your secrets to the press." Walter waited for a lightning strike. "Yes, I intended to write a story on you, but it would highlight your charitable work, the development of the exoskeleton, and the other things Gordon Industries is doing. I wanted people to see there's hope, that somebody is doing good in this rotten old world." He gazed into Chase's warm brown eyes—brown eyes with gold rings around the pupils, kind eyes, loving eyes... beautiful eyes. "How could you think...?"

Chase shook him off. "There were details. The initial story printed details, things they couldn't have known unless they'd been right there, in the room. You're a reporter. It's what you do."

"Like what?" Walter asked. "Tell me."

"Like a verbatim recital of things we said... I said...." Chase picked up that morning's *Courier-Express*. "Yes," he said. "'Do it like that. Just like that.' The witness claims to have been present at the Gordon residence when this shockingly intimate scene occurred...."

"What...? Who could have...?" Walter was dumbfounded. "Alec Pratt, maybe?" It hardly signified. Alec seemed like the sort of person who'd absolutely love to get his claws on some sordid gossip.

"It gets much better than that." Chase produced an earlier edition of the *New York Courier-Express*. The full-color front page showed Chase, lying on what appeared to be a pile of cushions. He was naked, except for the parts the *Dispatch* had obligingly obscured. Clearly the photograph was several years old. The headline read: CHASE GORDON SEX HOUSE, followed by, in smaller print, *Billionaire's Sumptuous Love Shack*. A young man in a FDNY uniform posed just below, his fireman's helmet tucked under his arm.

Holy crap. "That's *me*." Walter snatched the paper from Chase and stared at it. "What the hell…?" *Continued on page 6A*, it said. He paged through until he found it: a full spread, spilling across two pages, a collage of purloined photographs and comments taken out of context. FORMER FIREMAN'S BOOTY CALL: "*Gordon spent the previous weekend frolicking with his hunky new butler….*" The story had no byline, and no indication of the author's name; it could have been written by one reporter or by several. "This is utter crap!" Walter threw the newspaper down on Chase's bed. "You don't actually think I had anything to do with this, do you?"

"I don't know what to think," Chase said. "You didn't come here to work as a butler. I knew that, right from the beginning. Juliet knew it. We decided to take a gamble and let you into the house. I didn't think you'd write something this vicious. I even thought of you as"—he choked on the words—"my *friend.*"

"Jesus, Chase. I am your friend." Walter felt like he'd fallen through a hole into some strange, otherworldly dimension. "And yes, I did come here for a story, but not the one you think. I didn't write this." He drew a ragged breath. "My money's on Alec. And why the hell are you going to Honduras, of all places?"

"My parents funded the revitalization of a small Honduran village. It was intended to be a pilot project. That's where they were going when their plane went down. That's old news, thirteen years ago, nothing to do with now." Chase produced a much-read printout. "However, the church they helped set up was supposed to be perpetually funded. There's a special bank account just for that and nothing else."

Walter was having a hard time connecting "church" with "booty call." "I don't understand." The fax was entirely in Spanish and written in an almost indecipherable hand. "So who's this from?"

"The pastor of the church contacted me this morning. Lately— the past three months or so—they haven't been able to access the funds my parents left them. The bank refuses to recognize their authority. It's probably some glitch in their computer system." It wouldn't be the first time Chase's money hadn't gone where it should. Obviously something was up, and not just with animal charities like Shep's Place. He took the fax from Walter. "I'm going down there."

Walter stared. "You're going to Honduras. By yourself. In a wheelchair."

"I'm taking the exoskeleton. Despite what you may have heard, I'm not a complete invalid… and I'd rather be anywhere but here, feeding the paparazzi." Chase reached past him to retrieve an umbrella off the bed. "Excuse me, but my pilot is waiting." He was out the door and down the hall before Walter could speak. He moved to go after him, but was stayed by Juliet, who had a knack for appearing out of nowhere.

"Let him go," she said. "He needs to do this." She laid a gentle hand on Walter's arm.

"Juliet, he thinks—"

"We all know what he thinks. But he's wrong." She caught him in her gimlet stare. "Isn't he?"

"I would never write something like that." Not entirely true. Before he'd come here, before he'd met Chase and gotten to know him, he had been willing and eager to print whatever dirt he could get about the lonely inhabitant of Gordonstoun.

"Feel like helping me with the Thanksgiving decorations? I've got Alec fetching them down from the attic." She smiled beatifically. "It's filthy up there. I do hope he enjoys himself."

JULIET HAD cleaned up the kitchen after her latest foray into English baking, so there was little left for Walter to do. He swept the floor almost mechanically, still disturbed by the conversation he'd had with Chase. It bothered Walter that Chase suspected him of having brought the media to Gordonstoun. He wished he'd had time to make things better before Chase left for Honduras, but he was probably halfway there by now. It was four thirty by the kitchen wall clock, and Juliet liked to serve dinner around seven, so once he finished with the kitchen, Walter could take some time to himself.

He changed the blue bags in the recycling bins and tied up the kitchen garbage. Since Gordonstoun didn't get neighborhood trash pickup, Chase had enlisted a private firm to handle things. The company dropped off a dumpster behind the house, and when it was full, they came back and picked it up. It worked well.

He left the kitchen's back door ajar while he carried the trash to the dumpster. Juliet would pitch a fit if she knew, but the door tended to stick sometimes, especially in cold weather, and Walter wasn't interested in braving the fleet of paparazzi out front. He dropped the trash into the metal bin and was about to go back inside when a rustling in the bushes alerted him. He turned and saw three men dressed in hunting camouflage and carrying shotguns. "No hunting allowed around here," Walter said. "Sorry guys, but you'll have to go elsewhere."

The three kept coming toward him, and with a gut-deep flash of horror, Walter realized they weren't hunters at all. Hunters didn't wear dress pants and shiny black shoes with their camo. The only thing they were hunting was him.

He started back toward the house, but one of the men grabbed him and slapped a hand over his mouth.

"Make a peep and I'll blow your brains out," he said. His hand was cold and smelled of gun grease. He held his shotgun loosely in his other hand, but Walter knew he could cock the gun, turn, and fire before Walter had time to think. "Somebody back in the city wants to see you," his captor said. His breath hissed against Walter's ear and steamed out into the cold air. "He wants to see you. You've been a bad boy, Walter."

Walter wrenched free of his captor and yelled something incoherent as loudly as he could. The kitchen door swung back hard on its hinges and someone was there, someone Walter couldn't clearly see in the gathering gloom, someone—

—with a gun.

"Get out of the way!"

Walter reacted from pure instinct, stepping to the side as a bullet whizzed past his ear and struck the man who'd been holding him squarely in the throat. He dropped like a bridge fell on him. His two companions began backing away, firing random shots in Walter's direction, but the late autumn daylight was fading fast, and even professional hit men found it hard to shoot in the dark. Walter scrambled on hands and knees to the dumpster and hid behind its reassuring steel bulk, while what sounded like an Old West gunfight went on around him. The two remaining men weren't ready to give up, not just yet, and there was more gunfire. Walter decided none of this was real. He was dreaming a very vivid dream, and in a minute, he would wake up.

He risked another glance around the dumpster. One of the men was crouched on the ground, holding his shoulder. His companion fired back toward the house, then grunted in shock when something ploughed into his upper arm. Walter heard the distinct crack of what must have been a bullet breaking the bone before the two men broke and ran back into the woods.

A hand reached out and grabbed his collar, dragging him to his feet. "Come on," Alec panted—

Alec Pratt? Alec fucking Pratt?

—"they might come back."

He dragged Walter up over the stairs and into the kitchen, slamming the door behind him and pulling the bolt across.

The doors here still have bolts? Walter thought. *Why the hell am I thinking this?* "So, what?" he said. "Bullets don't penetrate wood around here?"

"They won't risk shooting you through the door," Alec said. "The place is crawling with reporters. The last thing he wants is for his goons to show up on the evening news."

"Who?" Walter asked weakly. He cleared his throat and tried again. "Whose goons?"

"Never mind." Alec wiped blood off his face with his sleeve. "You're better off not knowing."

"You're hurt," Walter said. He reached for Alec's face, but his hand was batted away.

"It's a scratch." Alec bent his head and scraped his cheek along his shoulder. "Bullet grazed me, is all. I've had worse than this."

There was a small commotion outside one of the swinging doors, and Juliet came barreling through. "What the bloody hell is going on? Is somebody starting a war out there, or what?"

"Some guys tried to snatch me," Walter said, "while I was taking out the garbage."

She nodded as if she'd only half heard him and turned to Alec. "Who were they? Do you know them?"

Alec shook his head. "Masetti's boys, probably. I don't know how the hell they found him." He nodded toward Walter. "Schrade figured he'd be safe here."

"He did. Are you hurt?" she asked Walter, who shook his head. "And you," she said to Alec. "Looks like you caught something in the face."

Alec waved a hand, then turned to check his gun, released the magazine, and smacked it back into place with his palm. "Scratch," he said. "I assure you, there is nothing whatsoever to worry about."

Juliet sent Alec off to the nearest bathroom so he could tend to the cut on his face. She put the kettle on and guided Walter to one of the tall stools set to one side of the kitchen counter. "You need a cup of tea. I can always tell. You've gone all gray." She took down the teapot. "You're the star witness if they ever get the Masettis to trial."

Walter nodded. "Schrade and Niedermeyer thought I'd be safe here. I guess they thought wrong."

CHAPTER SEVEN

THE SINGLE-ENGINE plane dropped steadily down through the thick band of clouds, descending slowly until Chase could just make out the dark green of the forest canopy. He'd been here before, when his parents first decided to fund the revitalization of Alanchito, a small Honduran village ravaged by a recent earthquake—but that had been over thirteen years ago, and his memories of the place were sketchy at best. This particular village had been intended as a test of the Gordons' plan to inject money into several other small settlements in the area. If Alanchito worked out, they would have proceeded to rebuild the others—but that never happened.

It was pouring rain when his plane touched down, turning the muddy airstrip into a filthy soup. The ground was uneven, and he worried the downpour might make wearing the exoskeleton—in its current configuration—problematic. It was still packed away in the back of the plane, and would be one of the last items removed with his other belongings to a waiting Jeep. Chase himself was carried to the vehicle by two large men with the hard muscles of lifelong farm workers.

A tanned man with a heavy black mustache reached to shake Chase's hand. "Dan Quinn," he said. His accent was entirely American, Kansas or Missouri, maybe. "I know," he said, at Chase's expression of surprise, "I look Honduran. I've just been here a long time. The local culture soaks into you after a while."

The trip from the airfield to the village—and Quinn's church—was no more than a mile or two, but the heavy rains meant the roads were nearly impassable. Eventually the Jeep cleared the last set of ruts and they pulled up in front of a typical Honduran house. A woman in a flowered dress was standing under an awning on the front porch; when she saw Quinn, she waved, beckoning them.

"My wife, Elena," Quinn said. "Be careful. She will want to feed you." He got out of the Jeep, and the two men who had originally helped Chase came forward again.

The wheelchair, he quickly saw, was useless, and he experienced a moment of panicked embarrassment: *What the hell were you thinking?* If he'd brought Juliet or even Walter, he might have made things easier for himself, but the current situation meant he'd have to be carried everywhere except for the main road of the village. Unless....

Chase waited until he'd settled in the Quinns' guest bedroom, his luggage with him, before getting into the suit and activating it. He'd been practicing using it—under Armand's direction—for several weeks now, using the long, empty hallways at Gordonstoun to improve his gait. He'd designed the thing, had supervised the construction of the initial prototype, and knew more about its function and operation than anyone. Maybe the muddy Honduran roads were exactly the test the exoskeleton needed.

And when you fall flat on your face in the mud?

It was an ugly thought, and he pushed it to the back of his mind. He wasn't a coward. Before his parents' death, he'd climbed, hiked, and kayaked most of the North American continent. He was an experienced spelunker whose cave dives made headlines. He surfed off the coast of Australia and raced costly, experimental bicycles in South Africa, and he'd been up Mount Kilimanjaro not once but twice. None of these accomplishments had come without failure, without sacrifice. If he fell flat on his face—in the mud or elsewhere—he'd get back up.

A test walk around the bedroom convinced him the local humidity was no impediment to the exoskeleton's operation. He'd be able to navigate the village easier if he were mobile, and the suit gave him that in a way that his wheelchair never could. Maybe he'd have a little look around when the rain stopped.

LATER THAT afternoon, after one of Elena's home-cooked meals, Dan drove Chase over to the local church, where he was the pastor. Chase expected a thatch-roofed, ramshackle affair, so he was surprised to see a beautiful modern building, with an internal environment optimized for the hot, humid climate.

Several local children were occupied in cutting leaves and flowers out of colored construction paper to decorate the Sunday school. When they saw Chase, they were struck dumb. Some of the younger ones hid behind the pews, unused to seeing a man with robot limbs walk into their church. The older ones, however, were fascinated and pressed forward, wanting to touch him, to reassure themselves he was real and not some fantastical machine. They gathered around him, murmuring to each other: *autómata... robot... sorprendente!*

Dan explained that Chase had come to help them with the church, and that he would only be staying a little while. "On Thursday nights we have general prayer here," Dan said. "We sing a few hymns and take tea together afterward. Perhaps you will join us?"

Chase hesitated. The last time he'd set foot inside a church was the Sunday before his parents' death. Never a regular churchgoer, he'd had no use for religion since then. "I... what I mean is...." He wavered, not wanting to give offense. "Of course." He'd have to sit there with a polite smile, enduring the proceedings while the congregation prayed to a god he didn't believe in. He supposed there were worse ways to spend an evening—but not many.

Dan offered to show him around the church. "This entire village was dying before your parents offered us their help. The people had always worked in the fields, growing coffee, bananas, sugarcane. Times change. The younger people found out they could get better jobs, make more money at industrial jobs in the larger towns and cities, so they left." He pointed to the main altar, at the front of the church. Instead of the traditional crucifix, there was a mural showing Honduran people walking among the myriad canes of a sugar plantation. The man at the head of the procession was dressed in the simple cotton shirt and pants of a farmer, but instead of a straw hat, he wore a stylized crown of thorns, knitted out of what looked to be barbed wire. The woman directly behind him held the hem of his shirt to her lips, weeping. It was a powerful, simple, and effective interpretation of the famous Via Dolorosa scene.

While Dan was explaining the mural, a trim dark-haired man made his way up the center aisle to where Chase was. He introduced himself as Eduardo Felicien, a reporter from the local television news program. "The only one of its kind in this area! We are on every evening at six o'clock," he said proudly.

Chase's chest tightened with anxiety. *I can't get away from them,* he thought, *even though I am halfway around the world.* He forced himself to smile as Felicien asked for an interview.

"Very brief only," he promised, "about the exoskeleton. We have lately been ravaged by bilharzia—you may have heard of it. A parasitic infestation that does great damage to the body, sometimes even the spine." He told Chase how the parasite, once it had infiltrated the spinal cord, caused paralysis, rendering its victim unable to walk, and in some extreme cases, unable to move at all. "Some recover," Felicien said, "and are able to go about their lives. Many others do not. We have been following your progress with the mechanical skeleton that allows such people to walk again."

Chase was impressed. Felicien had done his homework. "Your English is excellent."

"I completed a course of study at the University of Nevada some years ago," Felicien said. "Broadcast journalism, writing for newspapers, all these kinds of things."

"Thank you for your kind words about the device," Chase said, "but I'd prefer not to do any interviews. There's been too much of that lately."

Felicien's disappointment was writ large across his face. "To hear you speak of it would encourage people, and my cameraman"— he indicated a large young man standing behind him—"is ready at a moment's notice." He wouldn't beg—Chase saw this immediately, and it impressed him—but neither would he go away from here without a story of some kind.

Chase glanced at Dan, who stood quietly, saying nothing. Several of the children who'd been playing nearby left their construction paper and scissors and came near, drawn by curiosity.

"It is entirely your decision," Felicien said.

Chase sighed. "All right." It wasn't that he didn't want to help— that was his entire reason for coming here in the first place—but he'd had more than enough of the media lately. "A short interview," he added. "Please."

Felicien nodded and smiled, turning to speak rapid Spanish to his cameraman. Unlike American news media, Felicien didn't stick the microphone in Chase's face, but sat beside him on one of the pews and talked to him as if they'd met for morning coffee. "You are the only son of Elliot Gordon?"

Chase indicated he was.

"You loved your father very much."

It was an unexpected question, and it threw Chase for a temporary loop. "Yes," he replied. "I loved my father."

"And yet he was taken from you… is it fourteen years ago?"

He'd been in a hurry that morning to meet up with a couple of friends to go for a run. Besides, his parents were always flying off somewhere. Like as not, they'd be back in a day or so. Chase had said good-bye to them at the car just before they left for the airport. "Thirteen years," Chase said. "September 11th, 2001." He tried to smile, but his face kept tugging itself into lines of sadness. "That was a bad day for many people."

"And you became crippled," Felicien said, "immediately after the tragedy?"

Chase nodded. "I woke up one morning and my legs wouldn't work."

Felicien asked about the exoskeleton: how long had it taken to develop, was Chase in charge of the project or were there other developers, could anyone use it and was it easy to use?

"We've produced a prototype," Chase answered. "The suit I'm wearing right now. This particular suit is unique, one of a kind, but we are hoping to use 3D printing to manufacture an inexpensive version." Gordon Industries would be able to produce the suit in larger numbers and with greater frequency with 3D printing. This meant that many more people could make use of the exoskeleton to walk again. The printers could be set up anywhere in the world and used to produce the exoskeleton as needed.

AFTERWARD, DAN drove Chase back to the house. "I have to visit a sick parishioner in the village," he said. "You'll be all right here on your own?"

"I want to make some calls," Chase replied. "The sooner I get to the bottom of your financial situation, the better." It bothered him that both the Honduran operation and the animal rescue had run into financial problems at roughly the same time. Perhaps one had nothing to do with the other, but it suggested a fundamental lack of proper management at the most basic level—or the innermost circle of Gordon Industries. He wasn't directly involved with the firm's accounting, but he knew that some of the Gordon businesses shared one set of books using the same software. Theoretically, it wouldn't be hard for someone to shuffle money back and forth between them, funneling it to where he or she wanted it to go. Whoever had his fingers in the animal rescue funds probably had them in the other companies' funds as well.

"I've left the pertinent paperwork with Elena," Dan said, "and the telephone is in the kitchen… good for local calls. Anything else overtaxes the system." He grinned. "See you at church."

After greeting Elena and promising to drink the pitcher of cold tea she'd made, Chase settled down at a small table in his room and took out the satellite phone he'd brought with him. Most regular cell phones were equipped with GPS and could easily tap into satellites, but Chase didn't have a lot of faith in the local service. Maybe it was perfectly fine or even exceptional; he wouldn't know until he tried it. The table was at just the right height for his chair, so he unbuckled the exoskeleton and laid it on the bed. It looked eerily like some kind of movie monster, all snaps and buckles and articulated metal. Whoever wore something like that should be able to fly, or leap tall buildings and such. Chase grinned. When had he stopped believing in superheroes? Probably about the same time he swapped comic books for pulp fiction.

He opened his laptop and let it search for Internet connections. He was surprised to find the Quinns had Wi-Fi. He connected to their service and immediately set an alert on his e-mail program, which would beep if there were any incoming messages. Then he pulled up his list of contacts and began calling those members of the organization responsible for funding the various charities Gordon Industries supported. His first call put him in touch with the manager of the local bank, who was friendly and didn't seem to mind Chase's imprecise Spanish. He was willing to help Chase sort things out and offered whatever help was required. So why had the bank suddenly withdrawn permission? The problem lay in a missing signature: Chase's parents had signed the bank authorization forms at the beginning of the project, before their plane went down. The papers were intended to guarantee an amount of money be paid to the Honduran church in perpetuity.

Chase got hold of the family lawyer, who immediately drew up papers for the transfer of the account. From now on Chase would be responsible for the yearly disposition of funds to the Honduran project, something easily accomplished via Skype and fax machine.

He hadn't forgotten about Frey's disappearance or his role in the embezzlement of Gordon funds. He placed a quick call to private investigator Sam Jessup. Jessup, however, had nothing to report, which annoyed Chase, even though it wasn't the man's fault.

Whoever had been siphoning Gordon company funds knew his way around the accounting programs commonly in use—knew it well enough to escape detection, at least for a little while. The misleading entries in Frey's accounting were classic: skim a little off the top and rearrange the rest so nobody knows the difference. But the whole thing made no sense. Why would somebody with Frey's background and talents feel the need to steal from abused and neglected animals? Unless he was in dire financial trouble himself... maybe he had a gambling addiction? And if Frey was stealing from one company, he could very well have been stealing from them all. A forensic accountant would be able to pick up the threads more easily than Chase could. He'd get in touch with someone as soon as he was back in the States.

Chase sighed and poured a glass of tea from the pitcher that Elena had made. It was deliciously cool, with a hint of lemon and something that tasted like mint. It was pretty close to the way Juliet made it at home, when the summer heat made drinking hot beverages impossible. It reminded him of her, and he made a mental note to call her—*after* he looked up their relative time zones. Juliet coveted her sleep, and she wouldn't thank him if he woke her in the middle of the night. That made him want to call her just for the hell of it. The notion made him laugh out loud. He could just imagine Juliet at three or four in the morning, owl-eyed and sleepy, hissing into the phone. *What the bloody hell do you want now, Master Chase? Do you realize what time it is?*

He missed her... and he missed Walter Godfrey. He smiled, remembering the touch of Walter's hands on his naked skin, the way Walter had groaned and writhed beneath him the night they made love in the library.

Chase wasn't in the habit of sleeping with the domestic help, but there had been other servants before Walter, some of whom he'd shared a special understanding with. He'd flirted with them and they had flirted back, and once a visiting plumber had kissed him in the basement next to the main pipe stack, but that was it.

But Walter knew... at least, Chase amended, he knew now. That knowledge didn't panic him as it otherwise would, if Walter were anyone else. It wasn't true that Chase gave himself to whoever wanted him. Like most men his age, he'd had his share of crushes, affairs, even a forbidden fling or two while traveling in a foreign country, but he was never promiscuous. He enjoyed sex and he loved making love; sleeping with just anybody might be fun, but Chase could never get past that nagging feeling of emptiness afterward. He wanted more than just a quick fuck. He wanted a man who liked the same things he liked, but who was entirely an individual… a man who was intelligent enough to hold his own in a verbal argument, who didn't shy away from a fight just because it was dangerous or inconvenient. He wanted a man with laughing blue eyes and a strong jaw and wavy black hair cut short where it touched the nape of his neck… a man who kissed like his life depended on it, who made love with his whole body.

Chase sighed. What he wanted was Walter Godfrey.

His laptop beeped and he opened it to his e-mail program and scrolled through the messages to find the newest one from Emmett Till, another of the Gordon family lawyers. It was the amended contract for the Honduran project and the requisite papers from the bank. Although the Quinns' Wi-Fi was perfectly acceptable (if a little slow), his laptop had a satellite Internet connection so Chase could stay connected wherever he happened to be in the world. He clicked through the electronic documents, initialed and digitally signed them, then sent them back.

He closed his e-mail and pulled up a hidden, password-protected folder, identified only by a number. He waited for the prompt and keyed in the password. A newspaper photograph popped up in front of him. He clicked it and waited while the computer extracted files from the zipped folder. There were dozens upon dozens of clippings about the plane crash, some with detailed maps of the site where some locals had found the wreckage. There was nothing new here, and he was seeing none of them for the first time. Chase had assembled the collection from various media around the globe, and when he couldn't sleep—which was a lot of the time—he'd sit up and go through them, looking for something he might have missed, some small shred of evidence that had escaped the notice of the official police.

The first time Juliet had come upon him, hunched over his keyboard at two in the morning, she'd told him to go to bed. *Stop playing Sherlock bloody Holmes.* Later, she'd appear at his elbow, bearing a plate of sandwiches or a mug of warm milk liberally dosed with brandy. She expressed no interest in any of the displayed files, and she didn't ask what he was doing. She'd set down whatever she was carrying, squeeze his shoulder gently, and go away.

There was no mechanical reason for the plane to have crashed. It had been inspected two days before his parents' flight and pronounced perfectly safe and fit to fly. The Transportation Safety Board had gone over all the data from the flight recorder, finding nothing. The only thing of any note was that the plane's emergency locator beacon hadn't been activated. Private investigations had similarly turned up little information. Agents from some of the top security firms in the world had gone to the crash site and come away empty-handed.

It makes no sense, Chase thought bitterly. *Airplanes don't just disappear off the radar and fall out of the sky.*

Chase sighed and closed the file. He'd been over it so many times, he knew almost every article in there verbatim. Beyond what was there, in plain black-and-white, he knew nothing, absolutely nothing.

A light tap at the bedroom door claimed his attention. Elena was there, smiling. "May I come in?"

"Of course." Chase grinned. "It is your house, after all." He indicated the wheelchair. "Forgive me for not rising."

She went to the bed and sat on it, then beckoned to him.

What the hell...? His face flamed when he realized she merely wanted to talk.

"My husband and I have no children," she said quietly. Her accent was light, barely there except for the slight difference in rhythm, which gave her words a charming musicality. "I cannot have children."

Chase wondered where this was leading. "I'm so sorry."

She raised her hand, her palm toward him. "But you touch my heart." She drew a breath. "I love my husband. He also loves me. This kind of love between two people is, I think, important."

"I agree," Chase said, thinking of his own parents, who had loved each other devotedly. He pushed the thought aside as tears stung the backs of his eyes, and swallowed hard. Thirteen years, and it still hurt like hell. "It's very important."

"Sometimes we think we can go through life alone, you know? Do everything for ourselves, know everything we need, trust no one." Elena reached out, took hold of his wrist, and squeezed gently. "I think we get ahead of ourselves."

A bird sang in the sudden silence. Chase reached out to cover her hand with his. "It's not as simple for me. I'm… not like other men." He didn't want to offend her modesty by blurting out the truth of his sexual orientation. It wasn't the sort of thing one discussed with strange women, especially a pastor's wife. Elena seemed nice, but he knew from experience that as soon as he said the word "gay," some people pulled down a shutter in their minds, and that was that. End of discussion.

"I think there's someone back in America," she said carefully. She tilted her head to one side and regarded him with interest and not a little compassion. "The two of you dance around each other… it's still early. But… I think this man could love you."

Chase was stunned into silence. He opened his mouth to reply but could think of nothing to say. He ducked his head and tried to speak again. "How did you…." He coughed to cover his own awkwardness. "How did you know?"

"My husband says it's a gift from God." Elena shrugged, an elegant lifting of one shoulder. "He also says I am too inquisitive." She giggled, a refreshingly girlish sound. "I hope I haven't shocked you."

"No… you haven't shocked me," Chase replied. "It's unusual to hear someone say such things. Most people hate men like me."

"Jesus told us to love everyone," Elena said. "No exceptions." She patted his arm. "Come. It's time for church."

THE SERVICE was reassuringly familiar to Chase from his days of Sunday school, back when he was a young boy. The Honduran church followed an Episcopal form of worship, with a little Catholicism thrown in: hymns, a brief sermon, and communal prayer. When the collection plate was passed, Chase put in a check he'd written before he'd left the pastor's house. He would have preferred his donation be anonymous, but it couldn't be avoided. The only checks he had with him were his own—in his haste to get to Honduras, he'd forgotten most of the Gordon company files, including a corporate checkbook—and a folded slip of paper was less of a declaration than a fistful of Honduran *lempira*. Besides, he knew better than to carry large amounts of negotiable bills into an unknown—and possibly dangerous—situation. His father had instilled this practice in him when Chase went off to college, advising him to pay by credit card and then settle up at the end of the month. That way, he wasn't carrying large amounts of cash, which might make him a target for thieves and muggers.

Perhaps his father hadn't taken his own advice, Chase thought. Had he and Chase's mother been traveling with large amounts of money? Why would his father do that? Unless…. There were few banks available in this part of Honduras. Maybe his father—

You're grasping at straws. He sighed. Maybe his parents' accident was what everyone said it was: an unexpected tragedy, and nothing more.

"…we give one another a sign of peace," Dan said from the pulpit, jarring Chase back to the present. He turned in his chair to shake hands with—

Walter Godfrey.

Dark hair cut short, laughing blue eyes, that beautiful mouth. "*Que la paz esté contigo,*" he said, and the voice wasn't Walter's voice. The young man behind him was perhaps twenty, with the dark good looks of the local people. He was missing a tooth on the right side, which gave his smile a delightfully roguish aspect. He wasn't Walter. He didn't even look like Walter.

What the hell is wrong with me? I'm hallucinating now? He grasped the other man's hand and murmured something he hoped was intelligible. *Why would I think he's Walter?* Two older women stepped out of the pew and reached to shake Chase's hand. One of them patted his shoulder, as if in sympathy, and said something low and soothing in Spanish.

Chase was just about to leave when Dan came down from the altar in more of a hurry than Chase had ever seen. "Is something the matter?" he asked. The expression on the pastor's face was alarming to say the least.

"There must be some mistake," Dan said. He was on the verge of tears. He held Chase's check out to him. "I can't take this. It's too much money, after everything your family has done for us." He shook his head. "I can't take it."

"Please." Chase gently pushed away the hand that was trying to give him back the check. "I insist."

Dan looked at Elena, who had come to stand beside him. "I don't understand… why do you do this?"

Chase backed up his chair, ready to leave. "Because I can." He ducked his head for a moment as his cheeks grew hot. "I always think if I can, then I should." He reached out and clasped Dan's hand. "I know this will find its way to where it's needed most."

He went with them to the church hall, where tea and sandwiches were being served, but the chatter of so many people in such a confined space made his head ache. When Dan approached and asked if he'd like to leave, Chase readily agreed. Later, drowsing on the very edge of sleep, he wondered if what Elena had said was true. If so, who was waiting at home for him? *Someone*, he thought sleepily, *someone can love me... someone loves me already, maybe.* Someone.

The Honduran night was full of sounds. Tiny white bats flitted among the banana leaves, and occasional small monkeys made daring forays into the forest canopy. Croaking and peeping things croaked and peeped in the trees outside his window, and what sounded like crickets kept up an insistent cacophony in the darkness. It reminded Chase of a trip to Africa he'd taken with his graduating class, where they'd camped in deep grass alongside a river and listened to the incessant noises all night long. It hadn't bothered him the way it had bothered some other people. Chase liked the sounds of birds and animals and insects going about their business with their habitual disregard for humans. Their noises surrounded him in a comforting cocoon of warm sound, reminding him the night teemed with living things.

The undergrowth around the Quinns' house was thick—so thick it absorbed footsteps, the treacherous human sound of someone moving quickly in the darkness. Chase sat up, all pretense of sleep having flown, and strained his ears, held his breath, and listened acutely, waiting for the intruder to reveal himself.

"Señor Gordon, buenas noches." It was Felicien, the reporter. He stood in the open doorway of Chase's room. How he'd gotten past Elena and Dan, Chase had no idea.

"Buenas noches," Chase replied politely. "It's kind of late for a visit, isn't it?"

"I hope you will forgive my intrusion," Felicien replied, "except this good news I want to share with you."

Chase groaned inwardly. All he wanted was to go to sleep. "Can it wait till morning?"

"Señor, this news will not keep until the morning. I wanted you should know about it right away."

The thick rainforest undergrowth muffled the sound of footsteps as the two louvered doors at the side of Chase's bed swung open. The bulky figure of a man was framed there, a darker shadow against the night that pressed in from all sides. There was very little ambient light, but what there was allowed Chase to see the bulky man had a bulky gun in his bulky hand.

"My cameraman will help you from your bed," Felicien said. "He is ready to help at a moment's notice."

Felicien held the gun while the cameraman rolled Chase onto his stomach and cuffed his hands behind him. A black hood was fitted over his head, and then he was lifted bodily from his bed and carried down a short flight of stairs to the ground. He was shoved into a vehicle and the doors slammed.

Chase could hear two men talking rapidly in Spanish, but they didn't sound like Felicien and his cameraman. These voices were new. Chase hadn't heard them before. The situation, however, was amply clear to him. *I'm being fucking kidnapped*, he thought. *In the most dangerous country in the whole goddamn world.*

The vehicle he was in drove for some time, bumping over numerous ruts in the road and bouncing violently. Chase thought he might use that motion to his benefit, but then remembered he was in the middle of the jungle and would likely be eaten by insects before anyone came to rescue him. He sat back, his pinioned hands pressing uncomfortably into his back, and decided to take a philosophical approach. Until he knew absolutely what was going on, he'd stay still and keep his mouth shut.

He was alone in the backseat, but there were at least two men sitting up front, conversing quietly in a rapid Spanish dialect Chase couldn't really follow. They were friends, or at least friendly acquaintances, because their conversation often dissolved into laughter and short phrases that could have been teasing jeers. Where was Felicien? Where was his gigantic cameraman—if that's what he really was, and not just hired muscle.

"She won't pay it," Chase said. "If money's what you're looking for, my butler won't pay it. I gave her explicit instructions before I left."

This garnered no response. The two men fell suddenly silent. The car bumped over a particularly ferocious rut in the road, and then the wheels made contact with smooth asphalt. The transition was unmistakable. When Chase was a boy, he liked to ride in the car with his eyes closed, trying to tell by his other senses where he was. Most of the time this strategy failed him resoundingly, but he could almost always tell what kind of surface they were driving over.

Highway, Chase thought. *They're bringing me to somebody else.* So these were mere henchmen, drivers, maybe a couple of bored local boys. Asphalt meant they were on the two-lane road that ran between the major cities; odds were good they were taking him to Tegucigalpa, the capital. It wasn't a place he would have ever contemplated visiting: it was rife with every crime imaginable, and victims could expect no help, either from passersby or the official police. The Honduran jungle was infinitely preferable to the city. At least in the rainforest, there was cover. In Tegucigalpa, anyone could be attacked, any time at all, for various reasons or for none. Armed gangs controlled the city, funneling foreign currency into their underworld activities. Eighty percent of the cocaine that found its way to the United States had been shipped via Honduras. It occurred to Chase that maybe his parents hadn't died in the plane crash. Perhaps the plane crashed and they were murdered after the fact. It wasn't a pleasant thought. For several bleak moments, he wondered what he'd gotten himself into, and whether he'd get out of it alive.

An increase in the ambient noise level outside the vehicle alerted Chase that they'd driven into a larger metropolitan center. There were fewer bird sounds and hardly any insects; the auditory traffic consisted mainly of car horns, people shouting, police sirens, snatches of song floating from somebody's radio, somewhere. The air smelled of gasoline, spilled alcohol, and rotting food.

Chase was sweating under the hood, and his wrists ached from the handcuffs. "Where are we?" He didn't expect an answer and he didn't get one. Then the city sounds disappeared, replaced by the swishing of tires in an enclosed space: they were in a tunnel. The sounds reappeared. *No, a parking garage*, Chase amended, which meant they had probably reached the end of their journey.

The car stopped and was turned off. Chase's door opened, and someone shoved a hand under his knees and another behind his shoulders and lifted him out. After two flights of stairs and a ride in what felt like a very rickety elevator, a door opened and an American voice said, "Bring him in here." And, when the man carrying him swung Chase roughly into a chair: "Gently! For Christ's sake, can't you see the man's disabled?"

Retreating footsteps, and the door closed. Someone reached out and pulled off the hood. Chase blinked, trying to orient himself. The room he was in was a cross between a luxury hotel bathroom and a French fin-de-siècle whorehouse. Everything around him was red. Red lights ran up the walls in long strings like Christmas decorations and cast a lurid carmine glow against the flocked velvet wallpaper. The floors were mahogany, stained a deep and bloody crimson. A polished wooden bar of similar hue curved seductively along one wall, glistening wetly in the light cast by a series of chandeliers. All this was very interesting, but Chase was more interested in the man in front of him.

"I apologize," Franklyn Pratt said, "but this was necessary. I hope you weren't too incommoded by the journey?"

"It was perfect," Chase replied. "Very smooth, only I didn't like the in-flight snacks."

Pratt laughed, showing perfect white teeth. "Sarcasm. I like it. I think a man ought to be able to banter with his fellows, don't you?" Without warning, he stepped closer to Chase and delivered a stinging slap across the face. "Don't fuck with me, you little pissant. If it weren't for you and that bastard journalist, I wouldn't be here."

Chase fingered the warm spot on his cheek. "Why are we here?" He didn't see anyone else around, so maybe this was a personal audience. He didn't think Pratt's two goons were very far away—maybe eating *pastelitos* in the kitchen and sucking back a few bottles of Salva Vida while they waited for orders from the boss.

Pratt took a chair from a nearby table, turned it around, and sat on it, arms braced on the seat back. "You've caused me a lot of trouble, Chase—may I call you Chase?"

A cell phone rang somewhere in the building. Pratt cursed and got up. He seized an iPhone from the bar. "What?" He switched to Spanish, spoke a handful of words, and rang off. "I've been working for years... decades... to build something here, something profitable, something useful." He came back and sat in front of Chase. "Do you know what the average Honduran earns a month? Eight hundred dollars, maybe eight hundred and fifty if he's lucky."

"Lucky," Chase said, "or well-connected?"

Pratt ignored him. "I can get these people what they want: I can get them out of here. Do you know how many I move out of here a month?"

"I'm sure I can guess."

"Hundreds. I move women, girls, young boys, whatever there's a demand for." Pratt shrugged. "I've even filled special requests. Some people have unusual habits, you know: blind, deaf, amputees, scarred." He made a point of looking at Chase's lower body. "Even cripples. I send them off to America, to better lives."

Does Pratt really believe this, Chase wondered, *or has the old man finally cracked?* He shuddered to think the kind of life Alec and his sister must have endured, growing up. It was a wonder Pratt hadn't tried to pimp them out too. "I honestly don't care," Chase said, "why you do it. You're a sick old bastard." He waited for Pratt to slap him again. "I feel sorry for Alec, growing up with you as his father."

This last seemed to enrage Pratt. He stood and hurled the chair away from him. "My children are none of your goddamn business."

"But other people's children are my business," Chase said evenly. "In fact, they're everybody's business. I wonder if the State Department knows what you've been up to all these years?" He was reasonably sure the government had long since figured out what Pratt was up to; they were just waiting for the right time and the right situation to take him in. "You can't bribe everybody, can you? There has to be someone, somewhere, who isn't bent, and human trafficking is a serious offense."

The silence in the room grew almost as oppressive as the heat. Pratt walked to one of the windows overlooking the street. The air was full of the usual urban sounds, sirens and shouts and a loud conversation underneath the window. They were in the very center of Tegucigalpa, in the midst of a teeming city of nearly 800,000 people. Surely someone would hear him if he shouted, but would they bother coming in to see what was going on?

"Quite pointless," Pratt said, "I assure you. If you scream, everyone will hear you, but believe me, nobody here will give a damn." He returned to where Chase was, retrieved his chair, and sat again. "Besides, I haven't told you why we're here."

Finally, Chase thought.

"I have a little problem," Pratt told him, "and I very much need your help." He smiled as if he and Chase were best friends. "I've run into some difficulty here—business matters, you know how it is. Some associates of mine back in the States are quite adamant I pay them reparations for certain errors I've made." Chase said nothing, and Pratt continued. "Perhaps my calculations were off. It doesn't matter. What matters is my friends have been disappointed that a certain series of investments didn't pay off as much as they expected." He raised his hands in a "so what?" gesture and let them drop. "I need to return to New York to shore up some business interests there, but—"

"They know you screwed them over and they're waiting to kill you as soon as you set foot outside," Chase said. "Did I guess correctly?"

"You did," Pratt said. He didn't seem the slightest bit embarrassed by this fact. "These friends of mine have hired local men, members of certain organizations—"

"The mob," Chase cut in, "in other words."

Pratt shot him an irritated glance but didn't contradict him. "I need you to get me back onto American soil." He consulted his wristwatch. "There is a flight leaving from a private airstrip in the hills above the city. I can get there safely if I have you with me. I've been in contact with these local men, and I've promised you'll give them some money in exchange for safe passage out of the building and out of the city."

Human shield, Chase thought. *He wants to use me as a shield.*

"The State Department has been apprised of your situation," Pratt said, "and they aren't willing to risk your safety." He smiled thinly. "So we're a package deal, you and I."

"And you think the Hondurans will care?" Chase asked, incredulous. "You think they'll let you go because, what? You're with me? They don't give a damn. They don't even know who I am, for chrissakes."

"They do," Pratt said. "They know you're a rich *Americano*. They know who your parents were." He shrugged. "I'm sorry I had to dip into your family savings, but needs must, as they say. Money is always a useful commodity, and I needed to get you down here." He glanced at the window. "It'll be daylight soon. We'll have to stay here until it's dark again. Can I have someone bring you anything?"

"Who is it?" Chase asked. He'd figured out Pratt's predicament. "Fatty Veranda? One of the Masettis? You know they're never going to let you live."

"They will," Pratt replied. "You and I will be leaving this shithole together. You'll be quite safe. Masetti won't kill you out of respect for your late parents, and I can make a deal with him." His eyes narrowed to slits and he smiled like an evil gargoyle. "I understand your father and old Masetti were quite close. Quite close indeed."

"That's bullshit," Chase said, "and you know it." He gathered saliva in his mouth and spat on the floor.

WHEN THE devastation of 9/11 happened, Walter Godfrey, like all of the city's first responders, was deployed to sift through the rubble, looking for survivors—or, as was more likely, recovering the bodies of those who had died. Walter remembered everything about it: the dust floating in the air; the acrid smell of obliterated concrete; the general feeling that the chaos was only temporary; the belief that the world would return to its senses before too long. He was one of the first sent up the stairs after some of the elevators went—climbing endlessly through darkness, smoke, and confusion, looking for any signs of life, no matter how faint.

As he ascended higher, he passed seemingly endless hordes of people coming down, some horribly burned, the skin of their arms and faces hanging of their bodies in sheets, like wet laundry. It shocked him, and he'd seen some horrible things. *Don't look at it. Keep on going up.* The shrieking alarms, the dust, and the first faint whiffs of smoke coming down from the building's upper levels.... *This isn't right... there's something really wrong here. This isn't any ordinary fire....* His radio crackled with the voices of his colleagues, his friends, giving information about their locations, what the situation was where they were.

Someone shouted, "Oh my God, it's jet fuel!" It was running down the stairs as if it had been poured out of a bucket.

Keep going, he thought. *Just keep going, that's all you gotta do.*

He made it to the 58th floor when a series of explosions rang out above him. A group of perhaps twelve people, some of them wounded, were trying to get down the stairs, slipping on the spilled fuel, grabbing at the walls that were no longer there for support. Walter's radio hissed, crackled briefly, and died.

"Get out!" somebody shouted from above him. "The whole fucking building's gonna collapse!"

Walter was pushed back against the wall by panicked people trying to get past him and down the stairs. He righted himself and tried to calm them, stressing the need to progress in an orderly fashion, but no one was listening. The air filled with smoke as the lights in the stairwell blinked and went out. He forced his way up to the 62nd floor, but the stairs were blocked by fallen sheetrock and he could go no farther. Trying to chop through it would waste precious time, and there was so much of it, and so much other debris, that it was pointless.

Somehow, he was able to make his way down to the lobby command post, only to find all available personnel had been sent up the stairs, some even using the few still working elevators. Terrified people, some of them on fire, were streaming out of the building into the street. Walter patted out the fire in one woman's smoldering hair with his—he later realized—ungloved hands. He felt nothing, and it wasn't until sometime after the initial crisis that his hands started to hurt and he discovered he'd burned himself quite seriously. At the time, it hadn't seemed to matter.

He'd ended up in one of the first photographs from Ground Zero, taken in the hellish aftermath by a photographer from the *New York Times*. When he first noticed her taking pictures, he approached and asked her to please stay back for her own safety. Debris—and human bodies—were falling from above.

A perimeter had been established and was cordoned off with yellow tape, but in Walter's experience, members of the media tended to disregard such things. The woman was middle-aged or older—although the pall of fine white dust hanging over the site tended to settle on the skin and hair, obscuring a person's true features—and fiercely dedicated to her work. Walter told her several times to stay back, and when she didn't listen, he sent for police to escort her to safety. She wouldn't go. She insisted on staying where she was, shooting endless photographs of the carnage, taking pictures of him, of the police and other firefighters on site.

The photo that made it to the *New York Times* was a close-up of Walter in his standard firefighting gear, his face unrecognizable, smudged with dirt and ash under his helmet. His hands were raised in front of him, warning her back, and she'd caught him in midsentence with his mouth open. He looked fierce, determined, but also angry and tired, depressed and disappointed. Some part of him knew, even as he and the others struggled to find survivors, this was quickly turning into a recovery mission instead of a rescue. There was so much devastation, so much debris, the hopelessness of empty streets that resembled a war zone. Everyone would be touched by this. Even him.

It wasn't until much later, when he checked his voice mail that he learned Gary had died in the North Tower. "You know I love you," Gary had said, his voice heavy with emotion. "You are the great love of my life, Walter."

All these years later, he still couldn't bring himself to erase the message.

Her name was Diana Preston, the photographer. She'd sent him a copy of the photo, afterward. It still amazed him that one photographer could capture him so entirely, capture the mood of that day in the face of one firefighter, and the emotions that would stay with Walter for the rest of his life. Maybe it was morbid to come back here and visit the place where Gary and so many others had died, but Walter did it anyway, as a tribute. He liked the serenity of the two huge, cuboid fountains, and the rhythm of their falling water soothed him. Maybe it wasn't exactly smart to be walking around in the open, but he was tired of running scared from Masetti and his thugs. He needed to be here.

Today Walter had come to say good-bye. It was like ripping off a bandage that had adhered to the torn flesh beneath it. He slid his wedding ring off his finger and laid it carefully on the edge of the fountain. The small diamonds sparkled in the late autumn light, and Walter hesitated. It was the middle of the afternoon, gray and cold. The plaza was practically deserted, except for an old woman feeding pigeons and a small clutch of tourists, schoolgirls by the look of them, with matching uniform kilts and crazy Japanese backpacks.

Gary would always be his first real love, his companion and friend, his husband… but Gary was gone and it was time to move on. Maybe the priests and ministers were right and he'd see Gary in the afterlife, but that was a long way off. Walter wasn't interested in waiting. He was a different person now, a reporter instead of a firefighter, and somehow the inept underbutler to the scariest English woman he'd ever met. Chase was offering him a chance to love again, and Walter intended to take it.

What was it Billy had said to him, that day on the roof? *You're my friend and I love you. Don't be stupid.* Even if this thing with Chase turned out to be merely a fling, it was still time to leave the past behind him.

He reached for the wedding ring but didn't pick it up. He pushed it closer to the edge of the fountain, where it could easily be seen, hoping some other man or woman would have cause to wear it, would consider it a gift. Then he turned and left, walking quickly toward Liberty Street. He didn't look back.

IT WAS nearly dark when Walter made it back to Gordonstoun. Obviously someone had called the police or filed a court injunction, because the insistent press of media personalities was no longer in evidence. He hung his coat in the foyer and went into the great room, where Juliet had kindled an enormous fire.

"The wanderer returns," she said. "Enjoyed your afternoon, did you?"

Alec was underneath a huge, freshly cut fir tree the Gordons ordered from Nova Scotia every year. It was early to be trimming the tree, but Chase's father had always insisted on it being decorated in time for Thanksgiving dinner. All that could be seen of Alec were his feet and the hems of his pants. The tree shifted slightly, its limbs shaking as it was overtaken by a fit of shuddering. A muted voice came from beneath the tree. "What about now?"

"Stop shaking the bloody thing," Juliet said. She walked to the middle of the room and looked the tree over. "What do you think, Walter?"

At any time previous, Walter would have thought that here was a unique opportunity to put Alec through the kind of torture he so richly deserved. Alec Pratt, spoiled rich man's son and general irritation, had always struck Walter as someone who'd benefit from a good beating. The cut on Alec's cheek put paid to that idea—the cut made by a bullet intended for Walter. Alec had saved his life. If it weren't for him, Walter would be lying on a slab in the morgue about now.

His trip to the memorial, too, had sobered him, instilling in him a fragile sense of gratitude, tempered by loss. He felt winded and shaky, like he'd been crying, even though he hadn't. *Maybe that comes later*, he thought.

"It looks perfect," Walter said. "Good job, Alec."

The trousers came out from under the tree. Alec looked like he'd been dragged backward through a knothole. His clothes were filthy, and even his hair was standing more on end than usual, as if someone had run a garden rake through it and left it that way.

"Mr. Pratt was interested in exploring the house a little further than he has been," Juliet said. "He's been up and down the attic at least a dozen times, and that was before the tree arrived." She gestured at the remainder of the room, which had been decorated with long, looping garlands of spruce branches, accented at intervals by tiny silver bells.

"The bells were Alec's idea. I was going to put red bows like we always do, but he suggested this."

On a small table near the entrance, there was an arrangement of gourds, all different shapes and sizes. These had been hollowed out to receive the very last of the season's wildflowers and ornamental grasses, many of them as dry and fragile as old memories. The house's long, antique windows were dressed in sheer curtains of linen, complete with ties made of grosgrain ribbon in red, orange, yellow, or brown. Everywhere Walter looked, elements of the outdoors had been brought inside and used to decorate the house in imaginative and unusual ways. Even three old wooden chairs from the potting shed had been pressed into service, acting as temporary plant holders for some papery sheaves of ripened wheat.

"It's beautiful," Walter said. And it was. Who'd have ever thought someone like Alec had a knack for interior design? "You did this," he said to Juliet.

"Oh, no." She raised an eyebrow. "Mr. Pratt did this. All of it." She nodded at Pratt, who had suddenly turned a brilliant shade of red. "That'll be all, Alec. You can go." She studied Walter's face carefully. "I think you could do with a hot drink. Come into the kitchen." She filled the kettle at the sink and got out the teapot. "Have you heard anything from Chase since he went? Usually he'd have called me a dozen times by now."

Walter's heart sped up. "No, I haven't heard from him. He said he was going to Honduras, and he just… went." He peered at her more closely. "Do you think something's wrong?"

"I try not to leap to conclusions whenever I can," Juliet said. "Until I hear from him, I'm assuming everything is quite all right."

"Oh."

But Juliet looked worried, and that was very bad.

"I've called him," she said, "several times, in fact. It's not like him to not answer. Every call I've made has gone straight to voice mail." Juliet took the lid off the teapot and fetched down the tin of Twinings. "Earl Grey all right?" And, when Walter nodded, said, "You were gone quite a while just now."

"I went to the memorial… the fountains, you know." His ring finger felt shockingly naked. He supposed it would be that way for a while, until he got used to the absence. "It's… well, it's really beautiful… the fountains, I mean."

The kettle boiled, and Juliet wasted no time warming the pot and dousing the tea leaves with plenty of hot water. She replaced the lid and set the tea to steep on the countertop. "Walter, might I offer you some advice? Entirely unsolicited, I know, but...."

"Of course."

"We've all suffered losses in our lives. You, me, and the postman. It's a part of life." Juliet's gaze was faraway. "We tell ourselves, 'right, that's me, then' and resolve never to get involved, ever again. It hurts too much."

"I think I know where this is headed," Walter said wryly.

"Far be it from me to give you lessons on your love life." Juliet flapped one hand in the air like someone shooing flies. "But, Walter, don't shut the door on someone who wants to love you." She drew a slow breath. "Sometimes it's too late by the time we come to our senses, and that person is gone forever."

Walter wondered if he should venture a comment or keep his mouth closed. "You sound as if you're speaking from experience."

"Perhaps I am." Juliet's smile was just a little bit sad. "Now, then, drink up. The bathrooms on the second floor need a good going over, and that damned girl chose today to call in sick. Why today, I've no idea. Normally she clings round here like a barnacle."

ALEC CAUGHT up with Walter in the main foyer about half an hour later. "Can I talk to you?"

Walter turned. "It would appear you already are." Juliet's tea had warmed him, but he still wasn't in the mood for a complicated conversation with Alec Pratt. Walter was beginning to wonder if Alec ever had any other kind. He seemed to have no vocabulary for small talk.

Alec ignored the jab. "I trust you've suffered no ill effects from previous dumpster-related events?"

"I'm fine, Alec," Walter assured him. "You don't need to follow me around. I'm all right, seriously." He softened the remark with a smile. "I'm beginning to feel like I'm being stalked." He turned down a side corridor, Alec on his heels, and headed for the utility closet, where various cleaning implements were kept. Shrugging out of his formal jacket, he hung it on the hook provided and tied a long, butcher-style apron over his clothes. "Alec, come on. I'm just going to clean the bathrooms."

Alec ignored that, leaning on the doorframe. "You think nobody's ever been murdered in a bathroom?"

Walter huffed an exaggerated sigh. "Are you getting paid extra to be my shadow?"

"I'm not getting paid," Alec replied, "at all."

Walter stopped short. "Wait a minute… aren't you a cop?"

Alec's eyes widened comically in his too-pale face. He stared at Walter incredulously, then began to laugh. Walter wasn't sure what he'd said to provoke such an explosion of mirth. "A cop?" Alec said, between gasps of laughter. "A *cop*?"

Now Walter was really confused. "You're not a cop?"

"Oh, Walter." Alec took a moment to compose himself. "I'm about as far from a cop as you can possibly get."

Walter reached past him to fetch the mop out of the cupboard. "You're… a criminal?"

Alec screwed up his face. "Mmmmm, kinda. It's complicated."

Walter tried again. "You used to be a criminal but you're not now." He was beginning to feel like a quiz show contestant.

Alec narrowed his eyes, but his inability to keep from smiling took the edge off the gesture. "I was given an opportunity to pay for my sins. They were many and various." His gaze slid away, and he was suddenly very interested in the floor's tile pattern. "I'm still paying."

Walter didn't know what to say to this. He knew next to nothing about Alec, except what everybody else knew: he was Franklyn Pratt's only son; he had an older sister and an art history degree. "I… should clean the bathroom."

"Of course." Alec stepped away. "Forgive my intrusion." He made no move to leave, so Walter assumed this previous remark was just so much conversational filigree. He pushed open the door to one of the second-floor servants' bathrooms. He dusted the toilet bowl and the urinal with powdered cleanser, then did the same to the wash basin.

Pratt watched with feigned interest. "You told Eleanor you wanted to get an exclusive on Chase Gordon," Alec said. "You know, work that whole reclusive-philanthropist angle. When is he coming back from Honduras?" Pratt stepped to one side as Walter dragged a large white string mop out of its bucket and began slopping soapy water onto the floor.

"I don't know when he's coming back," Walter said, "and I'm trying to mop the floor." When Pratt didn't move, Walter cheerfully mopped him into a corner, then went to scrub the toilet and the urinal. He came back, lifted the mop bucket, and hefted it up to the sink.

Pratt stepped out of his corner and came over to watch. "I think you overfilled that bucket."

He was right: Walter had underestimated the weight of the water-filled bucket. He struggled to lift it up to the sink. "You might want to step back," he grunted. "This thing is heavy."

Alec didn't offer to help Walter, nor did he move away as Walter had requested. The bucket slipped out of Walter's hands, bounced on the rim of the sink, and, in one great tsunami of filthy water, spilled its entire contents over Alec.

He stared down at himself, his expression almost comically shocked. "I'm going to assume that was an accident," he said, gasping. "And that you didn't do it on purpose."

"I did tell you to get out of the way," Walter said calmly, trying not to laugh. Alec looked like a drowned rat.

"What am I going to do now?" He glanced down at himself, then back at Walter. "I'm soaked to the skin." He pulled a bath towel off one of the shelves and mopped at himself, making a disgusted face and sniffing elaborately at his sodden clothes.

"I told you to get out of the way," Walter repeated. He fetched a towel of his own and began patting Alec down. "Look, Pratt, some of us are here to work. It might have escaped your notice, but this is my *job*." He dabbed water off Pratt's face and neck.

Alec went still, and caught hold of Walter's wrist. There was something in his eyes Walter had never seen before: fear. "Nobody touches me," Alec said quietly.

"I'm sorry." Walter stepped back. "I didn't mean to be intrusive."

"No." Alec held on to his arm. "I mean, nobody ever... they don't want to, so they don't." He looked away. "I don't mean you should stop—"

Walter understood immediately. He discarded his wet towel and took another from the shelf, reached over, and began rubbing Alec's thick black hair. "I really am sorry. I didn't mean to dump the water on you." He pulled his hand back, holding the towel on top of Alec's disheveled hair. "I wouldn't do that." He couldn't stop the grin that spread itself over his face. "You really do look like somebody pissed all over you." He took down another towel and wrapped it around Alec's shoulders. "You should go change into some dry clothes. Juliet will kill me if you catch pneumonia." With his free hand, he reached out and squeezed Alec's shoulder, the touch lingering a moment or two longer than was strictly necessary.

Nobody touches me.

It was difficult to shake off a lingering sense of melancholy as he took the mop and cleaned up the mess. Why wouldn't somebody touch Alec? *They don't want to, so they don't.* True, Alec could be a bit… odd… at times, but surely he had friends, family who hugged him on holidays and birthdays?

Walter's pop had always been demonstrative, hugging Walter, patting his cheek, ruffling his hair. Needing his pop was something Walter had never grown out of. He was nearly forty and still loved it when Pop grabbed him and hugged him. *You're a good boy, Walter. Your old man loves you. You know that, right?* As Walter grew older, it got so he could lift his ageing father right off the floor. *I love you too, Pop. I love you more than….* He'd always try to think of something funny to say… *more than my luggage.* Growing up without his mother, Walter had depended on his father for almost everything. He could tell Pop anything, ask him anything. When at seventeen he had tearfully come out, Pop hugged him hard and told him, *You are my son, and I love you. The rest doesn't matter.* Walter didn't want to think about what would happen when Pop died. It was something he kept as far away from his thoughts as possible. He couldn't imagine a world that didn't have Pop in it.

Walter finished cleaning the bathrooms and dragged the vacuum cleaner over the rugs, to save Juliet the bother. She would, he knew, do it herself, and she shouldn't have to. He'd just stowed the vacuum back in its cupboard when Juliet buzzed him on the house phone.

"I've a call for you," she said. "They wouldn't say who, but it sounds like long distance."

Walter's heart thumped violently in his chest as he went to pick up the extension. "Walter Godfrey."

"You got two minutes," a man's voice said. "Don't fuck it up."

"Walter?"

"Chase, where are you? Juliet said—"

"Just listen." Chase sounded tired, his voice raspy and uneven. "Listen carefully. I don't have much time."

"What?" Walter grappled with the situation. "What do you mean?"

"Franklyn Pratt's got me. He had some of his boys snatch me last night. He's going to use me to get safe passage out of the country." Chase sighed. "He's playing every angle he can think of—the Hondurans, the Masetti family—"

"The mob?" Walter's pulse fluttered.

There was a long pause and then a burst of static. Chase's voice faded away, then came back. "...mob wants him and the Hondurans want him. I don't really give a damn. Franklyn Pratt is going back to New York, and I'm going with him.... I'm his insurance. Somebody will contact you."

There was a loud click and the line went dead. Walter stared at the phone in his hand like it was some kind of exotic animal. "Chase?"

Juliet appeared in the hallway with an armload of clean towels.

"That was Chase." He gazed at Juliet, then back at the phone. "Franklyn Pratt."

"Alec's father?" Juliet arched a brow. "What about him?"

"He's got Chase. He's holding him for... not ransom, but—"

Juliet's expression was incredulous. "He's been *kidnapped*?" She dropped the armload of clean towels on the floor. "Call Brian Schrade. Right now."

CHAPTER EIGHT

THE PRECINCT was relatively quiet, and most of the day shift had gone home. Brian Schrade stayed behind to tie up some paperwork. The days were so short now that it was often dark by five o'clock. Schrade had no need to leave early, and there was no one waiting for him at home. The precinct was hugely preferable to his tiny, dingy apartment with its narrow, uncomfortable couch and view of a brick wall. Niedermeyer and Jones had gone to the titty bar around the corner with some of the junior officers. It was somebody's birthday, and on Thursday and Friday nights, the bar put on a strip show it wasn't zoned for, but nobody really cared.

Juliet Lavish had appeared in front of Schrade's desk earlier that afternoon. She'd been her usual self, brusque and to the point. Chase Gordon had been kidnapped in Honduras and was being held by Franklyn Pratt.

"What the hell's Pratt going to do with him?" Schrade asked.

"He wants safe passage back to America," Juliet said, "and he's gambling that he can do that with Chase as a hostage. The man's an idiot."

Schrade's phone lines were all lit up, but he ignored them. "I'll get hold of the Feds." Maybe Pratt figured his mob buddies wouldn't bother him if he were traveling with Chase. This, Schrade knew, was incredibly naïve. Fatty Veranda would cheerfully kill Pratt and whoever he was with. Chase Gordon was probably already dead.

He wasn't about to tell Juliet that.

"There must be something I can do," Juliet said.

"There is." Schrade fumbled in his desk drawer for one of his business cards. "Go home. And take this." He handed the card across the desk to her.

"Yes, but surely there's something I can do," she persisted.

"Go home," he repeated. "Please." He lifted his phone's receiver and picked a button at random. "Detective Brian Schrade."

"Just in case you missed it, they were here." Alec Pratt sounded like he was standing in the bottom of a well. "Masetti's boys." There was a pause and then the click of a cigarette lighter. "Looking for Walter Godfrey. They took a couple of pot-shots at him, outside in the yard. I should have told you earlier but things… got a little busy."

"Are you smoking?" Schrade asked. "When was this, exactly?"

"Couple days ago," Alec said. "I only smoke when I'm nervous. I swear."

"Well, stop it." Schrade heard the note of fond concern in his own voice and cringed. "What did you do?"

"I neutralized the suspects." Alec uttered a short, sharp bark of laughter. "Don't worry. Nobody was hurt. Well, nobody who matters."

"What the hell does that mean?"

"One survived," Alec said. "I think I hit him in the shoulder."

"So Godfrey knows you're his backup man," Schrade said. This was turning into a real clusterfuck. Masetti had sent some of his goons out to Gordonstoun to try to finish Walter Godfrey; Alec had stopped them. Wonderful. "You've made yourself a target. That wasn't the plan. I wish you hadn't mixed it up with them. It's dangerous." He sighed. "I'll call you later," he said, and hung up the phone. He wanted to throttle Alec with his bare hands.

The surviving goon was almost certain to go back to Masetti and tell what he'd seen. So Alec was dead, or would be, just as soon as Masetti got his ducks in a row. Fatty Veranda would find out Alec had been working as a mole for Schrade, and somebody—one of Veranda's or Masetti's loyal henchmen—would take Alec somewhere and beat the shit out of him before strangling him and throwing his body in the river. He'd been afraid of this from the beginning, but when he'd told Alicia Mendes this, she'd laughed at him.

Why do you care? The mole's a throwaway. You know that.

Schrade picked up the small ceramic figure of an elephant that he kept on his desk, a gift from some long-departed girlfriend after he'd mentioned he liked elephants. He did like elephants. They seemed to know and understand things—like the time some "elephant whisperer" guy in Africa died and all the elephants from miles around came to him, as if they knew… as if they knew someone important to them had passed. Over the years of his long life, the man had faced rogue elephants, demented by pain and the abuses of mankind, had soothed and gentled them in startling physical ways that put him in extreme danger. What impressed Schrade most about the story was the man's courage, how he'd stood up to something fifty times his size without a second thought.

The mole's a throwaway.

It wasn't department policy to rescue guys like Alec if they got into trouble and needed help. Informants like him were easy to find, so their replacement value was almost nil. If Alec fucked up, say if he ratted on the wrong person and got himself bumped off by Masetti or Veranda or any of their buddies, the NYPD would simply shrug and go about its business as usual. No one would know what Alec had done. Nobody would care.

Schrade shouldn't care either, and it wasn't like he didn't have other cases to attend to. He'd been trying for five years to put Alec on the same footing as any other police informant. Somehow Alec had resisted being shuffled away like that, had insinuated himself into Schrade's mind. They weren't exactly friends, but if something happened to Alec....

He shook his head, scattering the unwelcome thought. The last time he'd seen Alec had been at the diner. Alec had been licking butter off his fingers, so slowly and deliberately that Schrade had been powerless to look away. He'd never denied his own appetites, but he hadn't gone out of his way to satisfy them either. He hadn't had a serious relationship in years, not since Toni left, and the few anonymous hookups he'd indulged in had scratched a physical itch, but that was all.

Alec Pratt was handsome enough... no, Schrade amended, he wasn't handsome; he was beautiful. He'd always been beautiful, but lately Schrade was having trouble keeping his hands off him. He wanted Alec in his bed, wanted to crush that pale, slender body under his own, suck that luscious bottom lip into his mouth, fuck Alec until he couldn't stand. He was even dreaming about Alec at night, for Christ's sake, powerfully erotic dreams that left him with damp sheets and an ache that wouldn't go away.

That's all it is, he thought, *physical attraction. It's only natural.* He and Alec were both single men, unattached, with no steady partner in either of their lives. Was Alec attracted to him? If Schrade approached Alec, would he accept the overture, or would he reject Schrade? He didn't know which was worse: being rejected by Alec, or falling for him, allowing himself to slip into a relationship with him and to hell with everything else.

Maybe hell was worth the risk.

He shook his head, scattering the thought. He wasn't about to jeopardize his career for a roll in the hay.

The phone on his desk rang; he reached out automatically. "Schrade."

It was Alec again. "We've got a problem."

"Again?" Schrade asked.

"My father."

It was an open secret that Franklyn Pratt's newspaper empire was bolstered and sustained by mob money in return for undetermined services that were probably illegal. Maybe he needed the dough. Maybe Pratt was a notoriously bad businessman who, left to his own devices, would run any reasonable business into the ground.

"What kind of a problem?" Schrade asked. He didn't really want to know. The paperwork on his desk seemed to be mutating into an unconquerable pile of dead trees; his phone never stopped ringing, even for five minutes; the horrible coffee he'd had from the machine was burning a slow hole in his stomach.

"Edward"—a lower-level snitch hired to pass information to Alec and from there to Schrade—"says there's a meeting planned for tomorrow night. But he doesn't know where. They're being a lot more careful. The whole thing is locked up tight. I can't get any information." He sighed roughly. "If you have any suggestions, now would be the time."

"Not over the phone," Schrade said. "I'll come to you."

"Tomorrow," Alec advised. "I'd rather we didn't meet up in the dark." He paused, and when he spoke again, something warm and teasing had crept into his voice. "At least not fully clothed."

"Tomorrow," Schrade agreed, ignoring the warm tingle Alec's voice ignited in him. "I'll meet you there."

"I'VE GOT a guy in place already," Schrade said, "college kid who runs messages for the mob." He shoved his hands into his coat pockets. They were walking, he and Alec, on the grounds of Gordonstoun. It was a cold day, but windless, and the frosty air cleared some of the city out of Schrade's head. "He says they've been moving the meetings. Somebody dropped a word in Fatty Veranda's ear that there's a mole." He shook his head. "They strongly suspect it's you."

"Not surprising," Alec said. "I wondered how much longer this was going to last." Their stroll had taken them around the back of the Gordon manor and into a little copse of naked birch trees.

"You don't sound as worried as I thought you'd be," Schrade replied. Maybe he'd misread the situation and Alec had resources Schrade hadn't considered.

"I'm only worried—" Alec stopped walking and turned around to face him. "—that my son of a bitch father will get away before you"—he stabbed an angry finger into the center of Schrade's chest—"catch him."

Schrade was surprised at this sudden fit of pique. Of course, Alec got angry just like everybody else, but he usually kept his feelings tightly wrapped. "No love lost there, huh?" Schrade asked.

Alec resumed walking at Schrade's side.

"Can I ask you something?"

Alec made an airy gesture with one hand, a gesture Schrade knew was meant to be sarcastic. "Oh, by all means. Ask me anything." For the briefest flicker of a moment, something passed across Alec's features, a fleeting expression that cut Schrade to the heart, and then it was gone.

"Are you scared?" Schrade asked. "This could all blow up in our faces. I don't know that I could save you." He clenched his fists. "I'm sorry." He'd had this same argument with himself more times than he could remember. Alec was a civilian. He hadn't trained for any of this: listening at doors, peering through keyholes, keeping careful watch on the chief players in his father's latest criminal drama. He did it anyway, as a way to scrub his own record clean. He'd been doing it for five years, long enough that his original debt was since expunged. Alec Pratt didn't owe Brian Schrade anything. Schrade, on the other hand, owed Alec a hell of a lot. Maybe it was time he stopped asking Alec for favors.

They stood now at the edge of the little stream. It was perhaps three feet wide. Alec gestured at it. "You go first."

Schrade stepped easily across the stream. "Your turn."

"My turn?" Alec asked. "Surely you know evil things can't cross water." He laughed, a self-deprecating laugh, pithy humor at his own expense.

Schrade ought to have been used to it by now, but he wasn't, and it jarred him. "Don't do that." He held out his hand to Alec. "Come on."

"Drop me and I'll kill you," Alec said. "These are good shoes."

Looking at Alec across the narrow expanse of water was like looking at him across a chasm. Schrade was on one side, the devoted servant of the people—here he mocked himself silently—while Alec was on the other, the criminal reformed by....

...by what?

Schrade reached across the gap and closed his fingers on Alec's wrist. "Deep breath," he said. "Think happy thoughts." Then he pulled Alec, laughing, across the stream. "So, are you?"

"Am I what?"

"Scared." Schrade was still holding Alec's wrist; slowly he drew his arm back, so their palms met. A prickle of warmth shivered up into Schrade's chest, and he unconsciously leaned closer. Alec's eyes were the calm, clear blue of an iceberg, and his skin was pale as paper, utterly unblemished. Schrade couldn't stop looking at his mouth, the Cupid's bow curve of the top lip and the soft cushion of the lower. The cold had painted splashes of red on Alec's cheekbones and stained his mouth a dark crimson. Suddenly all Schrade could think of was kissing him, sucking that bottom lip into his mouth, biting it, worrying it with his teeth.

"Yes." Alec drew a deep breath. "Yes," he repeated, "I'm scared."

Schrade tightened his grip on Alec's hand, his thumb lightly rubbing the skin around Alec's knuckles. "So am I." It was almost but not quite a whisper, and if Alec noticed Schrade's strange behavior, he didn't say anything.

"I should go. Juliet will kill me if she comes looking and I'm not there."

Schrade reluctantly let go of his hand. "Here." He handed Alec a scrap of paper. "Time and address."

Alec glanced at the paper. "This is really close to where you live." He smiled. "Maybe I'll come and visit."

"Be careful," Schrade said, as he took his leave. "And remember: no licking butter off your fingers."

AT TEN minutes past eleven, Alec got out of a taxi in front of La Grotta, an intimate little restaurant on West 44th Street. Modeled after a similar establishment in Palermo, it catered to theatergoers who preferred supper after the show and who weren't averse to paying more than a hundred bucks a head for the privilege. La Grotta had the best of everything: the best food, the best wine, extensive privacy, and mood lighting taken directly from a 1930s gangster movie. The interior was so dark, Alec was forced to grope his way to the table, bumping into other diners and hitting his shins painfully on the furniture.

"You're here." Fatty Veranda was seated at a banquette with a selection of meats and cheeses spread on a platter in front of him.

Alec, who hadn't eaten since breakfast, found himself gazing at the food longingly. "Yes," Alec said, "here I am." He didn't sit but waited to be invited. He'd learned the hard way that Mr. Veranda abhorred presumption.

"Sit," Veranda said. He gestured at the banquette. "You hungry?"

"Famished," Alec confessed.

Veranda raised his hand to summon one of the waiters. "Marco," he said when the man appeared at the table, "get my friend here something to eat, and bring some more bread, huh?"

"What would sir like?" Marco enquired in a dim, faraway voice. He was a thin, fragile-looking man in his midfifties. He looked like he'd rather be anywhere else but here, and if someone blew on him, he'd float away.

"Um, whatever's ready," Alec said. "I'm not fussy."

"The pork stew is excellent," Veranda said. "Bring him the pork stew."

The waiter left, and three men detached themselves from the shadows. They didn't speak, merely nodded at Fatty. Two of them sat next to Alec; the other slid in next to Veranda. Alec thought he recognized them, but it was so dark he couldn't be sure. They were Veranda's usual thugs, the kind of muscle-head goons chosen solely for their ability to follow orders, loyal to Veranda and to nobody else.

"Good evening, gentleman," Alec said. He fought to keep his voice level. "It's such a pleasure to see you all again."

They ignored him.

"I been hearing things," Veranda began. He pointed his knife at Alec. "These things I've been hearing, they don't make me happy." He forked a hefty portion of some unidentifiable meat into his mouth and commenced chewing.

The goons watched closely, obviously impressed by their boss's gustatory prowess.

"I'm sorry to hear that," Alec said. "Things are tough all over." He glanced at their impassive faces. "At least that's what I've heard."

"This friend of yours," Veranda said. He speared another chunk of meat. "This cop."

"He isn't a friend," Alec replied. "He's a useful source of information."

"You're not fucking him?" Veranda asked.

In my dreams, Alec thought. "No, Mr. Veranda, I'm not fucking him."

Veranda lifted his glass and drank some Chianti. "That's too bad. I figured he'd be just your type."

The goons laughed in unison.

"See if I set you up with anybody else."

The skin on Alec's face was suddenly too tight. "Sir?"

"I don't usually guess wrong, but you didn't take to this guy." Veranda shook his head. "That's so sad. I checked him out real careful too."

"Checked him... out?" Comprehension dawned slowly, as a burning tension in the pit of his stomach. "You—"

Veranda cut him off. "Don't be so fucking stupid." He refilled his glass from the Chianti bottle. "I see an opportunity, I go for it. This cop, he's interested in you, ever since he followed you to Spain." He sipped, lowered his glass, and laughed heartily. "So he's the one—him and that idiot partner of his—who took care of Walter Godfrey that night in Brooklyn when my guys roughed him up a bit." He laid his glass down with a thump. "So I give Godfrey a long leash." He shrugged. "I know where he is when I want him."

"Schrade wouldn't go for something like that."

"You think so?" Veranda paused to tear off a hunk of bread and stuff it into his mouth. "Guy follows you all the way to Spain because he thinks he's got something. He thinks if he keeps an eye on you, eventually you'll spill." He slurped wine. "You think I don't know cops?"

Alec didn't know what to say to that. Sometimes it was best to stay quiet.

"Franklyn Pratt is your old man. We do business together, me and him. This cop wants Franklyn Pratt." He paused to sip some wine. "He's been wanting him for years, long before you ever came into the picture."

"Mr. Veranda, I swear to you, I would never—"

"Do you think I'm fucking stupid?"

Rhetorical question, Alec thought. *Keep your mouth shut.*

"You think I don't know you been trying to play me?" Veranda thumped one huge fist hard on the table, rattling the glassware and cutlery. "This cop, he's got a line on your old man, thinks he can take him down. You can figure out what that means for me."

If—*when*, Alec corrected himself—when Schrade finally amassed enough evidence to arrest Franklyn Pratt, it would be like punching a hole in a balloon. The network of drugs and sex workers would collapse, leaving a huge space in Veranda's South American operation.

"So I gotta start all over again, find somebody else to take care of things on that end."

A steaming plate of rich stew was placed in front of Alec. He couldn't even look at it, but pushed it toward one of the goons.

"You don't want this?" the man asked.

Alec shook his head.

"You mind if I do?"

Alec shook his head again.

"Lemme break it down for you," Fatty said. He plucked another piece of bread out of the basket on the table. "Years and years the cops been watching me, watching my operation." He shrugged. "I don't worry. I got some safeguards in place. The information that the cops are getting all these years?" He tore off a chunk of bread. "It's nothing. See, you gotta be proactive. Me, I take control of situations."

Alec smiled thinly. "How very wise, to leave no stone unturned, as it were." He forced himself to look at Veranda, counted *one, two, three, four, five, six*, and looked away.

"It's a problem," Veranda said. "Let me explain it to you."

For years, Veranda and Pratt Senior kept the Central American police well in hand. It wasn't hard to do, especially in Honduras, where the cops were always on the take from somebody. "You drop a little money here, you drop a little there," Fatty said. He crumbled the piece of bread and tossed the fragments onto the table. "And then this…. Brian Schrade, he comes along. Son of a bitch takes this shit seriously. Pretty soon, he starts putting it together. I don't know why. It's something I can't figure out."

Alec swallowed hard. "I see."

"No," Veranda said, "you don't see nothing." He stuck his finger in Alec's face. "I got everything tied up, then you come along. Schrade and his buddies, they know what I let them know." He poked himself in the chest. "Everything is ship-shape, watertight. Until you."

"Mr. Veranda, I assure you, I would never—"

"Don't you lie to me!" Veranda made a fist. "This cop, this Schrade, now he's finding out things. He tells them to you. He's the only reason you're here, because I damn well didn't tell you where I'd be tonight. He's the only one who knew. How do you think he found out?" When Alec didn't reply, he continued. "I got a guy feeding him information. Some college kid too poor and too stupid to blow his own nose. Schrade thinks the kid's working for the cops." He laughed heartily. "We wanted Schrade, but he wouldn't play ball. Doesn't like to get his hands dirty."

So Fatty Veranda was playing Schrade, just like he played everybody. Alec wondered why he wasn't surprised.

"Where does that leave him?"

"Give you three guesses," Veranda said, "and the first two don't count."

Everything around Alec collapsed into hard space, immobile, unreal. Black spots swam before his vision, and his heartbeat boomed and thundered in his ears. The tabletop was sliding away, and he was on the floor, kneeling on the dark red carpet, carpet the color of blood.

Veranda leaned over. "I'm done with Schrade. By the time my boys are through with him, he won't know his own name." He nodded to the three goons. "Get rid of him," he said, gesturing toward Alec. "This guy's all used up."

The three men, Veranda's lieutenants, hauled Alec up off the floor and dragged him outside where a black late-model Lincoln was waiting. They shoved him in, and the car pulled smoothly away from the curb.

Nobody gets whacked in an alley anymore, Alec thought. *Nowadays they take you out into the country, or down by the river, made a big production out of it.* He knew he wasn't going to live beyond tonight, and that bothered him. He was sandwiched between Veranda's henchmen, one of whom had a gun pressed into his ribs. Even if he did manage to get out of the car, they'd shoot him before he had a chance to escape. *Think of something*, he chided himself. *Think! You're good at it.*

They left Manhattan's lights behind and crossed the icy East River. Alec wondered idly if he'd end up floating in it before the night was over; it seemed entirely possible. The car navigated a complex series of turns down narrow streets and into alleys, often doubling back to retrace previous routes. They drove for about half an hour, until the familiar shape of the Red Hook pier appeared.

"The East River," Alec said, trying for conversation. "I'm impressed, gentlemen. All this way so nobody hears me screaming."

They ignored him. The car pulled up at the end of a smaller container terminal adjacent to Pier 9, and the goons got out, dragging Alec with them.

He was shoved hard, stumbled, and fell to his knees, his hands on the filthy concrete. Someone kicked him, and he collapsed onto the ground, was struck repeatedly with what felt like iron pipes but was probably a baseball bat. He cowered, instinct making him cover his face and head, but they beat him until his arms fell away, and then someone kicked him in the head. *Let it be over soon*, Alec prayed, *let it be over.*

He'd been beaten before, as severely as this, and once, during his school years, a group of older boys had dragged him into the bathroom, where they had taken turns hitting him until he passed out. The janitor had found him the next morning when he came in to empty the trash and had called the principal, who had sent Alec to the nurse's office. Two black eyes, bruised ribs, and a broken jaw later, he had huddled in the local police station and refused to say who'd done it.

"Okay, that's enough," somebody said. "Pick him up." They hauled him off the concrete and threw him in the backseat of the car, bleeding from his ears and nose, his eyes swollen to slits. They'd broken most of the fingers on his left hand, and the pain in his back meant he'd be pissing blood for a while. *No*, he thought, *not pissing. Not doing anything.* He lay in a sticky puddle of his own blood and faded in and out of consciousness. He no longer cared what happened to him. He didn't have the strength to care.

"We should cut his throat," someone said. "The boss would want us to make sure, right?"

"Don't be an asshole," another replied. "He's already done. Anyway, I don't wanna get blood on my shirt. You know how that shit spurts all over the place."

"Too quick," a third voice said. "Boss said to make sure he suffers."

Alec lay with his cheek pressed against the car's expensive upholstery, bleeding all over it. This pleased him. Doing as much damage as possible seemed like an eminently achievable goal. If it cost Fatty thousands to clean Alec's blood out of the car, so much the better.

"…yeah, the cop lives up there," one of the men said. "Right on the doorstep, huh?" The car accelerated, its powerful engines whining, and the door on the street side opened, letting in a rush of cold night air. "Get him out of here!"

Alec was falling through space, seemingly weightless, and then his body hit the ground and slid along the asphalt. He crashed into the curb amid a cacophony of blaring horns and angry shouts and rolled into the gutter. The pain in his lower back was agonizing, and much of the skin on the right side of his body had been torn away, but he was alive. That surprised him, and he wondered how pleased Fatty Veranda was going to be when he learned his henchmen had fucked up. He sat up, gritting his teeth against the pain of his torn flesh, and pulled himself slowly to his feet. Directly in front of him was the well-lit lobby of an apartment building; if he could get to that, drag himself inside, he could call somebody to come and get him.

THERE WAS nothing on TV worth watching. *There never is*, Schrade thought sourly, tossing the remote onto the couch cushion beside him. His shift had ended at six and it was now eleven thirty. He should have been able to relax, but he couldn't. He was waiting for an agent to call him back from the FBI, because Chase goddamn Gordon had gotten himself kidnapped in fucking Honduras. Then Alec had gone into the midtown pit of vipers where his father's mob cronies met. It wasn't, Schrade knew, a nice place to be. The restaurant—La Grotta—was attached to a nightclub called—appropriately enough—Oblivion. On any given night, Oblivion hosted the city's worst drunks, murderers, and degenerates, who came for the floor show and as much booze as they could drink. The restaurant was the very model of respectability, but the club was a hellhole.

Schrade should have been in bed, except all he could think about was Alec. *This is nuts.* He'd never worried about an informant before. Snitches in this city were a dime a baker's dozen. If something happened to take Alec out of the picture, Schrade could have a minivan full of guys just like him within an hour. *He knows what he's doing. He's hardly new at this.* He couldn't shake the slow ticking of his intuition, just under the surface of his thoughts, pinging away like a drop hammer. He knew where the restaurant was; he could get in, extract Alec, and get out with a minimum of fuss. He could have Alec safe and out of there in no time. Alec had no business being there in the first place. The guy was a goddamn butler, for chrissakes.

He got up and paced the length of his living room for a while, his stocking feet sinking into the thick rug his sister had given him, a birthday gift from two or three years ago. At first he'd protested, arguing that she'd spent too much money, but she wouldn't take it back, and Brian had no idea where she had bought it. Similarly, the cocktail table and matching teak bookcases, also a gift from her, and the dining table that was far too big and ornate for his small dining room. Besides, he almost always ate in front of the TV. It was one of the perks of living alone.

He considered going to bed, but he was too wound up to sleep, so he decided to go down to the lobby and get the newspaper. It would give him something to do while he waited for the feds to call. The elevator being out of order, he took the stairs, which dated to the building's origins. The stairs started rather narrow at the top but flared wide at the bottom—wide enough, in fact, for a grown man to lie supine across one of the treads.

A man was lying across them now. At first Schrade thought it might be one of the elderly residents, until he got close enough—

Oh my God.

Alec Pratt had been beaten—savagely—and lay now in a bloodied heap at the bottom of the stairs. One side of his face was swollen, bruises darkening to a deep purple, and he had an absolutely spectacular black eye. His nose was bleeding, and blood from his ears had run onto his shirt, staining it a shocking red. His lower lip was cut and bleeding freely onto his collar, which had been wrenched violently apart until it tore. All the buttons were missing. He held one arm—the left—cradled against his body. Schrade strongly suspected the wrist was broken, maybe some of his fingers. "Alec?"

"Brian." Alec smiled. It must have hurt like hell. "I fell."

"Down the stairs?" Schrade asked. He wanted to touch, to offer comfort, but he was afraid to put his hands anywhere on Alec's battered body.

"Out of a car," Alec said calmly. "Actually, I was pushed."

"You have to go to the hospital. Can you sit up?"

"No hospital," Alec replied. Terror wrote itself in stark lines on his bruised and bleeding face. "Can you help me up?"

Schrade reached out and helped Alec to his feet. He was shuddering so badly that he practically vibrated. "Let's get you up to my place."

Slowly and painfully, they made the ascent, Schrade carrying most of Alec's weight. One of Alec's shoes was gone, and he limped like his back had been injured.

"What did they do?" Schrade asked. "You can hardly stand up."

"Baseball bat," Alec replied. "Louisville Slugger, I think, but don't quote me on that." He leaned against the wall while Schrade unlocked the apartment door. "You have to listen to me."

"Let's sit down on the couch and I can call an ambulance," Schrade said.

"No." Alec shook his head. "No ambulance. Listen." He let Schrade sit him on the sofa, then tugged Schrade down beside him. "It's you. I heard them planning it. They're coming after you. You have to leave town, now."

Schrade went into the kitchen to get him a glass of water. When he came back, Alec was leaning to one side, a hand on his ribs. "I'm not going anywhere."

"No. Listen—" Alec broke off to gulp water. "—they know about us."

The bottom of Schrade's stomach dropped out. "What do you mean?" he asked, even though he already knew. "They figured it out?" He sank to the floor in front of the sofa, sitting on his heels.

Alec gulped more water. "They did. I don't know how. I swear to God, I didn't tell them anything. The kid you've been using as a courier? He's dirty. Fatty Veranda has been feeding you information. They took me out to Red Hook." He gestured at his face with his one good hand. "This was supposed to kill me." Alec finished the water and put the glass down, nearly missing the cocktail table. "They'll try again. This time they'll make sure." He wiped his mouth on his sleeve. "So, it's been nice knowing you." He made to get up, but Schrade pressed him gently back down on the sofa again.

"No one," Schrade said, "is going to kill you." Something fiercely protective pulsed through him. "I won't let that happen."

Alec laughed humorlessly. "I don't see that you can do anything about it. As far as you know, my—"

Schrade leaned in and kissed him, effectively silencing whatever he'd been about to say. Alec's mouth was hot, like he was burning from the inside out. Schrade drew away, and Alec clutched at him, pulled him in, and kissed him again, like someone dying of thirst.

"I made your lip bleed," Schrade said, sitting back on his heels.

"It was already bleeding." Alec laughed, a little breathlessly. His injuries had to hurt like hell. "I feel like I was thrown under a bus."

Schrade gathered him gently into his arms and held him. It seemed the right thing to do now. "Please let me take you to the hospital."

"No." Alec shook his head. "They have to report things like this." He gestured at his face. "I… can't take that risk."

"Then let me call someone."

"I just need some rest," Alec said.

"I'm going to insist," Schrade said. "I think your ribs are broken… and you need to get that eye seen to." He snagged a throw blanket off the back of the sofa and wrapped it gently around Alec's shoulders. "Juliet Lavish is a doctor. You know she's very discreet. Let me call her." He pulled out his phone and started scrolling through his contacts.

Alec nodded wearily. "All right." He rested his head back against the couch. "I waited five years."

"Hmm?" Schrade looked up from his phone. "Yeah, five years." His brow furrowed. "For what?"

"I waited five years," Alec said, "for you to kiss me."

ALEC WAS sleeping when Schrade opened the door to let Juliet in. She carried her medical bag, a relic from her days as a young and sleepless intern, and her coat wasn't buttoned right.

"I didn't mean to wake you," Schrade said apologetically. "It's kind of an emergency." He hung Juliet's coat in the closet and ushered her down the hall to his own bedroom. He'd bathed Alec's injuries as well as he could, then stripped his torn, filthy clothes off and put him to bed. "Brace yourself," Schrade said right before he opened the door. "He's been pretty badly hurt." He opened the door.

The room was dark, a tiny nightlight the only spot of brightness in the space. Alec lay asleep under a clean white sheet, breathing harshly.

"How long has he been like this?" Juliet laid her bag on the nightstand and took out a stethoscope, all business.

"Earlier this evening," Schrade said.

"And you didn't take him to hospital?"

"He wouldn't go," Schrade replied. "He's afraid. He knows they can get to him."

"You're a damned fool. He could have internal injuries. Christ, the man could be bleeding into his brain." She sat on the side of the bed and took hold of Alec's right wrist. "What happened to his other hand?"

"They broke his fingers," Schrade said. "It's a specialty of Fatty's boys. They like to be thorough."

Juliet let go of Alec's hand and rummaged in her bag. "What with? He needs X-rays. He has to go to the hospital."

Usually Fatty Veranda liked to make his punishments last as long as possible. Schrade had heard of his goons stomping on the hands of a restrained man until the bones were shattered. If Fatty was in a hurry, he'd just use whatever tool was handy. It was rumored he had a special ball-peen hammer he kept for such occasions.

"Probably a hammer," Schrade said. "That's his style."

"A hammer," Juliet murmured. She lifted Alec's shattered hand gently, examining the fingers. Her touch seemed to be light as air, but he moaned, his ruined face twisted in pain. "Those cowardly sons of bitches," she hissed. "He's probably got internal injuries. He has to have X-rays, and I want to get him into a clinical setting." She laid the bell of the stethoscope on Alec's chest, listening intently. "One of his lungs sounds a bit wet. I don't like it." She tugged the earpieces out and stowed the stethoscope in her bag. "There's nothing for it. He has to have proper medical attention." Schrade opened his mouth to protest, but Juliet stopped him. "There's a small clinic out near Montauk. I can get him in there. All I need is a day or two to stabilize him, and then we can move him to a more remote location." Her expression said she wasn't making a request. "Have you got something warm to wrap him in? You can drive. I'll sit in the backseat with him."

Schrade stared at her.

"Well, go on, then!" Juliet snapped. "I've no time to be fannying about."

Schrade wrapped Alec in a woolen lap rug and took only the essentials with him: his cell phone, wallet, badge, and gun.

Juliet got into the backseat of Schrade's vintage Ford Granada and drew Alec in after her, making a nest of blankets for him. "He's already running a fever," she said, laying her palm against Alec's cheek. "Those bastards."

"What kind of a clinic is this place, anyway?" Schrade asked, strapping himself into the driver's seat.

"A clinic where he can receive appropriate care," Juliet replied. She would say no more.

Schrade pulled into the midnight urban traffic. They drove in silence, passing out of Manhattan's neon-washed landscape into the relative darkness of Long Island, while Alec slept on Juliet's lap and Schrade remained sunk in his own thoughts.

If he dies, it's your fault. No, Alec wasn't going to die. That wasn't going to happen. Alec was going to be fine. Juliet would see to that.

"Does he know?" Juliet's voice jarred Schrade out of his thoughts.

"What?"

"Alec. Does he know how you feel?"

Schrade caught her eye in the rearview mirror. "I... don't know." He swallowed hard. "I hope so."

"I understand he's been offering his services for some time now," she continued, "helping the police with their various investigations."

"That's correct."

"He's a brave man." She brushed Alec's hair back from his forehead. He was quite unconscious, his iron constitution having given way to pain and exhaustion. "The sort of man who often gets overlooked during the course of things."

"Oh?" Schrade didn't care for the insinuation in her voice. "What sorts of things?"

Silence grew between them until he assumed Juliet had nothing more to say.

"Dangerous things," Juliet said finally. "Detective Schrade, please don't make the mistake of assuming I'm merely a foolish old woman."

Schrade cut his gaze to her in the mirror. "I would never assume any such thing."

Alec stirred, moaning gently in his sleep, and Juliet tucked the lap rug more firmly around his shoulders and murmured to him quietly.

"In fact," Schrade continued, "I... I don't want him to feel like... like he's expected to reciprocate." He swallowed thickly. "I would never... I mean, I want it to be his choice. If that's what he wants—" He broke off, aware he was making an idiot of himself.

"Do you love him?" Juliet asked.

"Yes," Schrade whispered—hotly, desperately. "Yes, I love him."

WALTER WAS polishing silver—it kept his mind from worrying endlessly over what was going to happen to Chase—the next morning when the telephone rang.

It was Eleanor. She didn't bother with preamble or small talk. "Get your ass out here," she said, "and make it quick. I've had a phone call, and it's about you."

"What?" Walter pulled off his gloves and laid them on the table. "About me?" He glanced out the window at the morning, cold and gray and hinting strongly of a hard winter to come. It was the kind of day that made him long for the warmth of his long-vacated bed and the softness of his eiderdown.

"I'm not talking about it over the phone. Get out of that goddamn butler uniform and get out here."

"Yes, but—" Juliet had been gone since the night before, helping Detective Schrade with something she wouldn't talk about. Walter wasn't sure if he ought to leave the house until she got back.

"Do not 'but' me, Walter. I swear to God I will have your junk for meatball soup."

Walter caught an express train into the city and found himself in front of Eleanor's desk at the *Times* just after ten thirty.

She didn't bother to greet him, just shoved a manila envelope across the desk. "The big story is that Gordon Industries has somehow been funding the South American drug trade. Somebody got pissy and now Chase Gordon has gone missing."

"Yeah," Walter said. He wasn't sure what Eleanor wanted him to say.

"Some of the Associated Press people think he was kidnapped," Eleanor continued, "probably after his Honduran buddies turned on him."

The envelope contained several high-resolution photos taken with a zoom lens from a distance and printed from a camera's memory card. There were about eight in all, and they appeared to have been taken inside some kind of church or public building. "So what?" Walter said. "Everybody knows he went to Honduras on business." He wasn't about to tell Eleanor that he'd heard from Chase and that he had indeed been kidnapped. She'd want to fly him down to Honduras and drop him right in the middle of that shitstorm. More than that, he had no intention of using Chase's situation to grab some sensational story for the paper.

"Do you recognize the man in the picture with him?" Eleanor asked. "The man who is smiling and shaking hands with Chase? He's Señor Malo, that's who. 'Mr. Nasty' if you want it translated. Mean motherfucker." She shook her head. "Who knew Chase Gordon was dirty? Jeez, the guy can't even get out of his goddamn wheelchair. Where'd he find the time to get himself kidnapped?"

"He went down there to do some charity work," Eleanor said. "God knows why. I suppose somebody as rich as he is needs to do something to ease his conscience." Her gaze was faraway for a moment, and Walter knew she was strategizing, planning out her next move and the paper's next big story. "I'm gonna send a photographer out to the Gordon mansion with you." Her hard red fingernails clacked on the keys of her computer. "I think we can start with some kind of think piece. Interview the staff, get the dirt on Gordon. Maybe he doesn't pay them very much. Hell, maybe he beats them."

"I'm reasonably sure he doesn't beat them. Don't you think I'd know?"

Eleanor ignored him and picked up the phone. "Miles, where's Sam? Where? Tell him to get the hell back here. I've got something for him to do this afternoon." She laid the receiver back in the cradle with a noisy clatter. "Sam'll meet you there. You'd better go on back. I want information gathering, Walter. Information."

He opened his mouth to say something, then thought better of it. Besides, Eleanor was on the phone again. He knew better than to interrupt her when she was in the middle of a conversation.

CHASE HAD slept well, considering his predicament, at least Franklyn Pratt's Honduran flunkies had given him a decent room. He supposed it was to be expected, but who knew Pratt owned hotels in Tegucigalpa?

He'd risen early, jarred out of a sound sleep by the bark of an automobile horn outside his window, and by his body's insistence that he was still on Long Island, not some thousands of miles south of the border. A wheelchair had been left beside his bed, hardly the top-of-the-line model he used at home, but it would serve to furnish his mobility. He'd gone into the bathroom and sluiced his head with cold water from the tap. When he returned, a breakfast tray was waiting for him on the table in his room, complete with a carafe of fresh, hot coffee. The food was surprisingly good, and there was plenty of it; he ate everything on his plate and poured another cup of coffee from the pot. He took the tray to the door, which was—amazingly—unlocked. If he could get to the elevator, and from there to the lobby—

"Good morning, señor." A tall man with the sad face of a disappointed basset hound took the tray from him. He was at least six feet six inches tall, with a large frame and musculature to match. The hand that gripped the tray could have easily wrapped around Chase's neck and snapped it without so much as a moment's pause. "Is there anything else you require?"

Chase's plan of escape shriveled and died. "Not just now." He glanced up and down the hallway, but there was no one else around. "How about I scream and you run away? Would that work?" He went back into the room, closing the door on the man's reply.

The manila envelope had been delivered shortly after the breakfast tray. He'd opened it and understood immediately: these pictures of him with Dan Quinn and the Honduran reporter were damning in their own right—more so since the earnest Honduran "journalist" had been identified as a major player in the international skin trade.

He dropped the envelope and its contents onto the desk and squeezed his eyes shut. This was going to be a clusterfuck. Even if he hired the best lawyers in the world—and he could—it had the potential to be a long, drawn-out, painful, ugly situation that would leave Gordon Enterprises with one hell of a black eye. He pinched the bridge of his nose with one hand.

What would Philip Marlowe do?

Probably punch somebody, Chase thought. It was a nice idea, but not a very practical one. Finding whoever was responsible for this and then punching their lights out would only get him into more trouble. *I wish Dad were here.* Elliott Gordon would urge Chase to unburden himself, would listen without judgment, and then advise his son on what he ought to do. He wouldn't solve Chase's problem for him; he'd guide Chase so he could solve it by himself.

The photos had been taken by a local journalist, the one who had asked for a brief interview while Chase was in the church. A second set of photos showed Ken and Tracy Lloyd shaking hands with Chase over a groaning buffet table at some unnamed charity event.

The Lloyds were shysters so notorious, they were well-known even beyond the five boroughs. They'd started their career as male prostitutes working the Bowery district and graduated to working as runners for the mob on the Lower East Side. They were couriers, mostly, transporting drugs from point A to point wherever and taking a cut of the profits. Judging by their faintly addled expressions, they weren't above taking a few samples of the product. Their association with Fatty Veranda had elevated them to the status of minor demigods among the denizens of the city's sex trade; in exchange they sometimes did favors for Veranda and his friends—lap dances, private strip shows, or blowjobs in the back of somebody's hired limousine. Obviously they had graduated to their current association with Franklyn Pratt and were somehow involved in the New York aspect of the whole sordid business—the insinuation being that Chase's Honduran interests implicated him as well.

Of course, the photo had been doctored. Chase didn't mix with people like the Lloyd brothers, and a faint case of germaphobia meant he rarely shook hands with anyone, anywhere, unless it was unavoidable.

This entire situation cast Gordon Industries in a very bad light and threatened everything Chase and his parents had been trying to do in Honduras. He had to get a message to someone, but he very much doubted the behemoth in the hall would allow him to go outside the room. He couldn't wheel himself down the several flights of stairs leading to where he was, either... and he'd prefer not to jump out a window if he could avoid it.

Think, dammit. You can figure this out. It's what you do.

There was no telephone in the room and no Internet. The windows opened, but what was he going to do, stick his head out and yell? Most likely he'd be ignored by any passersby, and his chances of alerting a local cop were just about nil. His laptop and phone were back at the Quinns' house, so he couldn't count on modern technology to get him out of this fix. *I should have invented a set of goddamn wings*, he thought, *so I could fly out the window.* And he couldn't walk away. Pratt had taken the exoskeleton.

Bitching about his situation wasn't doing anything to solve it, so he poked around the room until he found a stub of pencil and some kind of local takeout menu, printed on one side. *So*, he wondered, *what's for lunch?* The menu advertised a variety of Honduran fast food, from *baleadas*—a kind of tortilla—for 7 *lempiras*, to *tajadas*—unripe plantain sliced thin and deep fried—for 25 *lempiras*. If you wanted refried beans or cheese, that was extra.

Chase knew very little about Honduran cuisine, but he'd sampled other South and Central American dishes and had developed a passion for them. He wondered if Walter liked South American food. It would be nice to take him to one of the fine Honduran restaurants in Manhattan, maybe Oulu, with its Art Deco surroundings and soaring white walls. No.... Oulu was fashionable and quite expensive, but when Chase wanted to eat, he went for one of the small neighborhood places, Casa Mama or Adele's, where the food was excellent and the portions just this side of enormous. He'd love to take Walter out for a really nice meal, with candlelight and flowers and all the rest of it—if he ever got home again.

The morning moved with all the rapidity of a neurasthenic snail. Chase sat looking out the windows for a while, but there was nothing of interest. The air was too polluted for him to see for any great distance, and the constant roar of passing traffic on the street below was like an ice pick to the skull. Chase got down on the floor and ran through the full range of exercises Armand had given him, contorting and stretching his muscles till his entire body was bathed in sweat. Lying flat on his back, he concentrated on trying to move his toes. A shiver of what might have been electricity ran up his right leg, but that was about it.

He got back into his chair and went into the bathroom to have a shower. The facilities hadn't made any particular impression on him, and he'd used them only when it had been absolutely necessary. He had the luxury of regret when he noticed the shower was nothing more than an extremely narrow stall—perfect for other people, but not for him. Chase sighed, his fists clenching in his lap. He had no doubt that was deliberate, that Franklyn Pratt had made sure to put him in a room where using the sanitary facilities was difficult or even dangerous. Pratt wanted to humiliate him, to try to break him down—not for any particular purpose, but just because he could. The enmity between Pratt and Chase's father stemmed from long-ago business transactions that had nothing to do with Chase. Since Elliott Gordon was no longer a viable target, Chase was the next best thing.

"Fucking asshole," he murmured. He'd be damned if a reprobate like Franklyn Pratt was going to get any such satisfaction out of him. Well, screw him anyway. Chase would have to bathe at the sink.

He washed himself quickly, not wanting Pratt or one of his goons to burst in and see him naked. He wasn't ashamed, and he knew his body was good to look at, but it was a sight reserved for others, one other in particular. The only gaze Chase wanted on him belonged to Walter.

He dressed quickly, the same clothes he'd been kidnapped in, and rinsed his mouth with cold water in lieu of toothpaste and a brush. He hadn't had a shave in several days, and he was sure nobody in Pratt's entourage was going to trust him with even a safety razor. Even if he could take a shower, there was no shampoo in the room, so his hair looked more like Alec's than Chase wanted to admit. Too bad. Franklyn Pratt would have to take him as he was, or he could blithely go and fuck himself.

Around eleven, there was a rapping at the door. "Come in," Chase called out. It was a formality only. Any one of Pratt's men could enter the room whenever they pleased, and there was nothing Chase could do about it.

The door opened to reveal a man Chase had never seen before. He was short and swarthy, with dark bags under his eyes. "What do you want for lunch?" His accent wasn't quite Honduran, but wasn't fully American either.

"It's not even close to lunchtime," Chase said. What the hell was Pratt up to, anyway?

"We get food from one of the local restaurants—Honduran food. It takes a while to get here after we order, so we call early." He recited this as if he'd rehearsed it. "Tell me what you want and I'll send out for it."

The printed restaurant menu he'd found lay on a nearby table. *Tapas de Lola*, the name was. He looked it over carefully. "What restaurant?" He held up the menu so the man could see it. "This place? I'd like to order from this place."

"I don't give a fuck, man. Far as I'm concerned, you can eat your own shit. Let me see the menu."

Chase passed it across to him.

"Yeah, I know this place. What do you want?"

"*Baleadas, tajadas* and… *pollo frito*," Chase said. "Tell them to hold the tomato sauce. Couple bottles of pasteurized water."

The man turned to go.

"And can I maybe get a toothbrush and some toothpaste, if nobody minds?"

Chase occupied himself with reading—or trying to read—a Spanish paperback Western someone had left in the room until the food came.

The book was called *El Furgón Negro* by Marcial Lafuente Estefania; the cover illustration suggested pulp fiction, Chase's favorite genre. It was easy to read, even with his seldom-used Spanish, with prose that suggested Louis L'Amour or Zane Grey. He became so engrossed that he didn't hear the knock at his door, and didn't look up until the door opened and someone stepped inside.

She was maybe thirteen, hollow-eyed and hollow-cheeked, with a face like a frightened rabbit. She held out a greasy paper bag and nodded at him.

"You want me to take it?" Chase asked, and she nodded again. "*Muchas gracias por este.*" Chase hoped what he'd just said was "thank you."

"I speak English," she said quietly. "I moved to Nevada with my mother and three brothers several years ago."

"For work?" Chase opened the bag. He wasn't really hungry, but the food smelled wonderful. "What kind of work do you do?"

"All kinds," she said. Her accent was vaguely Mexican, but Chase couldn't be sure. She shifted from one foot to the other, gazing around the room while Chase bit into something delicious rolled in a flour tortilla. "Do you want to buy me?"

The food he'd just swallowed seemed to stick in his throat. He coughed until tears came to his eyes.

The girl went into the bathroom and returned with a glass of water.

Chase waved it away. "Fine," he croaked. "Just went down wrong." He twisted the top off a bottle of pasteurized water and took a long drink.

"It wouldn't cost you very much." She thought for a second. "Seventy-five *lempira*."

The water seemed to congeal, turning to ice inside his stomach. Seventy-five *lempira*—Chase did the mental arithmetic—about three fifty American. The price of a hamburger at a fast-food joint back home. "What's your name?"

"Rosa," she replied, "but I can be any name you want." She wrapped her skinny arms around her torso, hugging herself. "What do you say?"

"Rosa, how did you get here? From Nevada, I mean." He looked her over carefully. "You can tell me."

She told him how she and her mother were taken from Nevada in a truck with other women and driven to the border in San Diego. Along the way, they stopped in various small towns where they were made to beg for food and personal items. Then they were loaded back onto the truck again and driven farther south. There was little water and even less food, and some of the women slept standing up because the truck was so crowded.

"Were there only women in the truck?" Chase asked. "Or were men there too?"

No men, except for the ones who were driving. "Some of the women had babies and small children with them. I don't know what happened to them."

"I do," Chase said grimly. He drew a breath. "Listen, Rosa… when you leave here, are you going back to the restaurant?"

She nodded.

"Will you do something for me?" He tore a piece from the takeout menu and scribbled on it with the pencil stub. He folded the paper into a tiny square and handed it to her. "I need you to do this one thing." He folded her hand over the slip of paper. "Is there a police station nearby?"

She thought for a moment. "Yes," she said. "Very nearby."

He tapped her hand, the one holding the slip of paper. "I need you to go inside and give this to them. Can you do that?" *This is ridiculous*, he thought. *She has no idea.*

"I know the station. The captain there is very friendly with me."

I just bet he is. He was suddenly absurdly grateful to her. "Thank you." He took out his wallet and extracted twenty dollars. "Please," he said, "take this."

The girl looked down at the money, then reached to take it timidly. "I don't understand. You said you did not want to buy me."

"I don't… do that," Chase said, with a grimace. "It's a present. Please keep it."

An hour later, a sullen teenage boy with a skateboard tucked under his arm brought Chase several more bottles of water in a cardboard carton. "*Bebida.* For later." He handed Chase the box.

"What happened to the little girl?" Chase asked.

The boy looked blank.

"*¿Dónde está la niña?*"

"Not here," the boy replied.

No kidding, Chase thought. "I gave some money to the girl. Did she give it to you?"

The boy shrugged. Either he didn't understand or he didn't care.

"Thanks for the water," Chase said. "*Gracias.*"

There was no refrigerator in the room, so Chase stowed the water under the bed. He opened one of the bottles and drank it slowly, conscious of the sun's position by the shifting shadows on the wall. When he was finished, he recapped the empty bottle and put it back into the box. No doubt Pratt would send somebody to take out the garbage. He was the type to think of everything.

At the bottom of the box, however, just as he'd requested, there was a new toothbrush, still in its wrapper, and a tube of what he assumed was toothpaste. He didn't recognize the brand, but he took it into the bathroom, eager to cleanse his teeth. He unscrewed the top of a bottle of water and used it to wet the brush, but when he squeezed the toothpaste tube, nothing came out. He huffed out an irritated breath and tried again, but whatever was inside the tube refused to yield. He found a sewing needle someone had obviously overlooked in the medicine cabinet and probed the opening, thinking the contents might have hardened from disuse. The needle caught on something—something that proved to be a rolled-up piece of thin cardboard. He tugged it out with the tip of the needle, careful not to prick his fingers.

He unrolled it and rubbed it clean. It was a business card. One side was brightly colored, advertising a nightclub: *Histeria.* The other side was blank except for a series of numbers: 504-151-511-1138, written in pencil.

A phone number, a local one. For the nightclub? But the number printed on the front was different from that written on the back. Clearly the penciled number was for something else. It hardly mattered, anyway. Pratt kept his iPhone on his person nearly all the time, and Chase's phone was back at Quinn's place.

The doorknob rattled, and Pratt was back. "Enjoying the local cuisine?"

Chase stared at him in silence.

"Well," Pratt said, "if you're going to be like that...." He fished out his iPhone and held it out to Chase. "Call your pilot. I'm going to need your private plane."

"Can't I use the bathroom first?" He pressed a hand to his abdomen. "I think the local food's done a number on me." He made a face. "Christ, this isn't going to be pleasant."

Pratt recoiled with a look of horror. "Fine, then!" he snapped. "But hurry up. I don't have all goddamn day."

Chase wheeled himself into the small bathroom and locked the door behind him. He knew Pratt wouldn't leave him alone for very long, so he needed to make the best of whatever time he did have. He retrieved the list of Franklyn's contacts from the iPhone's menu and flicked through them. Most of them were labeled with what appeared to be aliases instead of names: *B-Boy* and *InkyJ* and *BigStink*. Chase suspected someone besides Pratt had made up the nicknames. They were no one Chase knew, nothing he could use.

He dialed the number on the business card he'd gotten from the toothpaste tube. It rang seven times, eight, nine, and Chase was about to hang up when a gruff-sounding female voice said, "*Policia.*"

"Chase Gordon," he said. "I'm being held in a building in Tegucigalpa, near *Tapas de Lola* restaurant." He struggled to phrase it in Spanish: "*Estoy siendo sostuve contra mi voluntad.*"

The voice coughed. "Eh?"

"Chase Gordon," he repeated. "Americano. *Secuestrado.*"

"*Secuestrado?*" the voice said. "*No lo entiendo.*" *I don't understand.*

"Shit."

"Hurry up in there." Pratt pounded on the door. "This isn't some kind of game."

Chase leaned over, clenched his stomach muscles, and gave his best approximation of uncontrollable vomiting. He straightened, groaning, said, "Awwww, fuck," then flushed the toilet. He ran the water for as long as possible and flushed the toilet again, twice for good measure.

Pratt was waiting outside when Chase opened the door. He glanced past Chase, into the bathroom. "It's about goddamn time," he said. He gestured at the iPhone . "Call."

THE CLINIC was located at the end of a long, narrow drive lined with trees whose leaves had since drifted to the cold November ground and lay in piles like discarded clothing. The building was smaller than Schrade had expected, made of red brick, with a wide porch at the front and closely trimmed shrubbery on either side. He pulled the car up as close to the front steps as possible, then helped Juliet walk a groggy, barely conscious Alec into the building.

It wasn't like any hospital Schrade had ever seen. There were no gleaming tile floors, no signs warning not to smoke or block emergency exits, no intercom bleating messages overhead. The interior was tastefully decorated with forest-green carpet and cream wallpaper; the furniture looked like pictures he'd seen in chi-chi design magazines. A slight scent of coconut permeated the air.

"What kind of a place is this?" Schrade asked Juliet.

"It's a private hospital," she replied. "Very exclusive, catering to a certain class of clientele."

"Rich people," Schrade said.

Juliet narrowed her eyes at him. "It isn't a sin to have money, you know."

Schrade shrugged. "I wouldn't know. I've never had any."

He looked up as a smartly dressed young woman appeared from an inside office. She had one of the most perfectly symmetrical faces Schrade had ever seen, and her highly arched eyebrows and smooth forehead suggested an encounter with botulinum toxin, the injectable kind. Her long blonde hair was thick, shiny, and cascaded around her shoulders like a golden cape. Her eyes were green, almond-shaped and slightly slanted. They went well with her full red lips, the bottom an exquisitely soft cushion, the top a perfect Cupid's bow. Her nametag read: Alice O'Dea, R.N.

"Good evening," she said. "May I help you?" Her gaze flickered on Alec, a bloodied lump of bruises slumped against Schrade's shoulder.

"Juliet Lavish. I'm wondering if Dr. Chan is in this evening."

"He is. Let me page him for you." She turned away for a moment and pressed a series of buttons on the desk phone. Two male nurses emerged from a secondary hallway, rolling a gurney. "Darryl and James will take the young man for X-rays." They lowered the gurney so Alec could sit on it, efficiently bundled him aboard, and wheeled him away.

A trim Asian man in a white coat and wearing a stethoscope around his neck came to greet Julia warmly. "Please," he said, "we can speak in my office. I will need some information."

Juliet introduced Schrade as "a close friend of the patient." He accepted a cup of coffee from the doctor's sophisticated coffeemaker and sat in a ridiculously comfortable chair. He remembered seeing the coffeemaker advertised in magazines and on TV: *fresh coffee one cup at a time!* It didn't taste anything like the cheap, plasticky coffee he regularly endured at the precinct; this was something he'd actually want to drink. He only half listened while Chan and Juliet conversed in impenetrable medical-ese, using terms like *elevated intercranial pressure* and *subdural hematoma.* Then Juliet said "thirty-five percent mortality rate" and Schrade snapped to attention.

"Whose mortality rate?" His heartbeat thundered in his ears. "Who's going to die?" His inner vision was filled with images of Alec lying at the bottom of the stairs, horribly battered but managing a sort of smile: *I fell.*

"No one is going to die," Juliet said, but Schrade didn't believe her. He saw the look that passed between her and Dr. Chan, the silent consultation that doctors were particularly good at, even better than cops.

"I need to get some air." He stood and fumbled his way to the door. He remembered how to get back to the main entrance, which offered itself appealingly as he approached. Schrade smiled at the desk nurse. "Just going outside."

The automatic doors slid silently open and he stepped through. The night was cold, clear, and frosty, but it was exactly what Schrade needed to anchor himself. Ever since he'd found Alec, the temptation to rush to an unfavorable conclusion slid into his mind like a thread of smoke. Schrade had seen badly beaten people before; a lot of them died. Alec wasn't going to die, though.

He remembered the day he'd surprised Alec coming out of Joe Martel's place in Little Italy, and wondered when, exactly, he'd fallen in love with him. What quirk of fate had placed Alec in Schrade's path at just that very moment, and how did Schrade just happen to be in Little Italy in the first place?

Cannoli, he remembered. *I was buying cannoli.* Niedermeyer's mother was recovering from hip surgery, and Niedermeyer was due in the chief's office for a meeting, so Schrade had volunteered to go. He wasn't real familiar with the restaurant, but Niedermeyer had insisted they made the best cannoli in the tri-state area. It had been raining, and Schrade had run into Alec—literally—as Alec came out the front door, opening an umbrella. He'd managed to sidestep the umbrella's sharp ferrule, but only just, and it had irritated him that someone could be so careless.

Hey! Watch what you're doing with that thing.

The umbrella had lowered slowly, revealing a pale face with long-lashed, ice-blue eyes, a young man's face. *And you should watch where you're putting your big feet, detective.*

How Alec had figured him for a cop, Schrade didn't know. The two had stood facing each other, half in and half out of the doorway, sizing each other up like angry cats in an alley. Then Alec had stepped forward, raised his umbrella, and made his slow, dignified way down the street while Schrade watched him, feeling as if the earth had shifted underneath his feet.

Niedermeyer had commented on it later when Schrade showed up at his mother's house to drop off the cannoli: *You look like somebody kicked you in the nuts.*

Schrade always had some loose idea where Alec was and why; he'd made it a condition of Alec's release, all those years ago in Spain, that they work out some way for Schrade to keep tabs on him... for all the good it did.

I couldn't keep him out of danger, Schrade thought miserably. *I couldn't keep him safe.*

He pulled out his phone and scrolled through his contacts. He needed someone to talk to. Sure, it was the middle of the night—or early in the morning—but he'd long ago made a pact with one particular friend. *Any time you need me, you call. I don't care how late it is. I don't care where I am or what I'm doing.*

Seven rings had sounded on the other end before the call was picked up. "Niedermeyer."

"Jack?"

"Jesus, Schrade, what the hell?"

"I need to talk to somebody... I know it's late—"

"Just a second." There was a barrage of sound and then Niedermeyer's voice again. "I fell asleep on the goddamn couch. Hey, where are you?"

"I'm at the... I dunno, it's a private hospital on Long Island." Schrade took a deep breath, filling his lungs with cold night air. "Alec Pratt was beaten up tonight, pretty bad."

"So the only hospital you could find was on Long Island?"

Schrade laughed. "Long story. I'll tell you over a beer sometime." A poignant silence swelled between them. "I need help, Jack."

"What kind of help?" A pause, while Niedermeyer lit a smoke. Schrade recognized the succinct click of his antique Ronson. "You still there?"

Schrade began haltingly. "He drives me fucking nuts, you know? There have been times I want to strangle him."

"Yeah, well, you're not alone in that," Niedermeyer said dryly. "You want I should give you a list?"

It had crept up on him, Schrade said, slowly and insidiously over the years. At first Alec was no more to him than any other police informant or snitch for hire, and Schrade initiated contact only when he absolutely had to. Then, in the summer of 2012, a serial killer they called "The Mister" for his disgusting habit of spraying his victims with urine was wreaking havoc on the entire city. People were afraid to leave their houses. Radio call-in shows were flooded with outraged citizens who wanted to know why the police hadn't done anything to catch him. The mayor went on TV to make an impassioned plea, assuring people that the authorities were doing whatever they could. Public hostility got so bad, cops were routinely hissed and catcalled in the streets. Worse, The Mister seemed to find himself a whole new crop of victims, leaving their bodies scattered in the streets. As nightmares went, it was horrible, almost cartoonish in its violence, and Schrade found himself wishing for some kind of intervention, divine or otherwise.

Alec Pratt had called him, wanting to meet. Over drinks at an uptown eatery, Alec had handed him a list of names, written in pencil on a half sheet of paper. Schrade's first thought was *There's more than one?* But none of them were The Mister, Alec explained. They worked for him, and it turned out The Mister was a very wealthy real-estate tycoon who'd found himself bored and decided to spice things up a bit.

Schrade didn't know where Alec had gotten the list of names and he didn't ask. Within a week The Mister was in custody. He was eventually convicted, and the last Schrade had heard, he was headed for a supermax prison in Colorado. None of it would have been possible without Alec's help, yet he asked nothing in return.

We made a deal, he said, *you and I. I'm simply honoring our agreement.*

"He's a brave little bastard," Niedermeyer said. "I gotta hand it to him."

"I don't know what to do," Schrade said. He shivered. The chill was seeping through his coat, turning his feet to icy, leaden lumps inside his shoes.

"About what?" Niedermeyer paused to yawn. "You think you got a choice?"

"What do you mean?"

"You're in love with him, you dumb bastard. I've seen the way you guys look at each other, all goo-goo eyes. Makes me kind of sick, actually."

"I've never made goo-goo eyes at anybody," Schrade protested.

The clinic's outer doors slid open, and the desk nurse was there. "They're ready for you," she said.

"Listen, Jack, I gotta go."

"Call me if you need me," Niedermeyer said. There was a click, and the call disconnected.

THE WARMTH of the clinic felt strange after Schrade's recent sojourn in the cold. He followed a nurse down the corridor to a private room where Juliet and Dr. Chan were waiting.

"Dr. Chan has placed him in an induced coma," Juliet said quietly. "It's the best option under the circumstances."

Alec lay in bed, seemingly asleep. The blood had been cleaned away from his face, but it was still a mass of bruises, and one arm was in a cast.

"There are no internal injuries," Juliet said, "which is a miracle. He will need to stay in hospital for a while, but he should be able to go home as soon as the swelling goes down."

Schrade's breath went out of him in a rush. "Swelling?"

Chan exchanged a glance with Juliet. "In cases like this, where there has been a violent physical attack, the brain often swells, pressing against the skull. Untreated, this can lead to injury—brain damage—so we put the patient into a coma to give the brain a rest."

Schrade swallowed a hard, sticky lump of fear that was trying to crawl up his throat. "But he will wake up, won't he?"

"Of course," Dr. Chan said. "In a few days' time, we'll take him off sedation and allow him to wake up."

Schrade was violently relieved.

"You can visit with him," Juliet said, "if you like, but not too long. Talk to him. He may be able to hear you."

She and Chan stepped out, leaving Schrade alone with Alec. He pulled a chair close to Alec's bed and sat.

Despite his earlier conversation with Niedermeyer, Schrade found himself strangely tongue-tied. He wanted to look his fill of Alec, wanted to touch him, wanted to tell him things he'd never told another living soul... but he couldn't. Instead, he took refuge in useless small talk, chattering about how cold it was outside and how he'd have quite the story to tell his colleagues when he got back to the precinct.

"I suppose you think this is funny," Schrade said. He took hold of Alec's hand. His skin was cool, but a pulse beat strongly in his wrist. "I bet you're wide awake in there and laughing at me." Schrade's hands were trembling, and it felt like a small bird was trapped inside his chest, wings fluttering violently. "This is all my fault. I'm sure you know that." He turned Alec's hand and leaned to place a kiss in the center of his palm. "I'm the one who brought you into this. I'm the one who coerced you into doing this work in the first place." A strand of Alec's black hair had fallen into his eyes; Schrade reached to brush it back. "You know, I've been in a lot of relationships over the years. I've had lots of opportunities to make things permanent. Something always held me back." He squeezed Alec's unresponsive hand, smoothing the knuckles with his thumb. "I guess I should have known, huh?" He smiled. His face was wet. "What's that old song say? 'It Had to Be You.'" He leaned in and kissed Alec gently.

SCHRADE WAS scheduled to work an evening, the day after Alec's "accident." Niedermeyer found him in the armory around nine that night, carefully surveying the available weapons. "Whatcha doin'?"

Schrade glanced up from the 9mm Glock he was fondling. "I'm going after him, Jack."

Niedermeyer pretended not to know what Schrade meant. "Going after who?"

"Fatty Veranda." Schrade worked the Glock's trigger assembly, grunted, and put it back.

"Something wrong with your service automatic?" Niedermeyer asked.

"This has gone far enough." Schrade took down a Sig Sauer to examine it. "He's got the whole damn city under his thumb. It's got to stop."

Niedermeyer nodded. "Okay, Fatty's got the city by the balls. So, what? You're gonna take him on all by yourself?"

Schrade ejected the Sig Sauer's magazine, examined it, slid it back into place again. "Yep."

Niedermeyer digested this for a moment. Outside, the various daily noises of the precinct were merely a dull murmur. Telephones rang as if they weren't entirely real. Filing cabinets opened and closed again, the warped metal screeching in its track, and computer keyboards clacked frantically, adding to the din. "Are you out of your fucking mind?"

"Keep your voice down," Schrade hissed. "You want the whole goddamn precinct in here?" His eyes were red-rimmed, set in dark holes in his face. He looked haggard, irrational, and Niedermeyer knew tired men often couldn't think straight.

Niedermeyer shut the door. "Look," he said, "I know you're all upset because your boyfriend got knocked around a little bit by Fatty's boys. Just... don't do something stupid."

"I'm going after him, Jack." Schrade placed the Sig Sauer in the pocket of his shoulder holster.

Niedermeyer sighed. "Then take me with you." Schrade made to turn away, but Niedermeyer grabbed his arm. "I'm serious. Either you let me go with you, or I'm gonna tell everybody in the goddamn squad room what you're doing."

They took one of the big Chevys from the motor pool, Niedermeyer driving.

"When we get there, I'm going in alone," Schrade said. "I don't want him to think this is some full-scale takedown."

"God forbid," Niedermeyer said bitingly.

They drove in silence, navigating the dark streets, slipping past taxicabs and rickshaws and unwary tourists choosing just the wrong moment to cross the street. Theatergoers jostled for space alongside shouting men with hotdog carts, and a cluster of young girls in choir robes drifted past, singing an aria from *Lakme*. Niedermeyer recognized the tune; his ex-wife had liked to sing it while she mopped the floor.

He saw an open spot by a nearby Szechuan place and eased the big car in by the curb.

"There it is," Schrade said. "La Grotta." He pointed up the street to where a squat storefront space presided over the sidewalk. "I'm going in."

"Wait." Niedermeyer caught hold of his sleeve. "What are you gonna do if you get in trouble?"

"I'll yell," Schrade said. He got out of the car.

"Remember." Niedermeyer leaned over. "You're no use to Alec Pratt if you get your head blown off."

SCHRADE BLEW past the doorman, badge raised, barely breaking stride. He didn't bother to speak to the man. The inside of the restaurant was dark, owing to what Schrade supposed was mood lighting. Individual candles burned on each of the tables, and a girl was onstage, sighing her way through some vintage love song while two burly men the size of commercial refrigerators stood nearby, arms folded over their massive chests.

Schrade approached the nearest one. "Where's Fatty? Where's your boss?"

The man exchanged a glance with his companion. "What's it to you?"

"Friend of mine was hurt. I think your boss knows something about it."

"Sorry," the first man said, "the boss ain't here." He nodded to the other man. "Jerry, go and get Denice." To Schrade, he said, "She's the manager."

A very petite woman appeared from behind a curtain, like a genie summoned from her bottle. She was dark and beautiful, her eyes artfully painted in a plethora of colors that shimmered when she moved, like the delicate feathers of some exotic bird. Her fingernails were long and pointed, and her head barely topped Schrade's shoulder, despite her high-heeled shoes. "How can I help, Officer?" Her voice was mellifluous, smooth as warm caramel.

"It's Detective, actually," Schrade said. He held his badge in front of her eyes. "Where's Fatty?" Out in the street, a car horn sounded, a repetitive pattern of two long and two short. Schrade was reasonably certain it was Niedermeyer. "I need to speak to him."

She indicated a nearby banquette. "Let's sit down and talk like civilized people, detective."

"I'd rather not. Can you tell me where Fatty is?" Schrade wasn't about to snap and start screaming at a woman, but he'd take her in if he had to. The captain would be more than happy to accommodate her.

"Why do you want him?" she asked. It was a fairly neutral question, but there was acid at the back of it somewhere, a thinly veiled nastiness that spoke volumes.

"I believe Mr. Veranda is responsible for a serious assault that occurred on or near these premises a couple of nights ago." He glanced around. "I suppose I could have this place shut down, pending an investigation. That'd put everybody out of work, including you."

She drew a slow breath, probably turning this over in her mind. "I'm telling you the truth. He isn't here." She stood back, one arm flung wide to indicate the space just beyond the dining room. "You can go through the place if you want. You won't find him. He went out earlier and he hasn't come back yet."

One of the thugs detached himself from the shadows and came to stand behind Denice. "Are we going to have a problem here?"

Schrade shook his head. "No problem." He turned on his heel and started for the door, one of the thugs following.

Niedermeyer was standing on the sidewalk, smoking a cigarette.

"Your friend got a chip on his shoulder?" the thug asked from just inside the doorway.

Niedermeyer didn't even look up. "More like a plank," he said.

Schrade got into the car. "Might as well go back to the station. Fatty could be anywhere."

They drove in silence for a while, until Niedermeyer said, "You know, Chief would probably put some men on this if you asked him." When Schrade didn't answer, he continued. "Every cop in the city knows the department is gunning for Fatty... and not just cops. From what I hear, he's been a royal pain in everybody's ass."

Schrade nodded. "Mmm."

"Are you listening to me?" Niedermeyer shook his head. "Vice would love to sink their teeth into this one. They've been hunting Fatty for years, but every time they try to bring him in, one of his goddamn ambulance chasers springs something and the bastard wriggles out of it." He pulled the car to a stop at the next red light. "The way I see it, you could get two of them if you really wanted to, Pratt and Fatty together." He nodded to himself. "I'd pay good money to see Pratt go before a grand jury. You know he'd spill the whole goddamn thing to save his own ass."

"He used to hit him, you know."

The light turned; Niedermeyer nudged the big car forward. "Fatty used to hit Pratt?"

"No. Alec's father, when he was a kid... he used to beat them up, Alec and the girl."

"And you know this how?"

"It's not important." Schrade shook his head. "So what do you say we get Vice involved? I think the chief would put some more men on this if we asked him."

Niedermeyer turned to stare at him. "Do you ever listen to a goddamn word I say?"

THE BUILDINGS and storefronts of Tegucigalpa slid past the windows of the taxi taking Chase and Franklyn Pratt to the airport. Dark clouds piled up on the horizon; it was going to rain. Pratt sat beside Chase in the back of the car and commented now and then in Spanish to the driver while his .45 automatic bored into Chase's side.

At each red light, small children ran up to the car, holding bunches of flowers for sale. They wore ragged clothes and most were barefoot. Near the double doors of a large *farmacia*, four young boys played makeshift instruments while a small girl, no older than nine, danced and sang. She wore a dress that might have been pale green once but was now grubby with age and street dust. Her arms and legs were so thin they resembled brittle sticks.

"That child," Pratt said suddenly. "She's a good example of what I mean. Don't you think she would be better off in the United States or some other first-world country?"

"Doing what?" Chase asked. It what a purely rhetorical question. He knew damn well "what."

"She could be put to work, earning a decent living. She might even make enough to send back home to her family." He offered Chase a disingenuous smile. "A man like me could help her more than she perhaps realizes."

"You're a sick fuck," Chase said. He looked back at the girl as the car pulled away. In a way he was looking forward to being Pratt's ticket out of Honduras, since it meant his tenure as Pratt's hostage would soon be over. As soon as the Gordon Industries plane touched down in New York—

He didn't actually expect Pratt or his associates would let him go. "So, when we land at JFK, what's the plan?"

"We aren't landing at JFK," Pratt said. "Much too public. It would cause problems. No, there's a small private airstrip on Long Island we'll be using. Two or three of my associates will meet us there. I need this entire operation to be discreet."

"I see." Chase nodded. He didn't need to ask the second half of his question. He strongly suspected Pratt would hand him over to his mob buddies without batting an eyelash. Where things went from there was anybody's guess.

CHAPTER NINE

WALTER WAS waiting for his train when his cell phone chirped. "Yeah?"

"Is this Godfrey?" It was a man's voice. "Walter Godfrey?"

Walter asserted that yes, it was indeed Walter Godfrey.

"They ain't coming in to JFK," he said. "Franklyn P. and your guy. They're coming in at the old Euwtawka airfield, out near Massapequa Park. Quarter past midnight."

"Who is this?" Walter demanded. "How the hell do you know?"

"It's *me*," the man said, "Vinnie Barone." One of Masetti's goons—the gorgeous, stocky one in the expensive suit. "You got that? Euwtawka. Quarter past."

"Why are you telling me this?" Walter asked, but too late. The line was dead. He hung up and immediately called Schrade.

The detective answered the phone sounding like he'd been dragged behind a bus. "Schrade."

"Pratt's coming in tonight, the old Euwtawka airfield. Just after midnight." He disconnected before Schrade could ask for more details. Then he called Eleanor at the paper. "I've got a lead," he said, "on the Chase Gordon kidnapping. I want to follow it up myself."

"Where will you be?" she asked indignantly. "And what the hell kind of lead could you get out there? Are you holding out on me, Walter?"

The old Euwtawka airfield was close to Massapequa, so Walter packed a bag and checked himself into a hotel just down the road in Montara, a few minutes after five o'clock that same afternoon. It was a small hotel, family run and very clean, and even though Walter knew he wouldn't get any sleep that night, at least he'd be comfortable.

The room was decorated in shades of dark green, with a mahogany desk and chair and a matching wardrobe. A thick, fluffy bathrobe hung just behind the bathroom door, so Walter stripped and stood under a hot shower until some of the tension eased out of his neck and shoulders. He threw himself down on the bed and turned on the TV. Every channel, it seemed, was full of Chase Gordon. One of the local news affiliates had set up a satellite truck just outside the perimeter of the Gordon property, and a bleached-blonde with a spray tan and too much microphone kept up a running commentary on any vehicle traffic that looked like it might be headed up to Gordonstoun.

The shower had relaxed him, so he set the alarm and fell asleep on top of the covers, still in the fluffy hotel bathrobe, his cell phone resting on his chest. He dreamed he and Chase were driving in one of Chase's cars, flashing down an unfamiliar road at an astonishing rate of speed. Chase was a very able driver, though, so Walter wasn't afraid, merely fascinated as he watched Chase handle the big car with consummate skill. The countryside gave way to Manhattan, and they were stuck in traffic and surrounded by honking horns while a flock of geese flew overhead in a V-formation.

When traffic began to move, they ran up against a red light. *Stuck again*, dream-Walter said.

Just seems that way, dream-Chase replied, turning to smile at Walter. He was gorgeously dressed in a charcoal gray suit with a crisp white shirt. *This is just temporary.*

The light changed and they were moving again, driving at great speed down suddenly empty streets at night. Chase laughed as he guided the car—was it a Maserati?—through an urban maze of streets and alleys, knocking over trashcans and stacks of cardboard boxes piled up in the middle of the road.

Then the dream switched to Chase's bedroom, and he and Walter were making love while a horde of reporters pressed against all the windows, peering in at them, and Walter couldn't concentrate. He kept licking a mole on the side of Chase's neck, while Chase lay prone beneath him, seemingly asleep. *I'm being set up*, he said, eyes closed. *You know this is a smear campaign. Walter, you know I would never do that. I'd never do that.* His fingertips dug hard into one of Walter's arms, and he was trying to shake Walter but could only manage to vibrate.

Walter woke to find his phone had fallen off his chest and was digging into his left bicep. Its vibrating had woken him. He picked it up and peered at the small screen: Unknown Caller. "Hello?"

"Is this Walter Godfrey, the reporter?"

The voice was indistinct. It might have been male or female, old or young or somewhere in between. He suspected whoever was talking used a voice distortion app to throw people off. The journalist in Walter pricked up his ears and picked up a pencil. "Yes, this is Walter."

"This is Lindsay Granger from the *National Investigator*. What can you tell us about the allegations made against Chase Gordon?"

"How did you get this number?" Walter's hand—the one not holding the phone—clenched into a fist around the pencil he held.

"Is it true that while in Honduras, Chase Gordon solicited sexual favors from underaged females in exchange for—"

He hung up and occupied himself with a pulp novel he'd brought from Chase's private library: Jack Clark's *Nobody's Angel*, an excellent read featuring a wise-cracking cab driver with the ability to notice things nobody else did.

At eleven thirty the telephone rang: it was Barone. "They're coming in early. Tail winds or some shit."

"Maybe there's no plane," Walter sneered, "and you're trying to get me out there so you can whack me."

"I swear to you," Barone said, "on my grandmother's grave."

Maybe, Walter thought, *he was making the sign of the cross somewhere on the other end of the line.*

"How fast can you get there?"

"Depends on the cabdriver," Walter said. "Where are you?"

"Lemme come and pick you up," Barone said. "You ain't gonna get no cab around here, not at this hour. Beverley Hotel, right?"

"How the hell did you know that?"

"Hey," Barone said, "maybe I'm one of the guys who shot you in the mustard. You ever think of that? Ten minutes."

Walter threw together a ditty bag of last-minute supplies: camera, digital recorder, a gun his father had given him on one of Walter's frequent visits to their old apartment. He stuck his phone in the inside pocket of his coat, along with a box of bullets. He felt ridiculous, like some Old West cowboy all ready for a showdown at the OK Corral; he was glad Chase couldn't see him.

He locked his room door behind him and had just descended to the lobby when the sound of a car horn announced Barone's arrival. He was driving a 1965 Cadillac Coupe DeVille, metallic gold and about a mile long. It gleamed in the dim lights of the hotel parking lot like an advertisement for sin and excess.

"Wow." Walter ran a reverent hand over the door; the finish was like silk. "This is some car."

"Got it on eBay," Barone said. "Come on, get in." He burned rubber going out of the parking lot, and Walter wondered if this was for his benefit or merely for show. "Ain't that far," Barone said, "but I figure we're better off getting there early. Less chance of being seen."

BARONE DROVE fast, but not recklessly, and he seemed to know Long Island better than Walter would have expected.

"My grandmother, God rest her soul, lived out near Great Neck," Barone said. "When I was a kid, we'd spend summers out here. My old man liked to take long Sunday drives." He stopped for a red light. "Not what you expected, huh?" He smiled. He had a nice smile. "I bet you figured me for one of these hard guys, growing up on the wrong side of the tracks, that kinda schtick." The light switched to green, but just then an ambulance, lights flashing and sirens screaming, came racing through the intersection. "Somebody's not having a good night." Barone glanced behind him in the rearview mirror, then pulled ahead.

"Why do you do it?" Walter asked, by way of making conversation.

"Why do I do what?" Barone pulled up to a stop sign and turned right without signaling. They were driving parallel with the boundary of a civic park, an empty soccer pitch eerie now under vague orange streetlights.

"The… work you do." Walter coughed. "You know, the, uh, services you provide for your… your boss."

Barone turned and looked at him. "You got me wrong, kid. I ain't no button man." He shrugged. "What you saw in the store that night, that was intimidation."

Walter's skin crawled. "You shot a man in cold blood."

"No, I didn't." Barone shook his head. "You got me all wrong. That guy? The guy in the store? Joey Bananas. You ever heard of Joey Bananas?"

"Cha-cha dancer," Walter said sarcastically, "fruit on her head?"

Barone stared at him. "You're a funny guy." He stopped for another red light. "Joey Bananas ain't somebody you want to mess with. Trust me on that. That had nothing to do with murder. It was just business." His expression softened. "Not that I need to explain myself to you."

Walter didn't know what to say to that.

They rode in silence for some time. There were fewer towns now, and longer stretches of emptiness between, and Walter began to get a little bit nervous. Maybe this whole business was a ruse and Barone was taking him out into the country to kill him. Maybe Chase would arrive back home to find Walter's battered body clinging to the rusted mesh of some suburban storm drain, or lying in pieces across the railroad tracks. Maybe Barone planned to tie him hand and foot and lock him in the trunk of a car, drive around until he suffocated—

"You hear what I said?"

Walter blinked. "Huh?"

Barone nodded at the windshield of the car. "Airfield up ahead. They're coming in now." He pulled off the road, put the car in park, and turned it off. "Won't be long."

A small white light flashed from what seemed to be a very long distance, a mere dot in the night-dark sky. As Walter watched, it grew larger, resolved into the body of a small private aircraft with the Gordon Industries corporate logo etched on the side. A frisson of excitement ran through him, and his palms were suddenly damp. *Home, he's coming home....* He made to get out of the car, but Barone's hand on his leg stopped him.

"Wait," Barone said. "Don't make it look like you're too eager. That's always a mistake." He took a .45 automatic from his shoulder holster and checked the magazine. "Act like you don't care. It's better that way." He slapped the gun's magazine into place and sighted along the barrel. "Stay in the car and don't say anything."

Walter couldn't drag his eyes away from the plane. "Uh-huh." He reached for the door handle.

"Are you listening to me?" Barone snapped. "Stay in the goddamn car." He replaced the gun in his shoulder holster and got out.

Walter clenched his fists, annoyed. The small jet dropped gracefully and landed on the tarmac without undue fuss or fanfare. It took every ounce of restraint Walter possessed to stay where he was.

Franklyn Pratt was the first to exit the aircraft. He nodded as Barone came closer, said something Walter couldn't make out. A black limousine slid out of the darkness and drew up in front of Pratt, almost nudging him with its shiny chrome bumper. A man in a chauffeur's uniform got out and held the door for him. Pratt slid into the car, followed by Barone, and they disappeared from Walter's view. The chauffeur turned to look at the car Walter was sitting in. His gaze lingered, and then he slipped into the driver's seat of his own vehicle, and the big car slowly pulled away from the tarmac.

"We got Pratt."

"Jesus!" Walter said. Jack Niedermeyer was leaning into his window. "What the hell are you trying to do to me?"

Niedermeyer laughed. "Sorry, kid." He snapped his chewing gum. "Didn't mean to scare you."

"Where the hell did you come from?" Walter gestured at the chauffeured limousine, disappearing into the darkness. "And where's Franklyn Pratt going?"

"Oh, he'll be safe enough back in the city," Niedermeyer said. "We've got a cell especially reserved just for him. Once the DA gets through with him, he'll be too tired and too busy to get himself into any kind of trouble. Of course, guy like Pratt's got his slimy lawyers, ambulance chasers, you know...."

Walter didn't hear anything else Niedermeyer had to say. The plane's pilot was standing on the small jet's stairs, helping somebody out onto the tarmac—somebody standing tall inside a bionic exoskeleton—

Chase, it's Chase—

He was out of the car and running, running to where Chase was, shouldering the pilot aside to take Chase in his arms, metal skeleton and all, and hold him close, so tight, vowing never to let him go again.

"Home," Walter said, breathing in the scent of Chase's skin, his hair. "You're home. Oh God, you're home." He seized Chase's face between his hands and kissed him, right there in front of Niedermeyer and God, and he didn't care who saw or what they thought of it. "Where'd you...?" He looked down at the exoskeleton between them. "Pratt let you have it back?"

"He wasn't going to leave an expensive prototype lying around in some Honduran jungle," Chase said. "He figured the easiest way to get it home was to make me wear it."

BRIAN SCHRADE was still wearing his borrowed chauffeur's uniform when he went to visit Alec the next morning. Alec was lying just as Schrade had left him, unconscious and unresponsive in his hospital bed. An IV pole with three bags attached dripped various substances into the catheter protruding from the back of Alec's right hand. Schrade supposed they were medicines, vital fluids, maybe a glucose solution in place of the food Alec wasn't able to take by mouth.

He sat beside the bed and stroked Alec's cheek. "We got him," he murmured. "Your old man. I'm not sure if you'll be happy about that or not...." His own father had been a pillar of Schrade's life; he couldn't imagine having a father like Franklyn Pratt. "He won't be bothering anybody anymore."

Schrade had always found it hard to talk about deep emotional things. He was a tender-hearted man, but when it came to saying things out loud, he just wasn't built that way. If he'd thought Alec was awake and listening... but Alec was deeply unconscious—drifting, perhaps, in dreams or journeying elsewhere in the cosmos. Anything, Schrade knew, was possible.

He reached for Alec's hand and held it gently in his own, careful of the catheter. "When I first met you, you didn't seem like the kind of guy I'd pick for a friend, and I was right." He squeezed the pale, limp fingers, smoothed Alec's bruised knuckles. "You're so much more than that." Tears stung the backs of his eyes, and he swallowed hard, refusing to be unmanned by a show of ridiculous emotion. "I'm not the kind of guy who falls in love. I don't... let myself." He glanced at Alec's face, slack with oblivion. "I've had some bad experiences. Like everybody, I've gotten in too deep and fucked myself up."

His last relationship had been with Toni, a hard-driving criminal lawyer from Los Angeles, with honey-blonde hair and legs up to her neck. It had lasted six months—barely—before she realized he wasn't ready to be emotionally engaged and went back to California. Schrade had been devastated. Niedermeyer hadn't let him forget it. *You really stepped on your dick that time*, he'd said. After that, Schrade had given up on relationships and their associated complications. He'd closed himself off.

Then Alec happened: a smartassed, spoiled little rich boy with more than tenuous connections to the mob and enough attitude to fill Yankee Stadium. Alec, of the twelve-hundred-dollar suits and the Testoni dress shoes, of the casual cynicism and the impossible hair and the often unbelievable courage. Alec, who'd risked the ire of the mafia in order to warn Schrade he was in danger....

He pressed Alec's limp hand to his cheek and kissed it, leaned down, and kissed his forehead, his lips. "I just love you," he murmured. "I love you." He turned away to wipe his face in his sleeve.

"'M glad." The voice was drowsy, rusty with drugs and with disuse, but it was unmistakably Alec. "Wondered when you'd get around to it." He motioned Schrade close and kissed him, held him as tightly as he was able with one good arm. "I love you too."

"For the love of Christ." Jack Niedermeyer huffed out an irritated breath. "Can't you guys control yourselves?" He moved into the room and tossed a newspaper down on Alec's bed. "You're a hero, snitch. Rah rah and all that crap." He regarded Alec's battered face for a moment. "How you feeling?"

"Better," Alec said. He smirked. "Maybe later on I'll be a lot better, when you aren't around." He drew the newspaper toward him. "Anonymous Hero Uncovers Cross-Border Traffickers, Routs Masetti Mob?" He frowned. "Anonymous?"

Schrade and Niedermeyer exchanged glances. "It's safer that way," Schrade said. "The captain agrees. It's best if the Masettis think you're dead."

"So, what?" Alec asked. "Witness protection?"

"Something like that," Niedermeyer said. "Trust me. You'll like it."

"You won't just like it," Schrade said. "You'll love it. Honest."

CHASE WAS scarcely home a day when Sam Jessup called to say he had a lead on Frey and the missing money from the animal sanctuary. Chase took the call in the library. "Where is he?" Chase asked. "And what's he doing with my money?"

Mr. Frey, it seemed, had gotten himself in pretty deep with some gentlemen in Nevada whose business interests ran to nightclubs and casinos. It seemed that Mr. Frey owed a significant amount of money to these same gentlemen, money he wasn't able to pay. Being reasonable men, his friends sent for him and insisted he come out to Nevada for a vacation, to discuss some things. At first Mr. Frey was reluctant, but....

"They had some guys come here and pick him up. Drove him all the way to Vegas." The sound of Jessup shuffling papers on his desk was clearly audible at the other end. "Near as my sources can make out, he found himself on the wrong side of Joey Napier. You heard of Joey Napier? Big time wiseguy, operates out of New Orleans?"

Chase had.

"Well," Jessup continued, "some of Mr. Napier's boys took Mr. Frey for a ride, and on the way back, they rolled him off a cliff, up there in Red Rock."

Chase cringed. "Jesus." He'd wanted Frey to pay for what he did, but off a cliff?

"Got a copy of the official death certificate here if you want to see it," Jessup said. "Just so you got closure, there. No sign of the money. I'd kiss it good-bye if I were you."

Chase hung up with a small sigh. Some things you just couldn't fix.

There was a rap on the door. "Come in."

Walter peered into the gap between the door and the frame. "Are you sure?"

"Please. And lock the door." Then he wheeled over to the sofa and lifted himself out of his chair. "Come here."

Walter went to sit beside him.

Chase wasn't sure if they would pick up where they had left off or if Walter wanted to wipe that particular slate clean. "It's good to see y—"

Walter leaned over and claimed his mouth in a searing kiss. Walter moaned, surging toward him, cupping Chase's face in his hands. The kiss left them both breathless, their faces close together, foreheads touching.

"Not enough drama," Chase muttered. "We need a plot. Let's see…."

Walter laughed. "A plot?" He kissed Chase's neck, lips lingering on the space behind his ear and just above his shoulder.

Hot lust prickled along Chase's veins. "I know. We're sworn enemies," Chase muttered, "and we're locked in here, and it's a battle to the death, last man standing, that sort of thing."

"We're going to kiss each other to death?" Walter asked. "You look like you're broiling," he said, reaching for the buttons of Chase's shirt. "Is it hot in here?" He pulled the shirt off Chase's shoulders and pressed his face against warm, naked skin. Whatever anger or misunderstanding had been between them when Chase left was gone now. Walter gasped when Chase caught hold of his sweater and tugged it up over his head.

Chase slammed him back against the couch and kissed him brutally, his tongue thrusting between Walter's parted lips. He ran his hands down Walter's chest, found the button of his trousers, and tore them open, heedless of damage, eager to get at what he wanted. "You…," he murmured. "I missed you." He mouthed the rigid cock through the thin cotton of Walter's underwear, warming it with his breath.

Walter moaned softly and dug his fingers into Chase's hair, pulling gently, scraping Chase's scalp with his nails.

"Tell me what you want," Chase urged, easing Walter's underwear down. "Tell me."

WALTER ARCHED his back when Chase's tongue touched the tip of his cock. "I want you to fuck me," he grunted, "with your mouth. Fuck me." He raised his upper body, leaned on his elbows, and scooted his body backward, legs spread, pelvis angled so Chase could reach him.

Chase circled the head with his tongue, then licked down the shaft, swallowing him whole.

The world shattered into lines and curves, dark and light, and Walter was falling upward through a well, tugged by some invisible string that pulled pleasure from the marrow of his bones. He clenched the muscles of his thighs and buttocks, straining to hold back his completion, but there was no use. Chase's clever tongue found and tripped the invisible switch that dragged him over the edge, and Walter came hard, panting. He clung to Chase as the orgasm had its way with him, drawing thin steel daggers of pleasure through him, a keen, knife-edged kind of pain.

Chase drew himself up to lie beside Walter on the narrow couch. Chase's mouth was close beside his ear. "Was that what you had in mind?"

"You're killing me," Walter said, smirking. His hand found its way into Chase's pants, and then Walter found himself on top of Chase, their bodies rocking together, seeking that delicious friction even though Walter wasn't anywhere close to being ready again. He didn't care. Chase was his again, in his arms, warm and gorgeous and alive. "Maybe not sworn enemies," Walter murmured. "Maybe I'm your loyal sidekick and we're celebrating our victory over… um, somebody evil." He gasped when Chase's fingers dug into his upper arms.

"Harder," Chase gasped, "no, harder." And then his expression shut down, his gaze turning inward, on himself. He was right *there*, on the edge, just a tiny little push.…

Walter's hips moved, grinding against him, and Chase came apart, gasping, his body shuddering through all the delicious throbs and pulses of his completion.

They lay in each other's arms while the sweat dried on their bodies. Walter got up, fetched a wet washcloth from the adjoining bathroom, and tenderly cleaned Chase, erasing any traces of their lovemaking. He stroked the warm cloth over Chase's flat belly and the muscles of his thighs, dipping between them, handling his lover gently. He adored touching Chase like this, when they were alone together and Chase was entirely and wholly his, when he didn't belong to Gordon Industries or the world or anybody. Just Walter.

Chase sighed. "That feels nice." He caught Walter's hand and kissed the palm. "You feel nice."

Walter dropped the washcloth on the floor, snagged the throw blanket off the back of the sofa, and covered them both. He settled down, Chase in his arms, Chase's dark head resting against Walter's shoulder. He wanted to say something, to say the right thing—*I love you. I'm in love with you*—but it was too soon for them, too early in their relationship or whatever this was. Declaring himself, when he wasn't even sure about what he felt, would be disastrous. It was far too soon to take such chances. He was afraid of ruining it, upsetting the delicate balance of what they'd found in each other.

"You were a firefighter," Chase said. "Before, I mean." He clasped Walter's hand in his own. "Strong hands… fireman's hands." He stroked a finger down Walter's cheek. "Why did you leave? You seemed to be good at it."

"I lost my…." He felt tears threatening, pressing at the backs of his eyes like miniscule needles. "My husband. On 9/11. He worked at the World Trade Center, in the North Tower."

"I'm sorry." Chase shook his head. "I am so sorry. I can't imagine what that feels like."

"I kind of think you can," Walter said quietly. "When you kiss someone good-bye one morning and they don't—"

"It's all right, Walter." Chase caressed the back of his bare arm, gentle fingers trailing over naked skin. "You don't have to explain yourself to me." He sobered. "I had an argument with my mother that morning… the morning they left. I was training for a marathon she didn't think I should run. We'd been arguing about it for ages, back and forth, getting nowhere." He closed his eyes and squeezed the bridge of his nose with his fingertips.

Walter recognized the gesture: it was one you used when you were trying not to cry.

"She said I was wearing myself thin, I wasn't taking proper care of my health. I told her to mind her own goddamn business. I left and went out for a run. When I got back, they'd already left." He shuddered, his voice breaking on the next words: "And they never came home."

Walter held him, his own body shaking with the power of unvoiced emotions. His hands trembled on Chase's bare shoulders, trembled on his naked back, so vulnerable underneath the blanket. He was trying to hold back his own tears, the sense of hurt and despair that came roaring back over the distance of thirteen years. "I know," he whispered. He said it over and over again, into Chase's dark hair. "I know."

And then he was crying and he didn't care. He'd already done his crying over Gary; that was finished, over with. What he was feeling was fear—afraid he'd fall in love again, had already fallen in love again, and Chase would be taken from him the same way Gary was. He pressed his lips against Chase's warm and willing mouth, still half weeping, the kiss tasting of salty tears. They clung together and held on tight, both of them, grinding their bodies together, rutting blindly against each other, shuddering and weeping and kissing desperately.

"I—" Walter began, but Chase shushed him.

"No." Chase's face was wet with tears, just like Walter's was. "Don't say anything." He kissed Walter tenderly, then drew the back of his hand across Walter's face. "Don't speak."

CHAPTER TEN

THE DAY before Thanksgiving, Chase recruited George, the gardener, to drive him into the city. He took only Juliet. When they arrived at their destination—a Park Avenue deco masterpiece—she went up with Chase in the elevator. They rode up to the fourteenth floor together and went into a spacious, beautifully appointed office where three receptionists drifted gracefully about, greeting visitors.

"Patrick Benson," Juliet said, "is the best there is for this sort of thing." She smiled gently. "Are you sure you want to go through with this? It might not work on the first try—or it might not work at all."

"I want to at least try," Chase said. "I don't have any expectations."

Dr. Benson himself appeared to usher them into his office. "Juliet," he said warmly, "it's been forever." He was about sixty, with graying hair and penetrating blue eyes. He struck Chase as the sort of man it would be impossible to lie to. "Juliet explained your case to me last week when she called. And you want to know if I can help you." He examined Chase thoroughly, moving and flexing his legs and testing his reflexes with a small rubber hammer. "Normal reflexes," he said, and Juliet nodded. "And no impairment of bowel or bladder function." He looked into Chase's eyes with a bright light and tapped various places on his skull and face. "Conversion disorder?"

Juliet nodded. "That's what we were told, yes."

Benson was silent for a moment. "And this occurred after your parents' death? The next morning, you woke up and you couldn't walk."

"The morning after their deaths," Chase replied. "It literally came on overnight."

"And you've had psychotherapy before. It didn't work."

"No. It didn't work."

Chase waited while Benson consulted with Juliet about a treatment course. "Transcranial magnetic stimulation," he said. "It's definitely worth a try."

"Magnetic pulses?" Chase asked. "To reset my brain."

Juliet laughed. "Yes, that's a good way of putting it." She laid a hand on his shoulder. "Are you willing to try? There's no guarantee it will work. As I've already said, you might go through all this and, in the end, be right where you are now."

Chase nodded. "I know," he said. "If it works, fine. If it doesn't work…." He glanced away for a moment. "I'll deal with it. I'm good at that."

"When do you want to start?" Dr. Benson asked. "I'll get Renee, my secretary, to set up a treatment schedule."

"Let's start right away," Chase said, "after Thanksgiving. I'd like to begin as soon as possible."

"You made the right decision," Juliet said when they were in the car and on their way back to Long Island. "Patrick Benson won't let you down. I think a cure might well be in sight for you."

"It would be nice," Chase said, "to walk again, to run like I used to do." He gazed out the side window at the passing scenery. "But maybe that won't happen… and if this doesn't work, and I still can't walk…." He drew a slow breath. "This chair isn't who I am. It won't ever be who I am. I'm still me. I'm still Chase Gordon. The chair has nothing to do with that." He smiled. "Besides… I make an excellent argument for Gordon Industries' exoskeleton. If people see me using it, they might be willing to give it a try. I'd like that." Privately he thought there were lots of different people in the world, people with all kinds of skills and abilities, who often got overlooked because other people thought they weren't capable of anything. Different didn't mean "bad" or "useless." Different was… well, just different.

"Walter will be glad to hear it," Juliet said. "He really cares about you."

"I know he does."

He loved Walter too. It was okay to admit it. He wasn't afraid anymore. He didn't think Walter would ever hurt him, but even if he did, Chase could handle it. He was ready to trust Walter, to let him into every corner of his life. He was ready to risk it.

The next day, Gordonstoun hosted its first Thanksgiving dinner in a long time. A catering company had been hired to cook and serve the meal, and Alec had made sure the house was tastefully and beautifully decorated. Juliet supervised the caterer's assistants, none of whom—according to her—knew a damn about how to serve a meal.

Walter brought his father, who regaled them all with ribald stories of his time as a merchant seaman, pausing frequently to apologize to Juliet before launching into another horrifyingly hilarious tale.

Chase, wearing the exoskeleton, sat at the head of the table where his father would have been. Between dinner and dessert, he and Walter escaped to a small reading niche near the stairs. "I used to hide in here when I was little," Chase said. It was more a small room than a reading nook, big enough for two or three people to huddle under the stairs, out of the direct line of sight. "Especially if my tutor was looking for me." He pulled Walter in beside him. "It's very private. I like that."

Walter leaned close and gave him a scorching kiss. "I like it too." He leaned against Chase, who put an arm around him. "Chase, I love you." He drew back to gaze into Chase's eyes. "Maybe it's too soon, and maybe I'm putting you in an awkward position." It had seemed more natural to say it after they'd made love in the library, when they'd been lying in each other's arms. But he hadn't said it, and this was broad daylight, stone cold sober. "I'm in love with you."

Chase started to say something, but then Juliet's voice came from somewhere uncomfortably close. "What the bloody hell are you doing in there? Come back to the table right this minute."

Chase's face was hot when he and Walter clambered out of the reading nook. Juliet had obviously guessed what was going on.

"The coffee's getting cold. You two can—" She seemed to be looking for the right word. "—nuzzle on your own time."

After dinner, everyone followed Juliet into the great room for a game of charades, helped along by copious applications of brandy. By five that afternoon, everyone was drunk and Walter's father had missed his train. Juliet made one of the guest rooms ready for him.

"I think we should all live here together," Chase said when he and Walter were back in the reading nook. "All of us. You, me, and everybody." That Chase was more than a little drunk hadn't escaped Walter's notice.

"I think you've been into the sauce," Walter said. He turned Chase's face to his and kissed him.

Chase groaned, arching into the kiss, wanting as much of himself as possible to be touching Walter. "I don't give a rat's ass," Chase replied—drunkenly. "Take me to bed and ravish me already."

Walter smirked. "But I'm only the underbutler, sir."

Chase nodded sagely. "That's exactly where I want to be," he said, "under the butler."

"In that case," Walter replied, "I'm your man."

"You are," Chase agreed. "You're my man, Godfrey."

Epilogue

Charlotte Amalie, St. Thomas. US Virgin Islands
November, 2015

"ALEC? YOU in here?" Brian Schrade closed the front door of his Caribbean villa and yanked at the knot of his tie. "Alec?" It was just after seven; he'd been kept late at work, and they had dinner reservations for eight. "You here?"

"Out here," Alec called.

Schrade went through to the back of the house. Alec was sitting on the tiled steps in the pool, a glass of wine in his hand. "You look inordinately pleased with yourself," Schrade said, and bent down to kiss him. "What are you celebrating?"

"First batch of reviews are in. Jamie"—Alec's literary agent—"sent them an hour ago. *Seeds of Sorrow* is at number one." He grinned, and the smile transformed his pale, serious face into the very picture of glee. "I'm a *bestselling author*, Brian." He reached behind him for his smartphone and brought up the e-mail. "Look," he said, thrusting the phone at his husband, "it's all over the Internet."

"It is," Schrade said. He was proud of Alec, so proud he could barely speak. "'Author Oliver J. Fleming surprises once again with a potent mix of romance and suspense....' Nicely done, babe."

"Mmm," Alec said, frowning. "Oliver Fleming."

Schrade reached out to ruffle his hair. "You know why you can't use your own name... it's not safe, for either of us."

Alec rolled his eyes. "Safety... that's why we're living in a place with a higher murder rate than New York." He grabbed a handful of Schrade's shirt. "Why don't you get out of those clothes and come in here with me?"

"Jack Niedermeyer flew in this morning just to see me. We have dinner reservations," Schrade murmured, as Alec's other hand located the growing bulge in his pants.

"They'll hold the table." Alec stood and pressed his mouth to Schrade's. "For the chief of police, they will." He wrapped his arms around Schrade and walked him down into the pool, fully clothed but very compliant. "And you're the chief of police." He captured Schrade's mouth and began stripping off his sodden clothing.

"Alec," Schrade began when he was naked save for his boxers, "maybe we should take this to the bedroom."

The faint glow of a streetlamp filtered wan light into the room. Alec led Schrade to the bed, pushed him down, and straddled him. He rolled to the side and slid down till he was lying with his cheek against Schrade's hip. He mouthed Schrade's hard cock through the sopping underwear, infusing the wet cloth with heat.

Schrade writhed underneath him. "We have dinner reservations," he said, albeit without much heat. He threaded his fingers through Alec's black hair and tugged gently as Alec rolled Schrade's underwear down and took just the tip of his cock into his hot mouth. "Ah," Schrade said as Alec began to suck. "Ah, Jesus, Alec…." He moved quickly, throwing Alec off him and rolling him onto his back. "I told you to behave yourself," he said. He caught hold of Alec's wrists and pinned them to the mattress, above his head. "We don't have time for this." For a moment Schrade's muscular torso blocked out the light from the window, and then he was lying on top of Alec, pressing their naked skin together.

Alec wrapped his legs around Schrade's waist and rocked against him. He slipped a hand between Schrade's thighs and palmed his balls.

Schrade's urgent movements stuttered, slowing down, then speeding up, his hips losing their carefully tended rhythm. He thrust against Alec and came with a shudder, spilling himself in the darkness, crying out as the pleasure took him in its teeth.

A second later Alec followed, wrenching his wrists free of Schrade's grasp and reaching to hold Schrade almost brutally against him. He keened his release, his voice dying on a strangled whimper. They were silent together in the darkness.

"I love you," Alec said. He always said it after they made love. He rolled onto his belly, cheek resting against the rumpled bedspread.

"I love you too," Schrade said. He whacked Alec's naked ass with the palm of his hand.

"Ow!"

"Come on," Schrade said, "before we lose the table."

JACK NIEDERMEYER was nowhere in sight when the waiter showed Alec and Schrade to their table, close to the water and with the waves practically at their feet. Schrade had cut himself shaving and Alec's hair was still wet from the shower; maybe it was good that Niedermeyer hadn't yet arrived to witness their telling state of *dishabille*. The waiter reappeared with a bottle of white wine and two glasses, and placed them down in front of the two men before vanishing back into the restaurant's interior.

"Are you sure he's coming?" Alec asked. He looked through the menu, even though he almost always ordered the same thing: seared scallops for a starter, followed by either lobster or mussels.

"He'll be here," Schrade said. "He said he's bringing somebody with him."

Alec arched an eyebrow, the menu temporarily forgotten. "Somebody like who? A woman?"

"I don't know. He was pretty cagy when I asked him about it."

"So he's met someone locally?"

"Apparently this person came with him from the States. And since when are you so interested in Jack's love life?"

Alec smirked. "I just want everybody to be as happy as we are."

Schrade sighed, pretending annoyance. "Tell me again why I married you."

"Because I'm brilliant," Alec said, reaching for Schrade's hand, "and I'm sexy, and I make you laugh, and because it's legal now."

Schrade turned his hand and his fingers tightened on Alec's. "Regrets?"

"None," Alec replied, eyes shining. "Not one." He leaned across the table to kiss Schrade.

"For Christ's sake!" Jack Niedermeyer appeared, seemingly out of nowhere. "Can't you guys keep your hands off each other? Jesus, you're making me puke."

Schrade jumped up and hugged him, laughing as his old friend pounded him on the back. "You look great, Jack. How you been keeping yourself?"

"Good, I've been good." Niedermeyer nodded to Alec. "Heard your book's gone to number one. Good job, snitch."

"You were bringing someone with you," Schrade prompted. "You said this was a big deal, you were in love"—he wagged a finger in Niedermeyer's face—"don't bother trying to deny it."

"Oh, yeah." Niedermeyer looked suddenly shy. It was an incongruous look for him. "I want you to meet...." He glanced behind him and spoke into the darkness. "Come over here, would you?"

Vincent Barone stepped into the light, diffident but smiling. He nodded at Alec and at Schrade. He was gorgeous in a white tropical-weight suit, with a pale blue shirt open at the collar.

Schrade couldn't have been more surprised if the big, handsome mobster had dropped out of the sky. "This... you and...?" Schrade's voice failed him. "I mean, it's good to see you. Please, sit down, join us." He spotted the waiter hovering by a nearby table and beckoned him over. "Bring another bottle of wine, Geoff, and a couple of menus, would you?"

There was a long interval of silence as Niedermeyer and Barone sat. The four men all gazed at each other, and then Niedermeyer suddenly laughed. "Ain't this a kick in the head?" He reached for Barone's hand and held on. "We... after that whole business with the Masettis... you know, Fatty Veranda...."

Barone was gazing at him like... *like Alec looks at me*, Schrade thought.

"It got too hot in New York for either of us to stay there," Niedermeyer said. He squeezed Barone's fingers. "Vinnie figured we ought to go somewhere until the heat's off, so... here we are."

"I never thought...." Schrade coughed to cover his confusion. "I figured you... I mean, you only ever dated women."

Niedermeyer traced a scratch in the dark wood of the table. "That's what I told you, and everybody." His gaze softened when he looked at Barone. "What the hell does it matter? If somebody loves you and you... love them."

"It doesn't matter," Schrade said. "It doesn't matter worth a damn." He glanced across at Alec, who was busy pouring wine into the newcomers' glasses. "Love always wins, in the end."

J.S. COOK was born and raised on the island of Newfoundland. She holds a BA and an MA in English Language and Literature and a BEd in post-secondary education. She makes her home in St. John's, Newfoundland, with her husband Paul, and Lola, her spoiled rotten dogter.

J.S. Cook also writes as JoAnne Soper-Cook.

Twitter: @jsopercook
Website: joannesopercook.net

In 1942, Pearl Harbor has been bombed and the war is very much in evidence, but it would seem to have little to do with Frank Boyle, a respected Bronx born insurance investigator. He's a man who can keep secrets, and no one suspects that his boyhood friend—local mob boss Nicky Brooks—is his lover. When Brooks accidentally kills Frank's younger brother in a shootout, Frank must choose between his affair with Nicky and revenge for his brother's life.

After Frank betrays Nicky, police detective Sam Lipinski, a Bronx native who has long carried a torch for Frank, makes a move against the mob and lands squarely in the way of Nicky's plans. Sam smuggles Frank out of New York to keep him safe, and sets him up him in a small northeastern city. But there, a messy insurance investigation involving the Roarkes, who may or may not have killed their own mother for the insurance payout, places him in danger again. Dodging bullets, shady characters, and fallout from the war, Sam and Frank will need far more than luck on their side if they're ever to see a loving future.

www.dreamspinnerpress.com

Jacob van Willingen arrives in a remote Romanian village aiming for a short visit. A member of the highly secretive Society for Psychical Research, Jacob has been charged with exterminating Caleb Donnithorn--but the society's intelligence about the reclusive nobleman is less than complete. As he studies his target, Van Willingen is drawn to Donnithorn, enthralled with the nobleman's alluring brides, three of society's most luminous geniuses gathered from the corners of Europe to create a fantastical machine: a resurrection engine that can capture a human soul at the moment of death.

Caleb Donnithorn represents everything that is evil in the world, but there is more to him than is initially apparent. What he knows about van Willingen is a truth so shocking it will shake the young scholar's world to its very foundations. Cast out from his friends and his beloved Society of Psychical Research, Jacob van Willingen will jettison everything he holds dear to remain with one whose love commands the highest price of all.

www.dreamspinnerpress.com

OASIS
OF NIGHT

J.S. COOK

Heartache Café: Books One and Two

The Second World War touches Newfoundland in unprecedented ways, throwing spies and patriots together inside Jack Stolyes's Heartache Café.

Heartache Café

American expatriate Jack Stoyles embarks on a self-imposed exile to St. John's, Newfoundland. With good reason, Jack calls his place "Heartache Café." He's content—until Samual Halim walks into his life.

When a constable goes missing, Jack finds himself caught between a manipulative woman, a corrupt cop, and a sabotaged work site.

Valley of the Dead

When Egyptian diplomat Samuel Halim enters Jack's Heartache Café, Jack's life changes forever. Then Sam disappears along with the code key to decipher a Nazi radio command that will set Rommel's troops in motion, leaving Jack with nothing but a fragmented phone call.

In the teeming heat of Cairo—a city rife with romance, secrets, sex, and danger, where no one is who he seems and violent death waits around every shadowed corner—it's up to Jack to find the new love of his life and deliver the code that will change the course of history. But as Sam's secrets come to light, there's more at stake than the tenuous relationship forming between the two men.

www.dreamspinnerpress.com

J.S. COOK

SKID ROW SERENADE

In the tradition of novel noir, nothing is ever quite as it seems.

Novelist and war hero Tony Leonard sees private investigator Edwin Malory being mugged outside a seaman's mission in downtown Los Angeles, so he takes him home and gives him clean clothes and access to a hot shower. It doesn't take him long to discover Malory was hired by wealthy industrialist Linton Vanderbilt Stirling, the father of Tony's estranged wife, Janet. The reason for this is simple: Tony's father-in-law suspects him of drinking away his daughter's personal fortune.

On a whim, Tony drops in on Janet one night and finds her naked, dead, and tied up, her skull beaten in. Horrified, Tony flees the scene, knowing that as her husband, he is the number one suspect in the killing. He sees only one way out. He needs to fake his own death.

And who better to send his "suicide note" to than Edwin Malory.

www.dreamspinnerpress.com

Veteran police chief Eli Gallagher doesn't ask for much, but he does insist that his officers uphold the "serve" part of "serve and protect." Conscientious young Deputy Stan Leach takes Eli's motto to heart, maintaining a high standard of personal accountability.

When Eli's long-distance boyfriend, Gilbert Nees, telephones from Philadelphia, Eli thinks he intends to further cement their relationship. Unfortunately, Gilbert's news is anything but good. But Eli doesn't have time to wallow, because a violent act results in murder in the small town of Morristown, Mississippi.

But as Eli and Stan uncover evidence, their personal lives begin to unravel. Stan, working closely with Chief Gallagher, grows increasingly attached to Eli and learns what it really means to be an advocate of justice.

www.dreamspinnerpress.com